"Have you enjoyed yourself tonight? Charlotte asked. Her eyes were a shade of blue you could only find at the very bottom of the ocean.**

"I have," Loretta replied. There was no one to hear them, but they were barely whispering. It felt like if they spoke too loudly, they would shatter the moment and lose it forever.

"And do you enjoy me?" Charlotte breathed.

Here was the moment the sun peaked in the sky. Here in the darkest of rooms, Loretta felt brighter than she'd ever been before. Everything would go back to normal after this, but for just a few seconds more, she could let her wantfulness run ahead like an unbroken horse.

"I do." Loretta smiled.

"Fair Titania, benevolent monarch of the forest, may I kiss you?"

Loretta held out her hand, and Charlotte giggled.

"That's not exactly what I meant..." Charlotte said, then kissed Loretta's hand anyway. Then her wrist. Then her forearm, then her elbow, all the way up to the place where her sleeve met her shoulder. Her neck. Charlotte paused, leaned up on her toes, and suddenly the space between their noses could only be filled by a single grain of sand.

Loretta nodded.

And they kissed. The pirate king and the fairy queen. Their lips met and Loretta was wrong about this being like the kisses she read about in her books.

It was better.

Author Note

Here in the United States, *The Duke's Sister and I* comes just in time for LGBTQ+ History Month. October returns each year to remind us that women have always found ways to love women, men have always found ways to love men, and people have always found ways to exist outside the gender binary. The language and identity labels change with each new generation, but this simple truth endures: *we have always existed, and we always will*.

So much of the historical information we have on Regency London's underground queer culture comes, tragically, from police reports and court transcripts. It can be hard to see the romance in stories told through the lens of criminalization. It can be harder still to find the happily-ever-afters of the people who were never caught.

But if history has preserved more sadness than joy, it is fiction's job to find the joy there is and elaborate, expand, imagine. Loretta and Charlotte may be characters made from my own heart, but their love story did not begin with them. Their love story is timeless, it is transcendent, it is true.

And now their love story is yours to savor.

In solidarity,

Emma-Claire Sunday

PS: Follow me on Spotify to hear the music I listened to while writing *The Duke's Sister and I*.

spoti.fi/42ZxVxT

THE DUKE'S
SISTER AND I

EMMA-CLAIRE SUNDAY

Harlequin
HISTORICAL

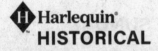

Harlequin®
HISTORICAL

ISBN-13: 978-1-335-53975-5

The Duke's Sister and I

Recycling programs for this product may not exist in your area.

Harlequin Enterprises ULC
22 Adelaide St. West, 41st Floor
Toronto, Ontario M5H 4E3, Canada
www.Harlequin.com

Printed in U.S.A.

Emma-Claire Sunday is on a mission to fill the world's libraries with queer happily-ever-afters. She has been a playwright, a filmmaker, a preacher and a competitive spoken word poet—always something different, but always a storyteller at heart. She lives with her partner in New Jersey, where they edit each other's writing, drink an abundance of whole milk and spend all their money at local bookstores. *The Duke's Sister and I* is Emma-Claire's debut novel and the winner of Harlequin's Romance Includes You 2023 Mentorship.

Connect with her on Instagram @author.ec.sunday.

Books by Emma-Claire Sunday

The Duke's Sister and I is Emma-Claire Sunday's debut title for Harlequin Historical.

Look out for more books from Emma-Claire Sunday coming soon.

Visit the Author Profile page
at Harlequin.com for more titles.

To all the women left out of history books:
the painters, the poets, the scientists, the lovers
whose names we should have remembered.

To Cami, to Sophia, to Patrick.

And to Henry, the best cat.

Chapter One

March 1824, London

There was no arguing the fact that Miss Loretta Linfield and the Duke of Colchester could have an agreeable marriage. Yet some deep and inscrutable part of her seemed to argue all the same.

As she gazed at him from her hiding spot behind a row of potted plants, Loretta was dismayed to find nothing immediately wrong with the tall, handsome Duke who stood in the conservatory, deep in discussion with her father. Broad shoulders, kind face, full head of hair—he was the very portrait of a desirable bachelor.

Loretta, of course, had to remind herself of the qualities she was supposed to look for in a gentleman the same way she had to recite her French lessons—over and over again. Never mind that when it came to courtship most ladies of the London season seemed native-born speakers—Loretta had read enough scandal sheets, romantic poetry and Jane Austen novels to navigate the language of love with near-perfect fluency.

A decrescendo from the string quartet afforded Loretta a moment to hear her father exclaim, 'You absolutely must meet my daughter tonight! She is a lovely specimen.'

Loretta felt her throat tighten and her jaw clench. She

loathed being discussed as though she were a scientific object…an impressive microbe beneath a microscope. She wanted a husband—or she *wanted* to want a husband—but anyone chosen by her ambitious father would most certainly be selected for his wealth and title above all else. Arthur Sterlington, Duke of Colchester, Britain's oldest city, would be no exception.

She slowly reached into the greenery and prised apart the purple wisteria petals, straining her neck to get a better view, her knees increasingly sore from kneeling on the stone floor.

A brazen, unfamiliar voice startled Loretta from her eavesdropping. 'I do hope that your chaperone doesn't find you alone and so intimately entangled with unmarried wisteria. I'm sure I'd *die* of the scandal.'

Loretta spun to look behind her and, her legs caught in her own satin skirts, tumbled firmly onto her backside.

The fashionable woman standing over her continued as though Loretta had not just entirely embarrassed herself. 'Though, given the gentlemen in attendance, I can hardly fault you.'

'I was simply—'

Simply what? Loretta couldn't exactly admit to spying on two members of the peerage.

She stammered out the first thing that came to mind. 'Simply searching for my dance card. I had dropped it amongst the flowers.'

Loretta's eyes climbed the lavender silk skirts before her the way ivy climbed a wall. Tendrils of lace and sequins led to a face adorned with rosy cheeks, stormy blue eyes and a mischievous grin framed by glittering amethyst earrings and a crown of golden curls. The woman before her stood nonchalant and contrapposto, in that pose made famous by the Grecian sculptors of old—with all her weight shifted to one leg, a hand on her protruding hip, in defiance of all things ladylike.

'I cannot fathom the loss of a dance card as anything other than a blessing,' the bold stranger said with a sigh.

Loretta didn't know what to say. She wasn't used to hearing people complain so openly about the rituals of society. She agreed that dancing could be quite tedious, of course, but she would never say so *out loud*.

Loretta must have looked confused, because the stranger continued. 'Are you the type of lady who *enjoys* dancing with all the prized gentlemen of the *ton*?'

The question made Loretta nervous. Saying yes wouldn't be truthful, but saying no would be impolite. 'What other type of lady could there be?'

'I merely saw you evading the night's festivities and wondered if I'd found someone as fatigued by society as I.'

The sudden squint of her eyes made Loretta feel entirely bare.

'I see now I was mistaken.'

'Indeed you were,' Loretta snapped, her face flushed with the rising heat of her temper.

She heard her own heartbeat, loud as a soldier's drum. And Loretta realised if she was hearing her heartbeat so clearly, she was not hearing the music. She clutched her dance card as the tune changed and scanned the list of hastily written names. The opening chord of the evening's first quadrille pierced the silence and announced to Loretta that she was late for her promised dance with the Earl of Hawick, a visiting Scot she'd met at last week's ball.

She frantically gathered her sapphire skirts and, with a cutting glance, strode with haste into the ballroom.

'Miss Linfield!' Loretta spun around to see the Earl approaching her from the direction of the punch table.

'My lord…' Loretta sank into a slow curtsy, in no hurry

whatsoever to lift her embarrassed face from the floor. 'I must apologise…it seems I had lost track of the time.'

The Earl gently reached out his hand to tuck a lock of copper-brown hair behind Loretta's ear—a curl that must have fallen during her race to the dance floor.

'Not to worry,' he said with a reassuring smile. 'The dance has only just begun.'

She took his arm and let him lead her, resisting the urge to turn her head in the direction from which she'd come.

Loretta was soon twirling around the polished floor, feigning interest in the Earl's unsolicited narration of his long carriage ride to London. She tried her best to grant his perfectly average face the polite eye contact years of etiquette lessons had prepared her for, but she couldn't stop her eyes from wandering around the grand ballroom.

Dresses of purples, pinks and greens spun before the powder-blue walls like a hurricane of colour. At one and twenty years of age, this was Loretta's third season, but she still found herself gaping in awe at the gorgeous gowns her peers arrived in, with their hair wound in elaborate patterns above their smooth, painted faces. She resented how fake and shallow the season could feel at times, but she had never stopped loving the beauty of it all.

'Wouldn't you agree, Miss Linfield?' the Earl asked with eager eyes.

Loretta plastered on her most polite smile and nodded in agreement. 'Most certainly,' she gushed, to fill the space between them, and prayed it wasn't too obvious she hadn't been paying attention.

As the dance reached its crescendo, Loretta saw a hand gesturing at her from the corner of the room. There, between two white pillars wrapped in decorative vines, stood her father and the Duke. Looking straight at her.

'Might there be room on your dance card for another…?' The Earl raised his eyebrows as the tune drifted into its final note.

'It appears my father has other plans for me this evening, my lord,' she said with relief.

'Another time, then,' the Earl replied—three words Loretta had heard a hundred times over from men who had failed to interest her in a second dance.

Most of her peers seemed to be enjoying themselves—not only tonight but in all aspects of the hunt for a proper husband. This was their duty, after all. Their purpose. Their very nature as members of the fairer sex.

Loretta lifted her chin high and glided towards her father, making a promise to herself then and there that she would greet the Duke with an open mind—no matter how difficult that might be.

'Loretta, darling,' her father said as she stepped into the admiring gaze of Arthur Sterlington. 'It is my honour to introduce you to the Duke of Colchester.'

'Your Grace.' Loretta curtsied, her eyes politely fixed on the floor.

'Your father has been singing your praises all evening,' the Duke said.

Had Loretta been less concerned with displaying the slowest and lowest curtsy a graceful lady like herself could manage, she might have noticed the swish of a lavender hem approaching. She might have caught a glimpse of the halo-gold hair and the devilish smirk that couldn't belong to anyone else, and she might have taken a moment to compose herself before rising.

Instead, Loretta was entirely helpless against the scarlet blush that bloomed up her neck and across her face like an invasive weed.

'You must also meet my sister, Lady Charlotte Sterlington,' the Duke continued. 'You may have met in a previous season?'

'I can't say that I recall.' Loretta shook her head and opened the fan tied around her wrist, cooling her face and avoiding Lady Charlotte's amused gaze.

'Charlotte is quite good at making herself unknown,' her brother said, with a teasing tone that indicated real frustration. 'But we all must leave the marriage market eventually.'

'And I intend to be a shopper in this market,' Lady Charlotte quipped with a venomous smile. 'Not a product.'

'A shopper or a loiterer?' The Duke shot his sister a conversation-killing glance, then turned to Loretta, completely unruffled. 'You'll have to forgive my sister. She has the unfortunate habit of leaving her manners at home. I assure you they are there somewhere.'

'I suppose there are worse places to leave your manners,' Loretta offered.

The Duke's sister raised an eyebrow in amusement.

'Ah, is that Lord Hoskins I see?' Loretta's father exclaimed, relieved at having found an exit from such an odd exchange. 'I shall find you at the end of the night.'

Lord Bertram Linfield, Baron Devonshire, had made his approval of the Duke unquestionably clear at breakfast, and there was no doubt in Loretta's mind that a dance with him was expected. Her father flashed his winning smile—the one he saved for a successful business transaction—and marched into the crowd.

Lord Sterlington held out his arm with the confidence one might expect of a Duke.

His sister rolled her eyes.

What on earth about this interaction could possibly be worthy of an eyeroll?

Loretta fixed her own eyes on Lord Arthur Sterlington

as he swept her onto the dance floor. He had an exception-
ally handsome face, a glowing head of bronze hair and the
commanding presence that came with such arrow-straight
posture. But as they twirled beneath the shimmering candlelight Loretta was struck with a most unfamiliar and unwanted
thought: she was somehow, inexplicably, undeniably, in the
arms of the wrong Sterlington.

Despite her unreserved disdain for society balls, Lady
Charlotte loved to dance. She adored the cool, crisp feeling of soft silk against her thin stockings, the sweet sensa-
tion of being swept up in the music. She was almost tempted
to join in tonight, but she could never indulge her brother's
hope that *this* would be the season, after twenty-five years
of spurning men's attentions, when she would blossom into
a suitable bride.

The punch table was the most interesting part of the ball
anyway, so she planted herself by an indigo velvet curtain
and sipped from a scandalously full glass, then turned her ear
away from the music towards the flock of gossiping mothers
gawking at the dance floor.

'This is Miss Beaumont's third dance with Mr Stanton,'
muttered a woman in a bright yellow frock. 'I imagine a proposal must be in the works.'

'She's nearing four and twenty,' a woman with a mountain-
ous amber hairstyle chimed in. 'I can't imagine she'd have a
chance beyond this.'

Charlotte clenched her jaw. She knew Arabella Beaumont.
They had never been close friends, but they had shared a passionate two-week affair after meeting at a private party for
Londoners whose romantic tastes could be described as…un-
conventional. Arabella didn't want a husband any more than

Charlotte did, and the thought of what she was giving up to be with Mr Stanton tugged at Charlotte's heart.

But had Charlotte any right to fault her? Women were given few options if they wanted stability, safety, financial security. Charlotte's brother could offer all that *and* a newly bestowed title. With marriage finally on his mind this year, he was bound to make someone very happy. It seemed Miss Linfield was angling to be that person.

The dance ended and a sapphire dress emerged from the crowd, shimmering and incandescent.

'Lady Charlotte,' said the Baron's daughter.

Her curtsy was impeccable—Charlotte knew an etiquette over-achiever when she saw one. The rigid posture, the easy smile and the insistent charade that they were speaking for the first time.

'Miss Linfield.' Charlotte forced a smile. 'Surely you're in need of punch after that performance?'

Loretta tilted her head as the slightest crease appeared between her eyebrows. 'I beg your pardon?'

'Don't tell me you find the company of my brother anything but tiresome? I'd never believe you anyway.'

'I assure you, that was no performance.'

'Well, a glass of punch nonetheless,' she said as she reached for the bowl. 'Allow me.'

Charlotte sank the ladle into the gold-orange liquid for a generous pouring. The crystal glass in her hand caught the flickering light of the chandeliers like a jar of glowworms—a sight lovely enough to divert both ladies' eyes until they rose to meet each other's.

That was when Charlotte noticed, for the first time, that Loretta Linfield was truly gorgeous. Her emerald eyes were striking, her soft smile inviting. Charlotte was certain Loretta would be just as stiff and stodgy as all the other women her brother had courted, but there was no harm in checking—just to be sure.

'I don't remember seeing you last year,' Charlotte said as she handed over the glass. She tried hard to recall if she'd seen her in years prior, but each season was a boring blur in Charlotte's memory.

'I stayed in the country,' Loretta responded. 'I was dreadfully ill.'

'I'm glad to see you're in good health now.'

This was quickly veering into small talk—a ritual that Charlotte worked hard to avoid. She'd give Loretta another minute before giving up and finding someone more interesting to talk to.

'Thank you,' Loretta said. 'I must admit, though, it was quite a lovely break. The season can be so tiresome.' She took a sip of punch. 'This is my third.'

Charlotte's eyebrows rose just slightly. 'Tell me more.'

Loretta tilted her head, looking confused, as if she wasn't used to saying more. Gentlemen didn't often ask for details.

'Well…' Loretta started uncertainly. 'My first season was supposed to end in a match with a viscount, but he—'

'Wait!' Charlotte interjected. 'Let me guess. He impregnated his mistress? Perished in a duel?'

'Goodness, no!' Loretta said with wide eyes.

'Aha! He realised he fancies men?'

'That would certainly have made *my* life easier,' Loretta mumbled. Her hand flew to her mouth. 'Oh, dear! I said that out loud, didn't I?'

Perhaps Loretta was not as boring as Charlotte had thought. 'Is he still after you?' she asked.

'He's not here any more,' Loretta said matter-of-factly. 'He lost his fortune to gambling, then disgraced his reputation with a drunken brawl at a club one night. My father decided he would no longer make a suitable husband. So he left.'

'And you agreed?'

'Excuse me?'

'With your father? That this viscount was no longer a decent suitor?'

Loretta wrinkled her nose. 'Lord Wrottesley was a decent gentleman before his fall from grace, I suppose. We grew up together, so at the time it seemed an easy match...'

She took another sip of punch, small and modest.

'Wrottesley sounds like a pest, and he doesn't deserve someone as exquisite as you.' Charlotte couldn't help herself...flirting with someone so unlikely to notice or reciprocate.

'You're too kind.' Loretta blushed, deflecting the compliment.

Had Charlotte been a man, some might have called her a rake, a rascal, even a scoundrel. But Charlotte was not a man, and there was no equivalent word for women with devilish desires.

There was no word for women with desires at all.

The music must have changed, because once again Loretta was hurrying to check her dance card. These high society ball tunes all sounded the same to Charlotte—sweet and mellow, like a cup of tea with too much sugar.

Loretta curtsied again, deep and slow. 'It's been a pleasure speaking to you, Lady Charlotte, but I must be off to my next dance.'

'It is my sincere hope that we don't meet again,' Charlotte said, and winked.

Loretta's eyes opened wide with astonishment. She looked much like a doe caught before a carriage.

'For that would mean that you've found a better suitor than my brother,' Charlotte continued.

The tall, slender woman in the deep blue dress blinked away her confusion and disappeared into the whirlwind of swaying silks and satins.

Charlotte had never considered herself the type to have a type, but if she had it wouldn't be Loretta Linfield. The Lorettas of the world were just too perfect. Beautiful, yes, but the kind of beautiful that left no stray hair uncombed. There was no glint of mischief in her eyes…no secret gap in her dance card for a tryst on the terrace.

Not that Charlotte looked much different from her tonight. From a distance, the dainty pearl beading at her neckline and the golden ringlets that framed her face made her indistinguishable from any other member of polite society. She knew how to dress the part—but the illusion was always shattered the moment she opened her mouth to speak.

'Ladies and gentlemen,' boomed the voice of Dudley Stanton, interrupting the music. 'It is with great pleasure that I must interject…' he paused for dramatic effect, a favourite conversational strategy of his '…to announce the happy news that Miss Arabella Beaumont and I are to be wed.'

The room erupted in applause, well-wishes and travelling trays of freshly poured champagne.

There was often a knot in Charlotte's stomach at these events, but it had just tightened beyond what she could bear. Her feet moved swiftly through the ballroom, her eyes staring straight ahead as she passed her brother and declared, louder than she'd intended, 'I've caught a chill. I'm taking the carriage.'

She reached for a glass of champagne and downed it on her way out the door.

Charlotte had never cared for rank, but there was something cruel about the knowledge that even a third son like

Dudley Stanton stood a better chance of landing Miss Beaumont than she did. Such was her fate.

The crisp air and the musty smell of horses was a balm to her senses, grounding her in the wideness of the world outside that ballroom. Sure enough, by the time she'd reached her carriage and settled in for the short ride home, Lady Charlotte Sterlington had done what she always did: forgotten. This engagement was no different from those that would happen all season.

Tired and numb, she dozed off to the sound of wheels on stone, then lazily climbed the stairs to her bedchamber and exhaled all her tension as her maid unlaced her bodice. While the sameness of nights like this exasperated her, the sameness of returning to her cosy bedsheets was a true comfort indeed.

Slowly but surely, the knot in her stomach unraveled.

It was simply another ball, Charlotte reminded herself, where nothing extraordinary had come to pass. She had once again spent an evening on the suffocating stage of society, where no one was diverted from their well-worn scripts and every stock character was played to perfection. This night would fade with sleep, as so many others had, and life would return the next morning unchanged.

Of this she was certain.

Chapter Two

An overlooked benefit of being a baron's daughter was the house full of treasures a baron needed to compensate for bearing the lowest rank of the peerage.

Loretta's morning walk from her bedchamber to the library was a tour of European art: the moody shadows of Rembrandt, the spacious landscapes of Callcott and the colourful bouquets of Moser all greeted her from elegant frames as she descended the wide stairs.

In the parlour hung field sketches of rare birds and peculiar plants, observed on the many expeditions her father was known to sponsor. The curio cabinet displayed a solid gold snuff box encrusted in rubies that had once belonged to the last King of Sicily—or so the Baron said.

At the landing, she paused to tilt her head upwards and take in the magnificent portrait that commanded the wall and shrank all other paintings by comparison. Her own face looked down at her with a visage of superiority she had practised in the mirror but never quite mastered. This Loretta stood confident and firm as the Roman pillar beside her, elegant and dainty as the English roses bordering the scene. Her slender figure and full breasts—a bit more slender and a bit more full than those of the Loretta who stood on the staircase landing—were draped in a flowing dress of finest silk, the deep purple of old royalty.

In the shadow of this perfect Loretta's glowing skin and effortless beauty, and the tightly styled hair that spilled no stray curl, the Loretta of the unpainted world felt bare. Inadequate. Scrutinised by a better version of herself. This was the image she was meant to portray and, with effort, the image she would someday become.

She continued on. The drawing room boasted porcelain vases of all shapes and sizes, a thick Persian rug and a tea set from France. The centrepiece was a large bust of Artemis gifted by an archaeologist whose success in Greece had cemented the Baron's legacy as a great patron of the natural sciences.

Loretta's father had filled his London townhouse with discoveries of extraordinary beauty and significance—and he truly appreciated none of them beyond the role they played in elevating his social status.

But Loretta was different. She never tired of marvelling at all the world had brought to her door. She revered the idiosyncrasies of her home, each room a chapel to the mysteries of life outside England—a life she'd become most acquainted with in her favourite room of all: the library.

'Good morning, Gulliver,' Loretta said to the taxidermy puffin in the corner. It wasn't her favourite of her father's acquisitions but, like most things in her life, she had learned to make peace with it.

Loretta settled into her mauve chaise longue, well worn to the shape of her body, and resumed the third volume of *A Simple Story* that sat on the end table. The floor-to-ceiling bookshelves towered over her, a forest of polished oak that bore poetry and prose, fiction and history, sermons and science. The collection was massive, but she knew the location of all her favourites by heart: *Robinson Crusoe* on the fourth shelf by the back window, *Northanger Abbey* behind the comically large globe, *Letters Written During a Short Residence in Sweden, Norway and Denmark* at eye level over the writing desk that held the very quill used—allegedly—by the Archbishop of Canterbury to sign the *Magna Carta.*

Though the morning had only just begun, Loretta was not two pages into her reading when her lady's maid entered with a thick bouquet of pink peonies, white roses and Queen Anne's lace.

'Just delivered by the Duke's own footman,' Bridget gushed as she set the freshly watered vase next to Loretta.

Bridget was a true romantic—so much so that Loretta couldn't tell if her giddiness was from Loretta's sudden prospects or a flirtatious exchange with the footman.

'These are lovely.' Loretta reluctantly set down her book. Flowers meant there would eventually be callers, and callers meant she wouldn't have time to read. 'Thank you, Bridget. Are you well this morning?'

'I am indeed.' Bridget brushed a strand of honey-coloured hair out of her face, then peered around the room conspiratorially before she continued. 'There were quite a few bouquets this morning—*ten*, to be exact—but just last week Mr Gillingham made *advances* to his sister's maid, who *promptly* found new employment with the Fitzroys and told their housekeeper, but was *overheard* by a gardener who told one of *our* footmen at the ball last night, who told Margaret—you know Margaret…the new kitchen maid—who told *me* this morning. And last I counted you had just *nine* bouquets, because I seem to have *lost* the one Mr Gillingham sent.'

Bridget exhaled as Loretta clutched her hand and smiled. 'I don't know what I'd do without you, Bridget. Everyone else's credentials are clean?'

'As far as I know—and if anyone would know it's me. The rest of the flowers are in the drawing room with your father, who requests your presence for tea and biscuits.'

Loretta could practically hear *A Simple Story* calling her from the table, longing to be held. Poets often wrote about the tender embrace of their lovers, but when Loretta read those words all she could think of was cradling a good book in her arms.

She stood tall and entered the drawing room.

The Baron looked up from his paper with a wide grin. 'It is a good morning to be a Linfield indeed!'

The overwhelming scent of a hundred flowers consumed Loretta. Colourful bouquets crowded the room, each one fashioned with a note from a suitor. Loretta sneezed.

Her father kept on reading the paper as he spoke. 'I can't say I'm surprised. There's not a lady in London with the poise, grace and sophistication that you have. Not unlike your mother in her season.'

Loretta smiled to hide her surprise—Bertram Linfield didn't mention his wife very often. 'You're too kind,' she said, and took a seat near him.

They were alone again for the London season. Elaine Linfield rarely left the country estate.

'Twice as many invitations arrived in the post. I sorted the ones who sent flowers—don't bother with the others. But if I'm being frank, the only invitation *truly* worth entertaining is the Duke of Colchester's.'

Loretta flipped through the stack of calling cards requesting her company for a promenade, a horse race, a night at the opera… She took special notice of the heavy cream paper on which *The Most Noble Duke of Colchester* was printed in an elegant font.

'We'll be going to Somerset House the day after next for

the latest exhibition,' Lord Linfield continued. 'You'll be there to win the Duke, and I'll be there to win the latest Nathaniel Fletcher painting and be the envy of Mayfair.'

'If a husband is something I'm meant to *win*, the way one wins an auction or a horse race, you must be terribly disappointed in how many seasons I've *lost*.'

She reached for her teacup. She was fond of the porcelain set that was out today—an eccentric collection of cups with handles shaped like butterfly wings.

'That's my fault more than yours, I assure you,' her father said as he bit into a lemon shortbread biscuit.

Usually mothers played the role of matchmaker in a young woman's life, but after one too many nervous breakdowns the Baroness had been prescribed a perpetual stay in the clean country air of the Linfield ancestral home.

Bertram folded his newspaper and sprang from his chair. He was spry and eager, even as his hair turned grey, and his every movement conveyed urgency—as though he were perpetually on the brink of discovery.

'My scientific exploits have diverted my attention long enough—this shall be the season you wed.'

And with that, the Baron left the room.

Loretta finished her sugary black tea as she read through the notes on each calling card.

They were lovely invitations, and they would make for entertaining outings. Then again, if her father was serious about the Duke, and the Duke was serious about her, it would not be wise to traipse around London with all these suitors.

All these suitors...

She grew light-headed as she tried to comprehend her own popularity—a trophy she had neither asked nor tried for.

She sneezed again.

'Not unlike your mother...' The Baron's words echoed.

The details Loretta knew of her mother's one and only season were sparse. Elaine had been beautiful, and sought-after, but her family had had no money for a proper dowry. They'd had a title, but no sons, no nephews, no male cousins. The Linfields had had nothing *but* sons, and enough money that gaining a title for Bertram was dowry enough. Elaine had many suitors, but Loretta was fairly certain that her mother never had a real choice.

She put her thoughts aside and returned to her bedchamber. She'd long ago made peace with the shambles of her parents' marriage, and the frail countenance and bottles of laudanum that fastened her mother to their country home.

In the shine of her giltwood mirror, she looked like no one but herself.

'The house smells like a garden today,' Bridget remarked as she wove ribbons into the waves of Loretta's hair.

'It won't for long,' Loretta said. 'This happens every year at the start of the season, and every year these men are snatched up by ladies with *real* motivation before I even get around to thanking them for their flowers.'

'There's nothing wrong with waiting for someone who truly catches your eye.' Bridget smiled. 'In the meantime, of *course* you'll attract suitors. Just look at you.'

Loretta straightened her posture and stared into the mirror. Her hair was long and graceful, flowing over her shoulders like a gentle stream. She had strong cheekbones, a dainty nose, a smooth, angular face. And her eyes… They were the most striking thing about her—not soft and muted, like moss, but bold and daring, like poison ivy.

'Thank you, Bridget.' Loretta sniffed, holding in another sneeze so she didn't ruin Bridget's handiwork. 'I know I'd make an excellent wife. I've done everything and become everything a lady is supposed to do and be… But every time a gentleman is interested, I just— *Ouch!*'

Bridget had found a tangle in Loretta's hair.

'I just don't find myself particularly interested in *him*.'

'I cannot fathom the loss of a dance card as anything other than a blessing,' Lady Sterlington had said at the ball.

It was the first time Loretta had heard anyone say out loud what she often thought to herself. And Lady Charlotte hadn't stopped there—she had given Loretta the opportunity to join her.

'I merely saw you evading the night's festivities and wondered if I'd found someone as fatigued by society as I.'

What if Loretta had said yes? What if she had confessed her fatigue and run off like the heroine in one of her adventure novels, leaving the ball and all its boring gentlemen behind?

An unfamiliar excitement stirred in her heart.

'So long as you avoid the likes of Mr Gillingham, I'm certain you'll find yourself in an agreeable marriage, no matter who you choose,' said Bridget.

'I'm not sure it will be much of a choice this year. My father has practically set his *own* cap at the Duke.'

Bridget giggled. 'It would be hard to do better than a *duke*.'

Indeed, there was no arguing with the fact that the Honourable Miss Loretta Linfield and the Duke of Colchester could have an agreeable marriage. And so long as she had a library full of wild romances and daring adventures, perhaps an agreeable marriage would be enough.

'It's just…' Charlotte mumbled as she inspected the latest figure in her sketchbook. 'It's not there yet.'

Her eyes scoured the page for imperfections like a hawk hunting mice in the wild. She'd captured Renée's sombre pose, leaning softly on the kitchen table and staring wistfully into the distance. Thick charcoal lines traced the folds of her skirt and apron, the arch of her nose, the delicate curve of her shoulders. It was suitable from a technical perspective, but something was just…*missing.*

'Renée, would you tilt your head up this much?' Charlotte stretched out her hand, her thumb and index finger half an inch apart. 'Yes, excellent. Now, set your eyes to look directly at me.'

Renée had a fierce and fearless gaze—the kind a person doesn't develop by accident. She held her pose unflinchingly as the rest of the kitchen staff swirled around them, carrying trays of food, filling pots and raising their eyebrows furtively at Charlotte.

And why shouldn't they? Here was the Duke's own sister, perched on a stool in the kitchen, with her skirts hiked up and her shoulders hunched over a sketchbook. She paused every few minutes to wipe the charcoal from her hands, dusting them on the dark grey dress that a proper lady would save only for mourning. But charcoal was indeed a kind of death… the charred corpse of a willow branch finding afterlife on an artist's page.

Charlotte wore the dress while sketching for the practicality of its colour, but also in protest of its very existence. For someone who had a far greater need for funeral garb than anyone should have had, to dirty it now would be to declare, *I won't need to wear this again any time soon.*

Renée had been with the Sterlingtons for just a few months, but she and Charlotte had quickly grown fond of each other and had got into a fair bit of mischief by helping each other sneak out for nights on the town.

The Duke was quite vocal with his disapproval.

'You spend God knows how many hours downstairs, bond-

ing with the servants, as if there isn't a perfectly decent group of gentlemen and ladies waiting in the hall!'

He was also quite easy to ignore.

Renée had become a muse, her long neck and tight black curls a worthy stand-in for the models that real artists—or, more precisely, *male* artists—would hire for their master-pieces.

'I saw Lady Cadogan at the ball last night,' Charlotte re-marked with an impish smile.

Renée, bless her, didn't react to the mention of her vile former employer, her face placid and smooth, so she could be drawn with ease. But Charlotte was after something else.

Something organic.

Something real.

'She was wearing a most *gaudy* maroon dress, with far too many layers and those unfashionably bulbous sleeves…and with those green feathers in her hair I dare say she looked like a bushel of beets.'

The corner of Renée's mouth rose in vengeful amusement, and the dimple in her cheek was like a soft thumbprint in a ball of dough. The change was barely perceptible, but it trans-formed the entire piece.

'Damn…' Charlotte whispered as she turned the charcoal over in her fingers, the chalky black stick too thick to illus-trate the subtle movement of muscle that had produced such an elusive smile.

'Lady Charlotte?' A stern-looking footman strode into the room, hands folded tightly behind his back. 'Your brother re-quests your presence upstairs.'

'Unable to find me himself, I see.' Charlotte blew the ex-cess soot from her page and closed the book, tucking it safely into the bottom of a linen drawer. 'He was always rotten at hide and seek.'

Charlotte climbed the stairs to find a brother who most definitely knew where she was hiding, but was far too snobbish to set foot in the kitchen himself.

She entered his study and rolled her eyes at the disappointed look on his face.

'Dearest Charlotte—' he shot from behind his desk '—the time to pack away your mourning gown was nearly six months ago.'

'I'm mourning all the more interesting things I could be doing if I weren't talking to you,' she said, with a voice sharp as vinegar.

Charlotte crossed her arms over her chest and watched the flame in her brother's eyes dim from hot irritation to lukewarm sadness.

'I've given you everything you could possibly want in this house,' he said slowly. 'And someday you shall have a husband who does the same.'

Arthur was not a wicked man. Charlotte could say with confidence that his morality towered above the likes of men like Mr Gillingham, the villain of the *ton*'s latest gossip. She knew her brother was as virtuous and chivalrous as any bride-to-be could hope for, but damn him for caring so much about his title and the social order that allowed him to profit from it.

Charlotte softened her gaze and sat in the chair across from him. She smiled at the portrait of her late father that hung above the fireplace.

'I've called you here to go over our schedule for the day after next,' the Duke said. 'You'll be chaperoning an outing between me and Miss Linfield.'

Charlotte opened her mouth to protest, but he continued.

'Before you complain, we'll be visiting Somerset House for their latest exhibition. Nathaniel will appreciate seeing us.

And you enjoy the arts, yes? You're always scribbling away in that book of yours.'

'I can't imagine I'll get the chance to enjoy much art while playing the role of watchful chaperone,' she countered. 'Is there truly no maid or aunt or cousin who is free?'

'Oh, there are plenty. But you need to see what a proper courtship looks like—and the gentlemen gathered at Somerset House need to see you. Father may have permitted your dawdling in the marriage mart, but I am the head of this household now, and it's my responsibility to see you respectably wed.'

And with that he rose from his chair, checked his pocket watch and marched to the door.

'It is time to see and be seen, Charlotte Sterlington,' he said on his way out. 'See and be seen.'

Charlotte sank back in her chair with a heavy sigh and gazed up at the portrait of her father. 'Oh, I *do* miss you,' she mumbled, catching a sob in the back of her throat and smothering it before it could escape. She sensed the rising tide of grief and left her brother's study before it dampened her soul.

Upstairs in her bedchamber, Charlotte's lady maid helped her out of the mourning dress and into something proper—a sage-green frock with delicate lace fern pattern throughout the skirt. When the mile of buttons on her back were finally fastened, and the large silk bow tied, she slipped out into the gardens behind the townhouse that her mother had once been so fond of. She strolled through the rows of hedges, along the stone path with its marble columns, and ascended the slight hill that would put her just out of sight from the back windows.

It was true that Arthur had never been skilled at hide and seek when they were children, but even the best of seekers would struggle to find someone who had had so much practice in hiding.

So Charlotte disappeared into the green...to where she always went when she didn't want to be found.

Chapter Three

Loretta would have been more than happy to accompany her father to Somerset House and join the Duke upon arrival, but the Baron had insisted she accept a ride in the Duke's carriage.

Glancing out through the window now, as the opulent black coach pulled up with its shiny red wheels and instantly recognisable family crest, Loretta understood it was the sight of the Sterlington family four-in-hand outside their townhouse that her father had desired—not the lack of company.

She gathered the skirts of her muslin day dress—creamy white with delicate pink embroidery and modestly puffed sleeves. Her copper hair was twisted elegantly to the top of her head, where it mingled with rose-coloured ribbons and bands of pearls, leaving two expertly sculpted ringlets to frame her lean face. Bridget placed a paisley shawl on her shoulders as a footman announced the coach's arrival, and Loretta stepped out to meet the early spring chill.

The Most Noble Lord Arthur Sterlington stood tall and cheerful by the carriage door, ready to take Loretta's hand and guide her up.

All of Mayfair seemed to be out for a stroll today—she could feel the heat of their curious stares, see their necks craning over fans in approval or jealousy or eager observation.

A stately coachman in elegant garb commanded the team of

hardy Cleveland Bays, uniformly reddish brown, with an air of dignity that suggested an awareness of their owner's rank.

'Miss Linfield,' the Duke said with a cordial smile. 'A radiant sight on such a dreary day as this.'

'You are too kind, my lord,' she responded reflexively.

'And you are too modest.'

Modesty came easily to Loretta. She'd always been effortlessly unaware of her own beauty—a virtue that compelled her to deflect even the most well-deserved of compliments. As a young girl she had once been chastised by her governess for looking in the mirror too long, and such self-admiration—or self-consideration, for that matter—had never seemed worth the trouble again.

Inside, the coach was dim and cosy, with velvet seats and gold-fringed curtains. So cosy, in fact, that it appeared to have lulled Lady Charlotte Sterlington to sleep.

'Don't mind my sister.'

The Duke nodded at the ocean-blue cloak in the corner, rising and falling to the slow rhythm of slumbrous breath. Lady Charlotte's face was half-covered by a thick woollen hood, her features uncharacteristically calm and gentle.

'No need to whisper on her account,' he continued. 'Wellington's own battalion couldn't wake her.'

A hundred questions raced through Loretta's head.

Had there been a ball last night?

How late must one be out to be asleep past noon?

Were these the kind of manners that had got Lady Charlotte so far in life without a husband?

But she blinked the questions away and turned her attention to the Duke.

'Are you an admirer of the arts, Your Grace?'

He broke into a bashful grin. 'I must confess little interest. But a good friend of mine has a painting in this month's exhibition. And from what your father tells me, you are quite the lady of culture.'

'I am of the opinion that there are few better things a lady could be,' Loretta said, reciting her old schoolroom adage.

'Then I have much about art to learn from you today,' said the Duke.

Charlotte released a thunderous snore.

Loretta jumped in her seat.

The Duke sat still as a statue, as though nothing at all had occurred.

They soon eased to a stop in the shadow of Somerset House's towering stone walls. Misty daylight poured into the carriage as the coachman opened the door. The Duke's sister jerked upwards, groaned loudly, and then—Loretta couldn't believe her eyes—*scowled.*

In their two interactions Charlotte Sterlington had managed to break every good habit of etiquette that Loretta had spent her whole life perfecting. This threw Loretta into a restless current of emotions which, due in part to the aforementioned good habits of etiquette, she could neither identify nor express.

The trio moved through the bustling courtyard and into the grand entrance hall. Loretta smiled at the playful centaurs who flanked the staircase. She took comfort in their stone faces, which could neither gawk nor whisper as she passed by. But even the attention of everyone who *wasn't* a statue was short-lived. The galleries of Somerset House were known to overwhelm the senses—even the most riveting gossip could not compete with the opulent paintings and grandiose sculptures that filled each room.

The clouds had just begun to part as Loretta stepped into the main exhibition room—a visual feast of paint and marble and gentle sunlight. A majestic life-sized portrait of Aphrodite claimed pride of place on the centre wall. The Greek goddess lounged half-naked in an airy meadow, her sandy blonde hair speckled with daisies.

A quick glance around the room confirmed for Loretta the prestige of this small but sumptuous exhibition, not nearly as crowded as the annual summer exhibition the Royal Academy was most famous for but every bit as impressive.

'A breathtaking piece,' the Duke remarked as he followed Loretta's gaze to the room's centrepiece.

'Oh, *Arthur…*' Charlotte sighed. 'If every painting of a bare, expressionless woman reclining in the woods is to take your breath away, I'm afraid you'll suffocate within the hour!'

Loretta clenched her jaw and resolved to spend the day entirely unbothered by Lady Charlotte's undignified behaviour.

Today the Duke's sister wore a striking gown of indigo silk layered with silver netting. A band of shimmering beads encircled her empire waistline, and a pair of dramatic silver gloves reflected the light from the room's high windows. Her glossy hair burst forth in wild ringlets from beneath a grey high-brimmed poke bonnet, the like of which was usually only worn indoors by married women and spinsters.

In the centre of this mane of curls was a soft round face, with gentle features that sloped into each other like melting snowbanks. It seemed her full pink lips couldn't decide if they wanted to smile or smirk at the room full of art. And her eyes… *How to describe her eyes?* Greyish blue or bluish grey. They held within them all the colours of the sea.

If realising that Charlotte was an Aphrodite in her own right wasn't enough to make Loretta blush, realising how long she'd been staring at her chaperone certainly was.

She quickly followed the Duke around the perimeter and dutifully stopped when he did, with his sister lagging behind and genuinely studying each work of art. They made light conversation as they gazed upon scenes from Waterloo and portraits of royalty, busts of philosophers and the occasional country landscape. While the Duke occasionally asked her thoughts on an exhibit, he mostly discussed the politics and particularities of the Dukedom in such vague and opaque terms that Loretta could hardly discern what it was a duke actually did.

While Loretta was not the type to insult a gentleman with accusations of boredom, she would at least admit—if only to herself—that the Duke's stories could not compete with the books in her father's library.

'But this!' His voice leapt in sudden excitement. 'This is what I have come to see.'

The trio converged upon a tall, lanky man with the dark ruffled hair and moody countenance one expected of an artist—a man who must be Nathaniel Fletcher. He stood beside a portrait of a woman that seemed, at first, to resemble every other portrait in the gallery. To the left of her opulent frame hung a triumphant portrayal of men and their horses charging into war, to the right, a sober depiction of young David standing over Goliath's body.

The Bible and the battlefield might be this era's favoured subjects for fine art, but the most enduring muse ever to grace the painter's canvas and the sculptor's clay had always been the woman. And row upon row they sat in their frames, charming and soft and enticingly untouchable.

They were the guaranteed guests of honour on any exhibition wall, draped in layers of royal cloth or bathing naked in a stream. Loretta pondered the timeless beauty of their rosy cheeks, their shiny curls, the slight lift of their unassuming smiles. She had never wondered if there was a different way to paint a woman until this moment, as she locked eyes with the subject of Mr Fletcher's grand portrait.

She sat in a winter garden, against a cloudy sky. Thorny black branches sagged under the weight of snow in a simple white-grey background that was interrupted, sharply and strongly, by a dazzling blue coat and a yard of tumbling orange hair. The quiet, placid smile Loretta had come to expect from portraits of women was replaced by a defiant smirk, with one corner of her pink lips lifted into a crease. The difference was subtle—unnoticeable from across the room but unmistakable from a few steps away. One fiery eyebrow was raised in a modest arch, her chin was tilted up and her misty grey eyes glanced down in amusement. Loretta felt that *she* was being examined by the woman in the portrait, not the other way round.

'I think it's strange,' Charlotte said bluntly.

Loretta snapped from her dizzying trance and gaped at the Duke's sister. Charlotte wasn't wrong—the woman was indeed stranger than her exhibit counterparts—but she was so much more. She was graceful, and challenging, and bold.

But the strangest thing, Loretta thought, was the pang in her chest that kept tightening the longer she looked at the painted woman. She wanted to stand in her gaze for ever, despite how it made her squirm.

'Always my most trusted critic,' Mr Fletcher said with a laugh.

'It is a daring choice indeed,' mused the Duke. 'But your mastery of the brush is undeniable. A truly marvellous work.'

Charlotte rolled her eyes and tilted her head to one side. 'The colours are quite clashing. It distracts from her face.'

Loretta felt the Duke's hand land gently on her elbow. 'My sister and I,' he explained, 'are old childhood friends of the Fletchers. Our London estates are next to each other.' He turned back to Nathaniel and continued, 'Do tell us about your piece, dear friend.'

The painter nodded earnestly and cleared his throat. 'I sought to capture the eternal warmth of the feminine spirit by positioning my subject within a biting London winter. It is only in the contrast between the barren snow and the female's nurturing, motherly nature that we come to appreciate the beauty that is earned in the face of suffering.'

The Duke squinted. 'Yes, I do see that quite clearly…'

'I have never heard such nonsense, Nathaniel,' Charlotte cut in.

'And you claim to know better?' challenged her brother. 'Your childish sketchbook makes you an artist no more than a saddle would make you a horse.'

Heat flashed across Charlotte's face as the siblings lost themselves to bickering, their tones hushed in awareness of the public's prying ears. It was amidst this bitter exchange that Loretta felt the painter's eyes on her, kind and tender and more than a little curious.

He spoke up. 'Miss Linfield, I would love to hear your thoughts.'

The Duke and his sister surrendered their fight to an apologetic silence. Loretta had barely spoken since they arrived, and her throat had gone dry. She inhaled slowly.

'I feel as though I know her.'

The two gentlemen blinked, their faces puzzled. That might have been enough to dam Loretta's stream of thoughts, which was always rushing beneath the surface but never shared. It might have been enough, that was, if not for the smile that curved into Charlotte's round face like a crescent moon in the early dawn sky.

And all at once, beneath that moon, Loretta's thoughts and wants and very being were as helpless as the tides.

'What I mean to say is, she's asking us to know her,' Loretta continued, pulled onward by Charlotte's encouraging eyes.

She had spent so much of her life observing the paintings,

books and artifacts from her father's collection, but she had never voiced those observations out loud.

'There are many portraits I admire, but I am often left with questions about the subject. What is she like? Is she clever? Is she meek? Is she witty? How does she feel in this moment? And does she know how marvellous she is?'

The orange-haired beauty with her impish grin and defiant posture seemed to look out at Loretta with approval.

'Mr Fletcher, this lady does not leave me asking if she is joyful or frightened or tired. She is showing us who she is with the bend of her brow, the tilt of her chin. She wants more than to be seen—she wants to be known.'

Loretta took a breath, and the confidence that had lifted her spirit vanished as quickly as it had come. She felt a great and mighty blush flood her face, her neck, the tips of her ears. She coughed lightly and opened her fan.

'That is certainly an interesting observa—' began the Duke.

His sister interrupted. 'I could not agree with Miss Linfield more.' Charlotte beamed, for the briefest of moments, and then settled back into the cynical countenance she wore so well.

Loretta buzzed with the unfamiliar thrill of speaking her mind. She wondered if it was something she would like to try again, and if it was a quality the Duke would enjoy in a wife. But for now she thought it best to return to her usual quiet demeanour. She knew how to nod along to the lengthy monologues of men, how to appear interested in their endless pontification. The routine was comforting in its familiarity, and she let it carry her through the day.

The Duke's sister, Loretta noticed, had no such routine. When she grew bored with her brother's commentary she openly rolled her eyes. When they approached sculptures and paintings of naked women Charlotte would grumble *'No one actually looks like that...'* from behind her fan. Loretta had promised herself she would not let Charlotte's impoliteness bother her, but as the day went on it wasn't feeling *bothered* that she had to worry about. She was, instead, intrigued.

And that was much worse.

As they left the building she heard the booming voice of her father describing how he had helped fund the invention of waterproof fabric. She squinted into the early-afternoon sunlight and found him chatting on the steps to another man. She craned her neck to see him…

Her stomach dropped as she recognized the thick black hair, broad shoulders and prominent chin of Cecil Wrottesley. She shivered, her body a snuffed candle, the pleasantness of the day a trail of smoke.

She pulled her shawl tightly around her.

'Miss Linfield! Your father!' the Duke exclaimed, as if the entire street couldn't hear the distinct voice of the Baron. 'How delightful. Shall we?'

Loretta let herself be guided down the steps, dread prickling at her skin. She kept her eyes low and tried not to trip.

'Your Grace!' the Baron bellowed, and reached out his hand. 'Always an honour when our paths cross. A fine day made even finer by your presence.'

'You are too kind,' the Duke said.

Loretta glanced up to see his bashful smile. He might be a rather boring conversationalist, but at least he was humble and polite—what more could Loretta ask for in a husband?

'I was just speaking with an old friend.' The Baron gestured towards Cecil. 'Or really, the son of an old friend. Lord Wrottesley, here, is in the prime of his life! And now he's full of stories from his adventures abroad.'

'Your Grace.' Cecil bowed dramatically, and Loretta knew when he arose he'd be looking at her. Her stomach was a whirlpool. She lifted her eyes.

'A pleasure to meet you,' the Duke said.

But Cecil was looking at Loretta. He stood taller than she remembered. More confident. His navy tailcoat with gleaming gold buttons looked expensive, and his stark white cravat aggressively reflected the light of the sun.

'It has been some time,' Cecil said with a flirtatious half grin.

Loretta extended her arm and silently thanked the weaver, the seamstress and the shopkeeper responsible for the glove that shielded her hand from Cecil's lips.

'It certainly has,' Loretta responded, and forced a smile of her own. She was supposed to have had more time before his return from exile—had it really taken him just three years to rebuild his fortune?

She turned then in search of Charlotte, to stand with and discuss womanly things so the gentlemen would forget they were even there. But Charlotte was long gone, having found another group—a more interesting group, most likely—to chat with on the other side of the stairs. Loretta ached to join her.

'He arrived from Rome earlier this week,' the Baron said. 'I'll be sending a dinner invitation shortly. I'm sure Loretta would love to hear about your travels!'

Loretta forced herself to face Cecil again and nodded. 'That sounds delightful.' Her voice was reliably sweet, years of practice coming to save her when she couldn't muster genuine affection.

'I apologise that I can't stay,' the Duke said. 'I have business to which I must attend after I escort Loretta home.'

Loretta noticed Cecil's charming visage wavered, resentment flashing across his eyes as he stared down at the Duke. It only lasted a second, and then his face was just as it had been before. They said their goodbyes, but Loretta didn't exhale until the carriage door was closed.

Charlotte sat with them, and Loretta was grateful for her presence. She wanted to say something smart, or witty—something that would make Charlotte react as she had in the gallery. She had *seen* Loretta, and her curious eyes indicated that she wanted to see more.

Instead, Loretta shrank into the corner of the carriage. She wasn't sure what there even *was* to see. She knew that when her father looked at her he saw the continuation of his success—potential generations of heirs and geniuses, patrons of the arts and sciences. When Cecil looked at her he saw redemption—a bride to reconfirm his standing in society, the final jewel in his homecoming crown.

When the Duke looked at her she hoped he saw a duchess. But as for his sister… *She* peered right into the core of Loretta's being—a place unfamiliar to even Loretta herself.

What would Charlotte find if she kept looking? Would she be disappointed if nothing of worth was there?

Loretta barely made it to her bedroom before her calm composure cracked. This was supposed to be a simple season—court the Duke of Colchester, get married and be done with the drudgery of the marriage mart for the rest of her life. It had taken mere hours for the season to become anything but simple.

She collapsed on her bed.

The first new variable she had to contend with was Cecil's return. He'd be angling for her hand in marriage, just as he had promised he would when he'd left all those years ago. And although Loretta so rarely knew what she wanted, she was confident in what she *didn't* want—a life as Lady Wrottesley.

The second variable was fuzzy…a vague, but still unpleasant feeling that she didn't want a life as the Duchess of Colchester either. The Duke was everything she'd been told to dream of in a husband, so why…?

Why doesn't my heart beat faster when I see him? Loretta wondered.

The signs of infatuation were supposed to blossom. She worried that there was something wrong with her that she never missed the gentlemen she courted when they weren't in the room.

But this was nonsense. She should be grateful even to be *considered* by the Duke.

She said it out loud, daring it to be true. 'I want to marry the Duke of Colchester.'

The words tasted bitter and strange. They spilled uncomfortably from her tongue.

She tried again. 'I am *enamoured* of His Grace.'

Just as bitter, just as strange.

'I have…' she spoke more stubbornly this time, as a governess might to an unruly pupil '…*romantic feelings* for Arthur.'

She placed her hands over her face. Against her better judgement she beckoned forth the image of Charlotte standing by Mr Fletcher's painting, beaming at her as she spoke her mind.

Loretta trembled. She sat up. She paced around the room. She could bring herself back to relative calm if she counted the window panes or recited an old poem, but the moment she thought of Charlotte Sterlington her heart leapt back into her ears and that pang in her chest tightened anew.

If the second variable was a whisper, then this third variable was barely a thought. She didn't know what it meant, but she knew it to be true: she wanted to stand in Charlotte's gaze again, despite—or because of—how it made her squirm.

Chapter Four

Charlotte Sterlington was nestled high in the branches of a walnut tree when the Duke bellowed from the balcony that they would be leaving for their promenade imminently and that Charlotte *must make haste*. She had been perched in this particular tree for nearly an hour and felt herself to be one with the bark, as though her very being had been grafted onto the trunk.

She let out a heavy sigh and slowly peeled her body from the gentle arms of her mother's garden. She closed her eyes and imagined she was an overgrown branch being carefully pruned from this old and mighty walnut tree.

The sound of the balcony door slamming shut elicited an eyeroll from Charlotte. 'Really,' she muttered into the sweet-smelling air. 'There's no need for dramatics.'

The climb down was cautious and clumsy, as Charlotte was still learning to navigate the garden in a dress. From when she was a child until her father had died there had been blissful tolerance for trousers in the privacy of their own home. So long as the garden had no visitors she could run and leap and tumble and climb in the kind of clothes that made running and leaping and tumbling and climbing easy.

'*There are only two Sterlingtons left,*' her brother had said on the carriage ride home from their father's funeral. *'And neither can afford to be strange.'*

All her trousers had been thrown into the fireplace that very day.

Charlotte hopped from the bottom branch and strolled past the brightly coloured pansies and sunny daffodils, the stunning white birch trees and drooping willows, the marble bird bath and the many Grecian statues. Everything was just as her mother had left it, trimmed and polished to preserve its original design. It was as close to a true wilderness garden as you could find in the heart of the city, with a winding layout far more common in country gardens. And to Charlotte it was a memorial as well—an altar to the botanist that the late Duchess of Colchester might have become.

As Charlotte ascended the steps to the house she could feel her grief drifting down like an autumn leaf to the base of her belly, where it lived most days unbothered. There it would stay like a sleeping beast until something awakened it, breaking her heart all over again for her mother, Catherine; her father, Joseph; and that other ghost, the one whose name she could not say.

Inside, the house was bustling with activity as the staff prepared for the exclusive dinner party to be held the day after next. Mrs Grant, their long-time housekeeper, was sparing no expense in dressing up the house for its first big event of the year. If Miss Linfield eventually agreed to marry Arthur, no doubt Mrs Grant would smile and say it was because she wanted to live in such a well-kept house.

There were many reasons Loretta might be wooed into Arthur's arms. Charlotte had wondered if her brief moment of outspokenness in the gallery would prove constant, but the rest of their day at Somerset House had convinced Charlotte that Loretta would make a decent match for her brother after all—Loretta was just like every other society lady, and Arthur was just like every other society gentleman.

A stern glance from Mrs Grant sent Charlotte flying up to her bedchamber. There were few people in this world who could inspire obedience in Charlotte, and none so quickly as Mrs Grant.

As much as Charlotte despised the pageantry of the season, she secretly appreciated the effort Mrs Grant put into making sure Charlotte didn't make a complete fool of herself each day. The woman had practically raised her after her mother had died, so Charlotte didn't complain as the maids stripped her of her garden gown, stuffed her into a boneless corset and laced her into a respectable day dress.

She hurried downstairs, transformed into someone worthy of being called a duke's sister.

Arthur's face, initially pinched in impatience, softened the moment he laid eyes on Charlotte. 'You look…marvellous.' He offered her an uncharacteristically sentimental smile.

'Don't sound so surprised,' Charlotte said with a wink.

'I've never doubted your place as the very diamond of London—only your willingness to claim it.' Arthur wore a proud smile on his face above the standard dark blue jacket and white cravat ensemble that made him blend into the crowd.

Charlotte raised her chin and extended her hand to be helped into the carriage. 'Your Grace…' she intoned as her brother removed his top hat and bowed comically low, taking her hand.

It felt nice to play like this, the way they'd used to before their titles and outfits and reputations truly mattered. But Kensington Gardens was no place to play, and in a moment any evidence that Arthur could still be humorous would vanish.

The sun was out, and so too was the entire *ton*, which meant it took the Sterlingtons a moment to spot Miss Linfield and her footman. But once she'd found Loretta, Charlotte had to admit, it was hard for her to find anything else. Loretta stood serenely beneath the shade of a tulip tree, beautiful enough to make even the flowers jealous.

'Try not to make a mull of this,' Arthur whispered in Charlotte's ear before he strode in the direction of his future bride.

With no time to form a retort, Charlotte sighed and drifted forth behind her brother.

'Miss Linfield…' the Duke bent politely at the waist and kissed Loretta's gloved hand. 'You are, like today's weather, a rare beauty.'

Oh, Arthur's a poet now!

Charlotte had no eyerolls left for her brother, so she turned her attention back to Loretta, who offered her a polite smile.

'Lady Charlotte, how nice of you to join us today.'

'I didn't—'

Have a choice, was what Charlotte wanted to say, but Loretta was too innocent to be caught in the crosshairs of a sibling feud.

'I didn't want to miss the first truly warm day of the season.'

And with that, their promenade began.

Arthur and Loretta took the lead, with Charlotte just behind and their footmen several paces back. The party turned more than a few heads. Perhaps because of the Duke, perhaps because of his spinster sister or perhaps because of the radiant woman draped in a smooth ivory gown that captured the sun's rays much as the moon.

Loretta strolled gracefully with her head held high—but not *too* high—and listened intently to everything Arthur had to say about the gardens, the weather and the latest local news.

He spoke only of matters that any other gentleman might have discussed with any other lady in a script that was playing itself out all across Kensington Gardens that very moment.

'A fine pair of horses,' Charlotte overheard a man with ridiculously large sideburns saying to his lady companion, 'makes all the difference on a long journey.'

'...but the opera isn't what it used to be...'

'...you simply must visit Greece if you get the chance...'

'...and that is why suffrage should be limited to the landed classes.'

The conversational drudgery of London's upper crust was interrupted, suddenly and blessedly, by the sight of Miss Imogen Barlow. The sweet memory of Imogen's firm hands around Charlotte's waist, of her eager lips and supple limbs, proved a worthy distraction from eavesdropping on the park's visitors.

They locked eyes as their paths crossed, and Imogen tilted her parasol to conceal her sly smile from her promenade partner. A flirtatious swish of Imogen's bright orange dress told Charlotte that the night in question—a mere fortnight ago—was a mutually fond memory. She made a mental note to call upon the Barlow townhouse.

Not every former lover was so chuffed to stroll past Charlotte. The newly betrothed and passionately pious Amaryllis Evans let slip an icy glare, before burying her face in her fan, clearly embarrassed by the reminder that she was not as virtuous and chaste as her carefully built reputation suggested.

Charlotte's heart felt sore at the memory, but she distracted herself by observing all the other beauties of Kensington Gardens. The soft black hair of Penelope Cott, the warm hazel eyes of Louisa St George, the voluminous thighs of the Dowager Countess who lived next door.

Were they, too, peering at Charlotte from beneath their hats and bonnets and savouring the sight of her?

Were they gazing upon her flowery pink dress, her crimson spencer jacket, her short lace gloves and yearning to tear them all off?

Were they—

'Loretta Linfield!' a cheerful voice called from just ahead.

Charlotte bristled to hear a man use Loretta's first name so casually.

The tall gentleman who approached them flashed a wide, dazzling smile, and bowed loosely before their party.

'What a wonderful chance encounter,' Loretta said, too quickly.

Her face was polite as she curtsied, but Charlotte sensed that this was not a wonderful encounter at all.

'Good to see you again, Lord Wrottesley,' Arthur said as the two men shook hands.

Wrottesley! Charlotte sucked in a breath. The man who had once set his cap at Loretta. The Viscount who had departed London in disgrace.

'Is this your sister?'

With earnest eyes he'd turned now to Charlotte. Lord Wrottesley seemed harmless enough, but when Charlotte glanced back at Loretta she knew this man was hiding something.

'My sister, Lady Charlotte Sterlington,' Arthur said flatly.

'Lord Cecil Wrottesley.' He bowed again. 'Loretta, I was just thinking about you.'

'Oh?' Loretta said.

'The pale dew-plant near our front door has just blossomed. Your favourite.'

Loretta nodded.

He continued. 'I'll have to bring you some when I visit for dinner.'

'That's very kind of you,' she said, with nearly convincing affection.

Charlotte didn't know Loretta especially well, but she knew when a woman needed an out. So she gasped—loudly. *'Ouch!'*

'What's wrong?' Arthur and Loretta said at once.

'I've been *stung*!' Charlotte moaned, perhaps a bit too dramatically. 'It must have been a bee. Miss Linfield, will you escort me to a bench so I might examine the wound?'

'Of course.' Loretta took her arm and guided her to a bench beneath a wide-branched tree, leaving Arthur to entertain Lord Cecil Wrottesley.

'Where is the sting?' Loretta asked when they were seated.

Charlotte opened her fan to hide her wicked smile from all but Loretta. 'There isn't any sting. But I wasn't going to leave you stranded in a conversation you so clearly had no interest in. You're *welcome*.'

Loretta opened her mouth, confusion and anger and gratitude flashing over her face before she spoke. She sighed, her shoulders sinking. 'You noticed my discomfort? That means I'm not as good at hiding it as I thought.'

'It has nothing to do with *you*, Miss Linfield. No one is truly good at hiding anything. Men are just uniquely bad at noticing.'

A quiet but sharp giggle escaped Loretta's mouth. Charlotte wanted to ask about Lord Wrottesley, who was supposed to be abroad last she heard, but Arthur was walking in their direction.

'The perfect spot for our picnic,' he said with open arms.

The footmen flapped open a wide blanket and unpacked a basket of snacks and sweets.

Loretta leaned her head back against the tree behind the bench. 'What a generous tree you are to cast your shade upon us,' she said playfully. 'I wish I knew what to call you.'

'Norway maple,' Charlotte said.

'Oh, really?' Loretta's eyes shone with interest. Arthur helped her to sit on the ground as she asked, 'Can you name all the trees here in the gardens?'

'I—I believe I can,' Charlotte answered, somewhat taken aback. She pointed across the field. 'Those over there are hornbeams, and the large tree to the left is a type of oak, though I'm not sure which. And if you come back next month...' she turned and caught sight of Loretta's face, absorbed in her every word '...you'll see those rowan trees in the distance bloom with flowers that look like clouds.'

Arthur tilted his head. 'When, pray tell, did you become an amateur dendrologist?' He said the word slowly, over-enunciating each syllable. With a knowing chuckle, he turned towards Loretta and added, 'Dendrology is the study of trees.'

'There is much you don't know about me, Arthur dear,' Charlotte said as her eyes drifted to a gorgeous, full-figured woman who was strolling past their picnic. 'Much indeed...'

Charlotte was used to keeping secrets from Arthur, and the discovery of their mother's journal was only the latest one. It was filled with botanical notes and sketches, the names of trees and how to identify them by the shape of their leaves, the hue of their bark. She'd found it in her father's study a few months ago, scavenging for keepsakes before Arthur claimed the room for himself. She'd taken her father's peacock quill, an old Jasperware vase and the journal that had been safely tucked away in the desk's bottom drawer. She couldn't yet bring herself to read the more personal pages—the ones that would tug on her heartstrings until they snapped. She stuck instead to the gardening schedules and the lists of flower species.

Arthur had already moved on to a new conversation with Loretta, who listened politely and laughed at all the right moments. She sat with practised posture in her layers of tulle and muslin, her neckline high and lacy and her straw bonnet tied with a robin's-egg-blue bow.

Of course the Duke would want her. Who wouldn't? She had all the charm and beauty of a future duchess and an air of confidence so believable even Charlotte couldn't tell if the whole thing was genuine or not.

This bothered Charlotte—because she could *always* tell.

As her brother rambled on about the various and vague duties of the Dukedom, Charlotte committed herself to cracking open the locket that was the Honourable Miss Loretta Linfield.

'What is it that you do in your leisure time?' Charlotte asked as she reached for the three-tiered serving stand and filled her plate with candied fruits, plum cake and chocolate biscuits.

Loretta's answer might have come from any lady of the landed class—embroidery, piano, trips to the theatre. But this only intrigued Charlotte more. She'd seen flickers of personality in Loretta the night they'd met, and later at the gallery, and she wanted to replicate whatever formula had dragged that part of Loretta to the surface.

There were few things Charlotte wouldn't do to amuse herself.

Arthur resumed his tiresome verbosity as Loretta nibbled on a dainty cucumber sandwich, and Charlotte began to imagine a life story for this woman who might someday be her sister.

Maybe she's a fortune-hunter.

But that wasn't exciting enough.

Maybe she's trying to cover up a pregnancy!

Charlotte entertained herself with possibilities until she arrived at the worst one of all—that the Linfield woman was exactly who she appeared to be: a stickler for all things prim and proper, who would spend her days as Duchess watching and reprimanding Charlotte's every move until she could marry her off to a greedy old widower who still hadn't produced an heir.

Charlotte bristled at the thought.

By the end of the picnic, the art of deciphering Loretta Linfield had gone from an amusing pastime to a dire emergency. Her every movement, every word, every breath was a clue into the kind of future Charlotte could expect from living with Loretta.

As they left the gardens and went their separate ways, Charlotte resolved to become the most vigilant chaperone all of London had ever known.

'You look just like her,' sighed Mrs Grant in a rare moment of sentimentality.

Charlotte stood before the floor-length mirror in her bedchamber, admiring the glossy violet gown that had been her mother's, returned from the modiste a few hours ago. The empire waistline had only just come into fashion when her mother had brought this dress over from France, no doubt stunning her peers with its heart-shaped neckline, beaded bodice and softly puffed sleeves. The skirt was far more simple than the embroidered fabrics currently in vogue and, with the crisp white gloves and a diamond headband, Charlotte looked strikingly like the woman memorialised in the old family portrait that hung in the library.

'I suppose I do,' she said as she turned her face this way and that, seeing her ferocious curls tamed and polished into a tight top bun.

'Your brother has asked me to remind you of tonight's guest list,' said Mrs Grant in her rich Scottish accent. 'These are important people seeking important matches, and many futures could be set in motion tonight. Especially your brother's.' She straightened the bow behind Charlotte's back. 'And perhaps yours as well.'

Charlotte couldn't help but roll her eyes. She almost felt sorry for whichever hopeless romantic her brother had dragged home from the House of Lords this time.

'You're relentless.' Charlotte shook her head, the corner of her mouth just barely lifted. 'All these years and you still think there's hope I'll find a match.'

'The last few seasons were just for weeding out all the unsuitable gentlemen.'

'But each new season even *more* unsuitable gentlemen come of age to take their place.'

Mrs Grant wrinkled her nose. 'I can't argue with that,' she chuckled, then sighed. 'You'll try your best anyway, won't you?'

Charlotte said nothing. She couldn't lie to Mrs Grant.

Within the hour she had taken her seat at a pompously decorated dining room table alongside fifteen of London's best-dressed and least interesting aristocrats. To her left was an earl who smelled like overripe fruit, and to her right was a different earl's brother who had the remarkable ability to segue any conversation topic into a story about his recent Grand Tour.

Charlotte was generally relieved that her brother's attempts at matchmaking were limited to seating charts and calling cards, but once he had a match of his own the stakes would most certainly be raised.

That particular match of his sat by his side in a creamy evening gown adorned with intricate lace and gilded edges. The candlelight drew out the reddish undertones of Loretta's russet hair, and for a moment—just a moment—Charlotte was struck by how perfectly her own lips would fit the smooth slope of her upper neck. But her desire for a woman, Charlotte knew, was worth nothing until that woman gave her a knowing wink, or a sly smile, or made some secret comment that would go undetected by the men around them. This hidden language that all ladies knew could convey an invitation, a rivalry, a kinship, an attack.

Charlotte was painfully aware that with just one glance Loretta could communicate what kind of duchess she would be.

'Gentlemen!' exclaimed Baron Linfield with such zeal that Charlotte was snapped out of her thoughts.

The men at the table had been discussing science for half an hour.

'Electrodynamics may be intriguing to the casual observer, but *geology* is the science that will come to define our era.'

'It is astonishing,' Arthur agreed, 'how we find ourselves in a time of such unprecedented discovery.'

'You continue to speak of nothing but rhinoceros teeth,' said the pungent earl in a stuffy voice.

'That hypothesis has been disproved!' A younger gentleman with a wispy moustache joined the excitement. 'Mantell has discovered an ancient species the likes of which we have never seen.'

'And his wife,' Charlotte interrupted.

She was met with a sudden, though not entirely unexpected silence.

The ladies and gentlemen at the table stared at Charlotte, some frozen with a forkful of food hovering near their mouths.

'The woman who does the fossil drawings?' piped up an older lady on the far end of the table.

'The very same,' said Charlotte. 'But she's a geologist in her own right, as well. Much like Mary Anning. Don't you gentlemen believe that the woman who gave us the first *ichthyosaurus* should be admitted to the Geological Society?'

'The halls of science are no place for members of the fair

sex,' said the gentleman to her right with a laugh. 'In fact, the ladies I met on my recent trip to—'

'Your halls of science are no place for God-fearing gentlemen, either!' spoke a mousy-looking man whom Charlotte recognised as the brother of a prominent clergyman. 'It is ridiculous to think a creature may have once walked this earth that now walks no more. A whole species cannot simply *cease to exist.* Utter nonsense.'

The men continued their lively debate as their wives quietly bit into chicken fricassee and buttered beans, chiming in occasionally to agree or ask questions.

Charlotte knew the Viscountess a few seats down to be a firebrand at ladies-only luncheons, who always had something to say about current events. They exchanged a furtive glance and the Viscountess arched one eyebrow, as if to say, *I too would prefer the company of lizard bones to men.*

Charlotte then set her eyes on Loretta, but found no such hint, no secret code relaying her true thoughts on science and fossils and dinner discussions. It seemed that Loretta was determined to keep her personality, her motives and her opinions behind a locked door.

'Have you attended any lectures on palaeontology, Miss Linfield?' asked Charlotte.

Loretta's eyes widened in surprise. She cleared her throat and looked around the table, her face going pale.

'I've never had a mind for the sciences, I must admit,' she said with a humble smile.

'Surely you're familiar with the ongoing controversy?' Charlotte pushed. 'Do you believe we're on the cusp of a remarkable discovery?'

Loretta bit her lip. Her father lowered his eyebrows, anxious at having lost control of the conversation.

'My father certainly seems to think so,' she said, looking

at everyone but Charlotte. 'And that has always been enough for me.'

'Here, here!' Her father's face relaxed as he lifted his sherry. The guests let out a good-natured laugh in approval.

Arthur turned to Loretta and offered a warm grin. 'I think it admirable when a lady refrains from crowding her head with gentlemen's affairs. My sister—' he directed a pointed look at Charlotte '—would benefit greatly from your tutelage.'

Charlotte felt her jaw clench and her chest grow hot. Conversations like this, where men did all the talking, were boring and bombastic, and women like Loretta didn't help by leaning into feminine meekness and letting the discussion go unchecked. Charlotte knew—she so frustratingly *knew*— that at any given moment there were a thousand forces at play convincing a woman to be quiet, to be proper, to be anything other than a threat to the nearest man's ego…and yet she couldn't help but feel lonely when she was the only woman at the table speaking up.

Charlotte decided the best course of action was to mentally and emotionally remove herself from the situation. Dinner was followed by dessert, and she grew increasingly restless for some time alone. But then the Baron boasted of his daughter's talent on the pianoforte, and the night was inevitably extended.

To the drawing room they went, and try as she might to remain as uninvolved as possible with all that was happening around her, Charlotte paid attention as Loretta shyly approached the chair. There was an ever-present quietness about Loretta that made Charlotte want to listen more intently.

Loretta was indeed talented. But the song she chose to play had no character, no style.

The gathered company was delighted, of course, but Charlotte was disappointed. This was boring. This was ordinary.

This was, once again, a perfect opportunity for Charlotte to tune out.

'Charlotte!' said Arthur pointedly, interrupting her inattention. 'You have quite a talent as well.'

He gestured to the grand wooden instrument, and Charlotte sighed. She wanted to speak to Loretta, to challenge her, to push her and see what she'd do. So she sank her fingers into a stormy arrangement of *Suite d'Etudes*, the first movement, far more fierce and expressive than the evening called for. It had been quite difficult to track down the sheet music, as print shops weren't exactly overflowing with female composers. But now Charlotte had got her hands on the work of Marie Bigot she rarely played anything else.

The music swelled like the sea, and the party around her disappeared. Charlotte loved to lose herself in this music, the only thing she could play with any semblance of expertise after years of forgotten musical instruction. The melody rose and crashed and resolved and crashed again, until she played the final haunting notes.

Jovial applause erupted nonetheless, as the guests had all been dipping rather deeply into their drinks. But this music had only been for Loretta—a defiant rebuff of the genteel womanhood expected of them both. Charlotte wanted to know if Loretta had anything at all beneath the surface she could relate to, or if she was instead a true believer in the societal customs Charlotte hated most.

Whatever the verdict, it would not be determined here in the drawing room. Loretta was nowhere to be found.

Charlotte scanned the room again to be sure. The other guests had turned their attention away from the piano. Arthur was engaged by the fireplace with Lord Linfield. No one seemed to have noticed that Loretta had left the room. No one, that was, except for Charlotte. She left to search the rooms of the ground floor with growing concern and without any success—until she heard the strangest sound coming from the veranda.

It sounded like weeping—the ragged breaths, the sniffling nose, the paper-thin sob from a tight throat—but weeping didn't fit any of the roles Charlotte had decided Loretta was playing.

So she stood in the doorway, waiting to be noticed.

What was there to say?

She took a careful step forward.

Loretta jumped when Charlotte's shadow shifted into view. She clutched her handkerchief to her chest as she whipped around, eyes pink and puffy, nose red and raw. Charlotte inhaled sharply; even like this, Loretta looked radiant.

'Have you not tired of mocking me?' Loretta sighed.

It was not an accusation, but a plea for mercy.

Charlotte had cried an ocean for each death that had plagued the Sterlington household, and the only way to stop herself from drowning had been to swear off tears—both hers and other's—for the rest of her life. Loretta was by no means bawling, but even the small round drops that fell down her cheeks made Charlotte go still. Her mouth was dry, and she didn't know what to say.

'I have tried, every day, to be nothing but kind to you,' continued Loretta through shaky hiccups. Exasperation rose in her voice. 'I may not be as clever or accomplished as you are, but I promise I can be a good wife to your brother.'

'Clever?' That was all Charlotte could say.

'I don't know about fossils! I can't name the trees!' Loretta threw her hands in the air. 'I can't stand those crowded, noisy lecture halls, and I can't play music with vigour and artistry. Perhaps that makes me a dull wit in your eyes, but...' She paused for a moment to catch her breath. 'But I like books, and I like strolls through the park. I have a quiet life, with quiet hobbies.'

'What books do you like?' Charlotte interrupted.

The dizzying shock of Loretta's emotions was wearing off, and as clarity returned Charlotte was beginning to see the woman before her not as a threat, or a riddle, nor even a locked door. She was a person, her pain and fear laid bare.

'It is of no matter.' Loretta sniffed and dabbed her handkerchief at her eyes. 'You would only list the far more impressive books *you* have read—just as you showed with your performance.'

'*My* performance?'

'Your performance in the drawing room! I am perfectly capable of entertaining on the pianoforte, but you had to… to…to embarrass me with your sophisticated music and…and I paled in comparison…'

She placed a hand to her forehead and leaned back against a marble pillar.

'Miss Linfield, I only meant to better understand who you are. To decipher why you're here. To…' She struggled to find the proper words. 'To determine what game you're playing.'

'*I am not playing a game!*'

Loretta looked as if she might apologise, but she drew her lips together firmly instead.

'But it's what we do,' Charlotte protested. 'To navigate the world of men. To insult each other or support each other. Or—' *Or want each other,* Charlotte thought. 'We learn to get by in the subtext.'

'Lady Charlotte,' Loretta responded, with slow and quiet resolve, 'everything I have said and done since the day you met me has been in earnest. This is who I am—just as any lady is.' She coughed, inhaled a shaky breath and continued.

'I want the same thing every woman wants. The same thing *you* want. I am no different.'

Charlotte took a hesitant step forward. 'What is it that we want, Miss Linfield?'

The redness in Loretta's face was slowly melting away. The last of her tears was balanced on the edge of her eyelid, and her brilliant green irises shone like morning dew. Her breath wavered.

'A husband,' Loretta said weakly.

Charlotte moved forward again and calmly, gently, slow as a sunrise, lifted her hand to catch the final tear that now spilled onto Loretta's cheek. The soft satin of her gloves absorbed the droplet instantly, but her hand lingered.

Loretta closed her eyes. She exhaled the first smooth breath of their conversation.

'Loretta!'

The lively voice of Baron Linfield called from deep within the house. Loretta's eyes flashed open. Without a moment's hesitation, she gathered her skirts and hurried inside.

Charlotte stood suspended in time, her hand raised as if still cupped around that moonlit face.

Here was the truth that Charlotte had failed to consider all this time—the truth that had been right in front of her since they'd first met behind the wisteria. It wasn't just that Charlotte didn't know who Loretta was or what she wanted.

It was that Loretta didn't know either.

Chapter Five

Loretta Linfield had promised herself that by the time Bridget knocked on her door she would have decided either to feign a head cold or face the day. After an hour of lying in bed and contemplating—in agonising detail—the unbearable situation she had found herself in, Bridget's gentle *tap-tap-tap* broke the morning's promise and left Loretta utterly unprepared.

'Come in,' she said weakly, making no move to emerge from the soft layers of her bed.

Bridget opened the doors and then all the curtains, allowing the sunshine to pour through the windows and remind Loretta that the day would begin whether she liked it or not.

'May I share an observation, Miss Linfield?' Bridget said with her hands on her hips.

She only addressed Loretta with such formality when she had something brutally honest to say.

'You may,' Loretta mumbled, and shifted deeper into her covers.

'You've practically been a ghost all week.' Bridget sat at the foot of the bed and smoothed out her floral muslin skirt.

'I haven't the faintest idea what you…' The rest of Loretta's sentence withered like a plucked flower in the heat of Bridget's stare.

'You've barely spoken a word to anyone,' Bridget continued. 'You aren't finishing what's put on your plate, and you've gone to bed early every night since you returned from the Sterlington dinner party. If something happened there—'

'Fine,' admitted Loretta. Something *had* happened, but what that particular something was remained stubbornly impossible to describe. So instead she blurted out, 'I do believe my father will be quite cross if this match doesn't work.'

This was not the primary reason Loretta lay in bed distressed, but it was true enough. She would not win the Duke's affections if his sister continued to disparage her character at every turn. Loretta was certain that Lady Charlotte had already divulged her embarrassing outburst on the veranda to her brother.

She was weeping like a child, Charlotte said in Loretta's imagination, laughing visciously. *All because of a silly tune!*

The Duke would chuckle and shake his head, then cross Loretta's name off his list and pursue the next woman who caught his fancy.

Her father, meanwhile, would feel like a failure. And that would make Loretta feel like a failure too.

'Today's invitation would have been revoked if this match was in any sort of peril.' Bridget smiled. 'Do you have a particular dress in mind?'

Loretta sat up as Bridget fetched some choices. 'Perhaps today is when he'll tell me…' She slid out of bed, hesitant. 'What I mean to say is, I don't think his sister likes me very much—and, while I don't have a sibling myself, I can't imagine he would marry someone his own sister finds displeasing.'

Bridget helped Loretta into a simple pea-green day dress with a matching shawl and asked, 'Has the Duke's sister said as much?'

'Not exactly,' answered Loretta slowly. 'But she is fond of drawing out my flaws—especially in company. And sometimes she will ask me a question, and then, as I answer, she will make no attempt to hide her boredom, or her disappointment, or whatever emotion causes her to stop paying attention to the rest of the day's events.'

Loretta could feel her face turning pink, but once the words had started to spill she could no more contain them than a cage could hold the wind.

'And *she* has the audacity to accuse *me* of playing games! As though I were sending *secret messages* across the room or pretending to be someone I am not. Does she think me an actress? Or a fortune-hunter?' She was growing dizzy with the speed at which her thoughts were tumbling forth. 'What is so suspicious about simply wanting a husband? Is that not the most *natural* thing for a woman to want?'

Bridget placed a hand on Loretta's shoulder, and Loretta noticed for the first time how heavy her breathing had become. She took a moment to compose herself, but the knot in her stomach reminded her of the words she had not said. How could Loretta explain to Bridget—to *herself*, even—how her heart had raced when Charlotte had reached out and caught her tears?

Loretta had seen paintings and sculptures from around the world; she had felt every fabric the modiste sold; she had read every book in her father's library—but nothing had prepared her for that moment when Charlotte had cupped her hand around Loretta's face, gentle as a cloud over the moon.

'Sisters can be very protective of their brothers,' Bridget said as she helped Loretta into her dress. 'Especially, I imagine, when that brother is a duke. It's nothing personal, Loretta. She'll see who you really are soon enough, and all her worries will melt away.'

'Who I really am?' Loretta repeated.

Right, she thought. *And I know who I am.*

A baron's daughter. An avid reader. A proper lady in a proper home and soon to be a proper bride. There wasn't much to be other than that.

'Thank you, Bridget. I'm fretting over nothing.'

Loretta continued to fret for the entire carriage ride. The Duke had been away on business since their last meeting, and his absence at the week's social events had confirmed that he was genuinely gone, and was not simply snubbing Loretta. Even so, his first request to see her was this, to meet in his private garden—the perfect place to let a lady down gently, outside the critical gaze of the public. No one would be there to witness the disappointment on her face.

No one, that was, except Charlotte.

The journey between houses felt like an eternity until the moment they arrived—at which point the whole trip felt much too fast. Loretta tried her best to believe that Bridget was right, that there was no use in overthinking things, but to little avail. She clasped her hands to stop them from trembling, then took a deep, slow breath. Her footman opened the carriage door to a cool, sunny day, and she tilted her straw bonnet forward to intercept the sky's harsh light.

'Good morning,' said the last voice Loretta had expected to greet her.

Charlotte Sterlington stood at the front door with a calm grin spread across a face that more often sported mischief, annoyance or outright displeasure. Today she looked amicable, and it caught Loretta entirely off guard.

Loretta blinked quickly as her eyes adjusted to the sun. Lady Charlotte wore a day dress the colour of raspberry jam. It was fraying just a bit around her wrists and ankles, and it sported no pattern on its simple muslin. The Duke's sister looked far less regal than she had on their previous outings—

no tint on her cheeks, no colour on her lips, no fancy ribbons to temper her buttercup curls. Loretta was struck by the easy beauty of the woman who stood before her. She would have been content to continue to forget the reason she had come at all…

Where is the Duke?

As if reading her mind, Charlotte said, 'My brother has fallen ill upon his return from his trip to the country—as he always does.'

'Oh, dear,' Loretta said worriedly. 'I do hope there's no cause for concern.'

'None at all!' Charlotte laughed. 'I'm not sure what is in the air on the way to Colchester and back, but each journey leaves him unwell and each time he makes a quick recovery. Though he often forgets that part.'

Charlotte's face fell for a moment, as if in remembrance of something more menacing, but she blinked hard and recovered her smile.

'Please send him my warmest regards,' Loretta said earnestly. 'I shall return at his earliest convenience.'

She curtsied, but before she could rise and re-enter the carriage Charlotte took a step forward.

'Wait,' she said. There was a pause. 'The garden is still in good health.'

The confusion on Loretta's face must have been apparent, because the Duke's sister continued awkwardly. 'Well—you came to see the garden—did you not? There is no illness there. She—the garden, I mean—is ready to receive her guest!'

This light-hearted humour seemed uncharacteristic of the Charlotte that Loretta had come to know. It wasn't entirely strange, but it didn't quite fit either—as though Charlotte were a child, trying to dance in her mother's gown. She was tripping over her words the way one might trip over one's skirts.

'I see,' said Loretta. She, too, paused. 'Are you proposing we tour the garden without His Grace?'

'Yes!' Charlotte exhaled. 'I am proposing exactly that.'

Loretta was disarmed by this sudden and unexpected olive branch, but she held on to her suspicion nonetheless. Charlotte might very well be scheming to corner Loretta in the garden and scare her away from the Sterlington home for ever.

'I…well…all right.'

Loretta was hesitant, but intrigued as Charlotte led her to the side of the house and down a path of large, flat stones to an enormous wrought-iron gate.

Already Loretta could smell the sweetness of the garden, wafting in on gentle breeze. Behind the gate and the tall hedges that surrounded the garden was a spectacle of colour and light and beauty. Her senses were wholly and completely overtaken; the rest of the world disappeared and all that remained was the garden.

Loretta closed her eyes and listened to the trickling fountain, the rustling leaves, the crunch beneath her feet as the path turned to gravel. She breathed in the floral, earthy scent of the humid air. Another breeze, stronger than before, rippled through the soft cotton of her shawl.

'This is extraordinary!' she proclaimed. 'It's quite different from what one usually sees in London.' She opened her eyes and there was Charlotte, watching her closely.

Loretta blushed.'

'My mother always preferred the country,' Charlotte replied, finally turning away. 'Shall we?'

Loretta followed Charlotte into the grounds and gazed admiringly at all that lay before her. To their left was a sweeping range of vibrant blossoms—*rosa rubiginosa*, as Charlotte called them—alongside flowers that Loretta recognised as daffodils and peonies, and to their right was a towering stone statue of Demeter, goddess of grain and harvest. She carried a basket of wheat and smiled down at all who crossed her path.

The pair walked in silence through a narrow gap bordered by birch trees. Their sudden closeness startled Loretta—she had been so dazzled by the garden that she'd momentarily forgotten the bitter confusion that stung her heart whenever she looked at Charlotte. Their walk had been pleasant so far, but there must be a catch.

The wind whistled through the trees, and a cloud muted the sun, but soon the path opened up.

'These are the walnut trees,' Charlotte said, and pointed ahead. 'There's a young woman in the kitchen, Renée, who coats the nuts in caramel to make a delicious sweet.' Suddenly she kneeled in the soft earth and stroked a dainty white flower with her fingers. *'Anemone nemorosa,'* she said. 'They enjoy the shade.'

The grass beneath the walnut trees was covered in luminous white petals, fallen walnuts and greenery of various shapes and sizes that Charlotte continued to name in an even, scientific tone of voice. She gestured for Loretta to join her on the ground, her greyish blue eyes fixed on something moving in the grass.

Loretta bent her knees and leaned over Charlotte's shoulder to see a small, blackish green snake slither away from them.

'Natrix helvetica,' whispered Charlotte.

Though it went against everything she knew a proper lady should do, Loretta let her knees relax and sat beside Charlotte on the bare ground. 'Where did you learn to identify such species?' she asked.

Charlotte was quiet for a long moment. She stared out at the walnut trees, then turned and faced Loretta. 'I've been reading my mother's journal. I found it after my father died. I already knew she loved plants, but it turns out she really wanted to be a botanist. She *was* a botanist, in her own way. She wrote about all the flowers and trees and fruits in the garden…sometimes the creatures too…'

She seemed lost in thought for a moment, and then her face shifted into a smile, wide and amused.

'All the Latin names make me sound more knowledgeable than I really am. I truly don't know much about plants or snakes, or any of my mother's words, but they are precious words to me.'

'Did you know her?' Loretta asked.

'I was three when she died.' Charlotte sighed. 'Though I feel I am getting to know her now.' She sprang up from the ground and offered a hand to help Loretta stand. 'And what of your mother? I noticed she wasn't at the dinner party. Do we have maternal death in common?'

Loretta was taken aback. 'Are you always this forward with your house guests?'

'Only the ones who interest me.' Charlotte chuckled.

Loretta could feel heat rising to her face even as the air around her cooled. She looked up at Charlotte, whose hair continued to shine, though the sky was now blanketed in pale grey clouds.

'My mother is very much alive,' said Loretta as they resumed their stroll. 'But the country is better for her health. She's quite frail, I'm afraid.'

It wasn't a lie…not really. But for the first time Loretta wondered what it would feel like to tell someone the whole truth.

'I'm sorry to hear that,' was Charlotte's simple response.

She didn't pry, but curiosity was clear across her face. Loretta was alarmed by how much she wanted to satisfy that curiosity— to answer every question Charlotte might have about her life, about herself. She looked away and said nothing.

They walked in silence for a while, passing a stone bench surrounded by gooseberry bushes. It overlooked a grassy slope that dipped into a pristine duck pond and a grove of weeping willow trees.

Charlotte picked a bright red flower from the bushes that lined the top of the slope and handed it to Loretta. Five petals like tiny fans were painted with white at their edges. 'It's called Sweet William,' Charlotte said. 'Or *Dianthus barbatus*. And that's the last I will say of my amateur interest in botany. Are there any places in this world *you* love as much as *I* love my mother's garden?

'My father's library,' she said with a smile, finally warming to their conversation. 'I sometimes believe that books are my dearest companions.'

'Which books do you read?'

Loretta sucked in her breath and bit her lip. She was more than happy to discuss general interests, but her specific books…they belonged to *her*. They were among the only things that belonged to her.

They stopped to admire a patch of hollyhocks, tall and radiant, and the trellised sweet peas behind them.

Loretta changed the subject. 'What's beyond there?'

'The Fletcher property. We've been neighbours since childhood, and Nathaniel—the painter you met at Somerset House—is a dear friend of mine. What books do you read?' asked Charlotte, changing the subject back.

Nothing Loretta read was scandalous or improper, but her father's library had always felt like her own private world. What would it mean to let someone in?

The wind picked up around them and a low rumble resounded above.

'I read the same books that any young lady reads,' Loretta said, avoiding Charlotte's steady eyes. 'I read…' she paused.

'I read books about—' But her opportunity to open up was interrupted by a forceful burst of wind. *'Oh!'* she cried as it carried her shawl off her shoulders, over the Sweet Williams, and down into the willow grove. She clung to her hat and searched in vain for some steps.

'There's a path—'

But Charlotte too was thrown off by the howl of nature. Thunder roared and dark clouds gathered. Charlotte turned to look at the shawl, then reached for Loretta's hand and led her to a small path hidden in the bushes.

Two layers of fabric separated their palms, but Loretta could still feel the warmth of Charlotte's hand. This was unlike the gentle clasp of dancers. This was not the graceful clutch of a gentleman helping a lady to her carriage. This was firm and deliberate, fastened like a button. Loretta felt… *grasped*. And as she trailed after Charlotte she felt certain that lightning could strike them this very moment and Charlotte would not let go.

The hill was steeper than it looked, and Loretta kept her eyes on her feet as they raced over roots and stones. Full dandelions lined their path, bold and sunny in the gloomy shadows that now spread over the garden. The wind picked up and sent a thick pink ribbon flying into Loretta's face. She looked up just in time to see Charlotte's hair tumble out of its bun as the first warm raindrops plopped onto their heads.

'By Jove!' Charlotte muttered in frustration.

They reached the weeping willows and found shelter in their leafy canopies. Charlotte untangled Loretta's shawl from the branches and shook it clean before wrapping it around Loretta's shoulders. They were closer than they'd ever been, enveloped by long swaying branches and drooping green leaves, damp and quiet and unsure of what might come next.

'What books do you read?' Charlotte asked again, earnest and eager.

'Adventure,' Loretta finally said. 'Travel. Drama. Faraway places. And stories about women, and how they come to know themselves.'

'Do you know yourself?'

Loretta considered for a moment, her forehead wrinkled in concentration, and then blurted out, 'It's hysteria.'

'What?'

'My mother.' Loretta knew her face must be bright red but she was determined. She wanted someone to know. She hadn't realised until now that she had always wanted someone to know—she had just never met a *someone* quite like Charlotte Sterlington.

'She's always had a tendency for melancholy,' Loretta continued, 'but a few years ago she had what the physicians called a *"nervous breakdown"* and her list of symptoms grew from there. Headaches, fatigue, sorrow, sleeplessness, despair… Some days she's fine, and some days she's like a ghost. Eventually the doctors decided it was hysteria.'

Loretta hadn't been aware of looking away on purpose, but she noticed now that she was watching the lazy sway of willow branches in the rainy wind. She turned to face Charlotte.

'My father says it just happens to women sometimes and that there's nothing we can do about it and we aren't to tell anyone.' She lowered her eyes, embarrassed.

'You have told *me*,' said Charlotte.

The two women jumped at a loud crash of thunder. Rain began to pour through the branches in heavy sheets.

'Back to the house?' Loretta shouted as their cover gave way to the sudden deluge.

She turned towards the hill, which was quickly becoming

a mudslide, then peered doubtfully at her shoes. She cast a worried look at Charlotte, who seemed deep in thought.

'All right!' yelled Charlotte over the deafening torrent. 'Follow me!'

Loretta opened her shawl above her head and pressed next to Charlotte to cover them both as they turned and ran—farther away from the house.

Charlotte led them to an old greenhouse, small and covered in ivy, hidden beneath the trees. She pulled a key from within her dress and unlocked the door. They rushed inside and tumbled to the ground, drenched and panting.

Loretta couldn't see Charlotte in the dark, but she could hear her breathing hard nearby. The running had stung Loretta's lungs, and she placed her hands on the smooth stone floor to steady herself. Charlotte stood to light some candles, and Loretta began to wring out her dress as her breathing slowed.

'Here,' called Charlotte, tossing her a length of cloth.

It was rough, and covered with something Loretta couldn't quite make out, but it dried her face well enough. She untied her bonnet, which had kept her hair blessedly dry, and peeled off her sopping gloves. Charlotte sat down next to her with a towel of her own, her gown drenched through and clinging tight to her body.

In the soft light of the candles Loretta could now see that it was dried paint that caked the cloth in her hands, that streaked the ground beneath her. She looked up at Charlotte, who was squeezing the rain from her thick hair, and couldn't stop herself from laughing. A long stripe of turquoise paint stretched across much of Charlotte's face.

'What is it?' Charlotte asked.

'I'm terribly sorry...' Loretta breathed, and steadied herself for a moment. But the giggling burst forth uncontrollably once more as she pointed to Charlotte's face.

Charlotte grabbed a mirror from the top of a nearby cabinet and studied the band of blue that now ran from her ear to her nose. *'Oh, bollocks,'* she said—and then as if remembering her company, stared at Loretta with wide, worried eyes.

The tension of such impropriety hung in the warm air for just a moment before both women erupted in laughter. Loretta couldn't remember the last time she'd laughed like this, with mirth rising from deep in her belly until her ribs were sore from convulsing.

'I think it's quite fashionable,' said Charlotte, puckering her lips at the mirror.

'Anyone who's *anyone* will be wearing it at the next ball,' said Loretta.

Her eyes had adjusted to the dim lighting, and she took a moment to survey her surroundings. The greenhouse was filled with rolls of canvas and stacks of wooden panels, cases of paints and colourful powders, bundles of brushes and dirty rags. And the room was something of a gallery—full of paintings, some small and some large, many unfinished, but each one breathtaking.

Loretta stood, mesmerised, and slipped out of her dripping shoes to get a closer look at the artwork. Charlotte followed close behind, and together they left a trail of water.

There were landscapes and still-lifes propped against the wall, but most were portraits. Faces that were troubled, yearning, hungry. Passionate. Lonely.

The few paintings that were finished bore a familiar signature in the bottom right corner, and Loretta remembered then that she was sheltering on the edge of the Fletcher property.

Nathaniel surely lived on his own somewhere in town, but this, on his family's land, must be his studio. Loretta marvelled at her enviable position—she was taking refuge from the storm amidst paintings that would soon be some of London's most sought-after pieces.

'Why do you have a key to…?' Loretta began, but she stopped when her eyes landed on a sketch in the corner.

It was of her own face, gently smiling, but there was sorrow in her eyes. And there, next to the sketch, was a half-finished painting of her on the night she had first met Charlotte. Loretta stared at herself painted from behind, at her painted form crouched beneath the wisteria in her sapphire-blue gown, the pencil strokes showing her father and the Duke off in the distance.

This Loretta looked angelic…as if she was peering through the veil of heaven onto the mortals below.

This Loretta had not been seen by Nathaniel Fletcher. To the best of Loretta's recollection, he hadn't even attended the Fitzroy ball.

This Loretta, sly and clumsy in her eavesdropping, had only been seen in that particular place at that particular time by one particular person.

The rain pelted the greenhouse roof like a thousand drums as each woman waited for the other to speak first.

Chapter Six

It took all of five seconds for Charlotte to decide that she was not going to speak first. She knew Loretta was trustworthy enough to keep this secret, but she didn't know what Loretta would think of *her.* Would she accuse Charlotte of being a liar? A coward? A fraud?

She would be right, Charlotte thought.

She held her breath and waited.

Loretta's eyes were still fixed on the unfinished painting of herself when she said, quietly, 'My hair looks quite good from this angle.'

Charlotte was certain she hadn't heard her clearly, but Loretta continued.

'One rarely gets a proper look at one's appearance from behind, and if this is truly how I wore my hair that night, then Bridget is even more of an expert than I realised.'

Loretta slowly turned to face Charlotte again, their gowns still dripping onto the drenched floor. They stood like that until a crash of thunder caused them both to jump.

'You must think me terribly boring...' Loretta sighed as she ran her fingers through her wavy hair.

This was not the reaction Charlotte had expected. Loretta was supposed to admonish Charlotte, not herself.

'What—?'

What does this have to do with you? Charlotte wanted to ask. But the moment was too delicate for a question so rude.

'Why would I think you're boring?'

'At first I wondered if you *detested* me…' Loretta began to pace around the cluttered studio. 'Perhaps because I didn't meet your standards for what a duchess should be. Then I wondered if you simply *enjoyed* mocking me—if it had become a hobby of yours. Or perhaps it was just a sister's duty to be protective of her brother's marriage prospects…'

The words spilled forth quickly, like a snapped string of pearls, and Charlotte scrambled to pick them up.

'But *now* I see what has happened. What has *been* happening this entire time.'

Loretta stopped her pacing and looked squarely at Charlotte. She laughed, but it was a bitter laugh, entirely unlike the sweet, full laugh they had shared just moments ago on the floor.

'I don't…' muttered Charlotte. 'I don't understand.'

'You're *remarkable*, Charlotte,' she said slowly, earnestly. 'And remarkable people want remarkable company.'

Thunder roared from all sides. Rain pelted the greenhouse as the storm reached its peak.

It was so loud that Charlotte could barely hear her own thoughts. 'I'm not remarkable,' she said with a weak laugh.

'Name one thing I've done that comes even *close* to this.' Loretta gestured at the towers of paintings that surrounded them.

'I *can't*!' Charlotte said, louder than she'd meant to. 'I can't because you don't show anyone who you really are. I know you said—on the balcony—that this is who you really are, but sometimes it's like you're a character cut from a ladies' magazine. You said you were being genuine, but I don't believe you.'

'What's the difference?' Loretta resumed her pacing. 'What's the difference between the *me* I show you and the *me* that I am?'

That difference, for Charlotte, was everything. She had built a stone wall between the Charlotte she was and the Charlotte everyone got to see, and every day was a careful negotiation over how high to pile the stones of that wall or how many of them to knock down.

No matter how many times Loretta tried to tell Charlotte that she didn't have such a wall in her own life, Charlotte just couldn't imagine any other way to live.

'Tell me something about you that I don't know,' Charlotte said. 'I know you read books, I know you're a decent pianist and I know you're...' *Kind. Beautiful. Inquisitive.* 'Tell me something no one knows.'

'All right...' Loretta raised her chin, rising to the challenge. 'I dislike embroidery.'

'That's it?' Charlotte giggled. 'You *dislike* embroidery?'

'I hate it, actually.' Loretta crossed her arms. 'I hate the way the needle slips and stabs my fingers. And I hate the way it isn't taken seriously, like other artforms. How it's never framed and hung in museums because it's *women's work*, and I hate how that makes *me* not take it seriously.'

Listening to Loretta think so deeply about the gendered politics of art sparked an attraction in Charlotte that overtook everything else she was feeling.

'I agree,' she said excitedly. 'Men scoff at embroidery, but they couldn't handle the pain of it for a second.'

Loretta laughed, strong and clear, a sound warm enough to thaw the icy tension that had formed between them.

'So that's the difference,' said Charlotte. 'Between the *you* that you show the world and the *you* that you are.'

'My disdain for embroidery?'

'No.' Charlotte took a step closer. 'Your thoughts. And the way you share them.'

Loretta inhaled deeply. A flash of lightning revealed the

deepening pink of her cheeks. 'Tell me something about yourself,' she said quietly. 'That no one knows.'

Charlotte looked around the greenhouse, at the paintings and sketches haphazardly arranged along the walls and tables, at the bottles and tins and rags of all sizes.

'Everything worth knowing about me is in this room.'

Loretta nodded, then began to roam.

Charlotte felt exposed and sensitive, like a peeled fruit. There was no tough exterior to protect her now and, depending on what Loretta said next, she could end up bruised.

'You *are* remarkable,' Loretta said as she studied each canvas. She lifted her dripping skirts to step over a pile of reference books, then pointed to a dusty charcoal sketch of two bodies twirling around a dance floor. The woman had Arthur's sharp jaw, and the man holding her had Charlotte's unruly hair. 'Are these your parents?'

'Yes.' Charlotte nodded. 'I was too young when she died to have seen them dance, but I like to imagine…to sketch out the memories I would have had if—' Grief shuffled in the pit of her stomach, summoned from its slumber, blinking open one eye. 'If things had been different.'

When Loretta turned her face back to Charlotte, she did not wear the mask of pity that others so often wore when talking to the Sterlingtons about death. Oh, how Charlotte had hated those years, when curse after curse had befallen their house and the only thing people had been able to say was, *'How unfortunate…' 'Truly sorry…'* Or, worst of all, that infuriating epithet: *'Have you heard what's happened to the Suffering Sterlingtons this time?'*

'I'm sure you know all about what happened.' Charlotte tried to hide the pain in her voice. 'Everyone always knows what happens to the family of a duke.

'I may know what the gossip columns *say* happened,' Loretta responded, 'but that is not the same as knowing what *actually* happened.'

Charlotte smiled, but she didn't elaborate. Grief had both its eyes open now and was starting to stretch. She needed a change of subject.

'Why is Lord Wrottesley in London?'

'Oh!' Loretta said, startled. The sky rattled with more thunder.

'If you don't want to—'

'No, it's all right. It was always his plan to make a name for himself on the Continent and return redeemed. And he has, apparently, and now the *ton* is ready to welcome him back as if nothing happened...' She sighed.

Charlotte took stock of Loretta's clenched jaw and raised shoulders, and she felt protective. 'Why don't you like him?'

'It's not polite to speak about someone behind his back,' Loretta started. 'But if you must know... Cecil—Lord Wrottesley—has always been...ambitious. When we were children he had to win *every* game—and he did. By cheating. When he got older, he just... He's always had something to prove. Someone to impress or defeat. And now...' She sighed heavily. 'Now he's back, and he has *everything* to prove.'

'But he's already done that,' Charlotte said. 'He's proved himself. What else does he—?'

'Me.' Loretta turned away, facing Charlotte's artwork again. 'He wants to marry me, I think. Just to prove that he can. He came to dinner earlier this week, and the way he looked at me...as if I was a piece of art to collect. My father will always prefer a duke to a viscount, of course, but he and Lord Wrottesley's father were the closest of friends...'

Charlotte spoke after a pause. 'Is pale dew-plant really your favourite flower?'

'Hmm?'

'Wrottesley pointed it out in Kensington Gardens. He said it was your favourite, but I'm guessing—'

'No, it's not. He doesn't know me at all.'

The heavy pulse of rain on the roof filled the space between them. Charlotte didn't know what to say. Her brother seemed quite taken with Loretta, so Wrottesley was unlikely to be a bother for long. But anyone bothering Loretta—even a little bit—bothered Charlotte too. Now that she was actually getting to know the woman she had so badly misjudged, she couldn't imagine why anyone would do *anything* to upset her.

Then again, she couldn't imagine why men did most of the things they did…

'This is stunning,' Loretta said as she pointed to a snowy landscape Charlotte had painted in the country.

'Thank you.' Charlotte appreciated the change of topic. 'But I'm really more of a portraitist.'

'Oh, like this?' Loretta laughed as her eyes caught a charcoal sketch of Arthur, with large, curved boar tusks jutting out of his face.

Charlotte grinned. 'Yes, that's some of my finest work!'

'Please tell me your brother isn't under some sort of fairytale curse that makes him look like this after midnight.'

'You'll just have to find out for yourself.'

'I hope to,' Loretta said with a genuine smile.

Charlotte found she was warming to the idea of having Loretta around.

'Who is this?' Loretta stopped in front of the only watercolour in the studio.

Damn. Charlotte had almost forgotten the grief that was still lurking within her. Now it unfurled entirely. It arched its back like an old, mangy cat and began to climb up Charlotte's ribcage.

'My brother,' Charlotte said. And then, when Loretta looked

confused, Charlotte clarified. 'My brother Thomas. He died when he was fifteen.'

She couldn't say his name out loud without tears pooling in her eyes, but she was well-practised in blinking them away.

'Oh...' Loretta said, clearly remembering whatever version of the story she had heard.

Grief clawed at Charlotte's heart. *It's been seven years,* she reminded herself. *It was so long ago.*

Charlotte could feel her throat tightening. 'Everyone said he was beautiful when he died.'

Consumption paled the skin and reddened the cheeks... turned its victims into elegant ghosts. It was caused by too much genius, too much passion...

'What a romantic way to die,' people had said.

But they'd been wrong. There was nothing romantic about death.

'He was the best of us.' Charlotte smiled bitterly. 'The best of the Suffering Sterlingtons.'

'I never liked the way they called you that.' Loretta shook her head. 'The Suffering Sterlingtons. I remember overhearing people referring to your family that way at parties.'

Thunder echoed, but farther away now.

'We *did* suffer.' Charlotte stepped closer to Loretta. They stood next to each other now, staring at Thomas's handsome face as the rain softened. 'But it would be nice to be known for something other than the worst things that ever happened to us.'

It struck Charlotte that this might be where Arthur's sudden push for marriage was coming from. If he had a wife, and Charlotte had a husband, they could start again with their new families and leave all those epithets behind.

'You loved him...' Loretta muttered.

'More than anyone,' said Charlotte.

But she realised Loretta wasn't just saying that because Thomas had been her brother. She was really *looking* at this painting…*seeing* it…and Charlotte was intrigued.

'How can you tell?'

'The imperfections,' Loretta said confidently, and then—as if surprised by herself—retreated into bashfulness. 'I spend a lot of time at home, and living with my father means there's always something new to see. He fills the house with paintings, sculptures, maps, field sketches, books… *Observing* is a favourite hobby of mine.'

'Tell me,' Charlotte said. 'Tell me about the imperfections.'

No one ever understood her artwork—not at first. No one really understood *her*—not beyond the surface. She didn't make it easy, of course, and she felt sickly satisfied whenever people stopped trying. But Loretta…

Loretta didn't need to try. She saw and she understood.

'I think a paid portraitist wouldn't have included that faded birthmark above his eyebrow, the slight crookedness of his nose, the dent in his right earlobe…'

Charlotte just stared. The greenhouse air was humid in her lungs. Droplets of water from her dress still splashed onto her feet. She noticed the tiny freckles scattered across Loretta's face, a miniature Milky Way rising and falling over the bridge of her nose. The rain must have washed her powder away.

'I never thought of them as imperfections,' said Charlotte.

'I can tell that by the way you painted him. Why watercolour?'

'It was his favourite.'

Boys didn't typically learn watercolour. But if Thomas's affinity with the medium struck Loretta as odd, she didn't show it. They stood there, still and quiet, for what felt like a long time, until the rain sounded more like the footsteps of a mouse than the war drum of an angry god.

Their bare hands were so close. Charlotte wanted more than

anything to lean over and wrap her fingers in Loretta's. She told herself it was only her grief, her need for comfort.

She let her little finger flick outward, ever so slightly, and inched her hand closer...

Loretta's arm shot up to her face to catch a sneeze.

Charlotte jumped at the sound. She was suddenly aware of the mellow light trickling in from the wide windows.

'I would never forgive myself if you became ill in my company,' Charlotte said, and walked towards the door. She had no attention left for grief now that there was someone to take care of.

'I'm quite all ri—' Loretta started, but was interrupted by another sneeze.

Charlotte opened the door to a slightly sunnier day. The scent of damp earth rushed into the greenhouse as the two women wrapped painting rags around their feet and blew out the candles. They said very little to each other as they braved the muddy path back to the house, any intimacy Charlotte had been feeling shrivelling in the sudden sunlight.

Once inside, Loretta was whisked away to be warmed and dried, and undressed and re-dressed, and presented with a basket of biscuits for her journey. Charlotte watched from her bedroom window with her hair wrapped in a towel as Loretta's carriage trotted away.

The cosiness of feeling so known and understood lingered in her heart.

But that feeling also scared her. It rarely ended well.

Charlotte made sure the rest of her day would be too busy for contemplating the consequences of opening her heart to Loretta Linfield. She went to a dress fitting, played the piano and even doted on her dramatically melancholy older brother.

She savoured the grilled salmon served at dinner. She played cards with Renée.

But when all she could think to do had been done, when all her clothes had dried by the fireplace, when all the candles had been snuffed out for the night, Charlotte drifted off to sleep unable to stop herself remembering how all the shades of green in her collection of paints looked like the thin broth of cabbage soup beside Loretta's verdant eyes…

The sun had long ago sunk beneath the horizon, but Loretta's eyes remained open and wide as the cloudless, dark sky. Her bedchamber was faintly lit by the dying embers of the fireplace, enough so that Loretta could find her way to the mantel and retrieve a thin strip of wood to transfer what was left of the fire to her candle.

With one hand raising her crisp white nightgown and the other holding her candle aloft, she sneaked down the stairs, tiptoed through the hall and stopped finally at the entrance to the library. The heavy door creaked open, threatening to give her away. She held her breath and slipped inside, immediately comforted by the smell of old books.

What would she say if someone found her?

I have a busy mind, that's all.

But busy with what, exactly? She was fairly certain there was no more ire between herself and Lady Charlotte.

Loretta no longer had reason to fret that her chaperone would disrupt her courtship with the Duke. They had made a strange peace, Loretta and Charlotte, and would carry on as if their initial misunderstanding had never happened.

Then why, Loretta asked herself, *won't the image of her smirking face leave my head?*

Their goodbye had been quick when the storm had finally stopped. Charlotte had been rushed away to a warm bath, and

Loretta had been given a dry dress for the ride home. Neither had got the chance to say anything of substance before they'd parted ways.

Loretta had moved awkwardly in Charlotte's amber dress, too short in the hem and too loose in the waist…too enticing in its floral scent. As her carriage had traversed the busy streets of London she'd pulled the skirt up to her nose and breathed in the sweet scent of peonies and oil paint. She had breathed in Charlotte.

Loretta reached for a random book of her father's that might lull her to sleep—something dense and boring and unromantic. Gulliver the taxidermy puffin looked eerie in the flickering candlelight—almost alive—so Loretta chose a cushioned chair that faced away from him and nestled into its arms.

It was in this way that she spent her night, dozing in and out of sleep as she flipped through the musty pages of *The Theological and Miscellaneous Works* of Joseph Priestley.

'Miss Linfield?' said a gentle but startled voice.

Loretta opened one eye to see Bridget standing over her with concern painted over her face.

Loretta blushed, embarrassed by the lingering suspicion that she had dreamt of Charlotte and Bridget somehow knew.

'Are you quite all right?'

The room was bright now. Loretta had no idea how long she'd been asleep. She cleared her throat and said, 'A restless night, I suppose.'

Bridget placed a hand on Loretta's forehead. 'I'll have someone draw you a mustard bath, just to be safe. No need to catch a chill from the rain.'

She handed Loretta a letter sealed with the Sterlington family crest, opened the curtains and left for the kitchen.

Loretta, blinking in the harsh light of morning and stretching her stiff joints, resolved to open the Duke's missive after a cup of head-clearing tea. She glanced down at the open book on her lap and wondered if Joseph Priestley had anything interesting to say now that she was awake.

In completing one discovery, she read, *we never fail to get an imperfect knowledge of others of which we could have no idea before, so that we cannot solve one doubt without creating several new ones.*

And all at once the events of the previous afternoon rushed back into Loretta's mind like a riptide. In discovering that Charlotte was secretly the next big thing in London's art world, Loretta had opened a scandalous box that held more questions than answers.

How long had Charlotte and Nathaniel been putting on this ruse?

Was her painting career the reason she hadn't yet married?

And was she hiding all this from Arthur?

But there was another mystery that had been solved yesterday, and this was where Priestley's words hit home. There was no longer any doubt that Loretta and Charlotte could get on—her courtship with Arthur would not be sabotaged and the mockery would not continue—but with the resolution of *this* doubt came the creation of several new ones. Doubts about the role of women in society. Doubts about how women were to feel for one another. Doubts that were, Loretta decided, too troublesome to dwell upon.

The Duke's letter would set her straight.

She walked briskly to the writing desk and, without waiting for her tea or her bath or anything to calm her nerves, she broke the seal.

Loretta's eyebrows rose as she took in the dramatic curves and inky loops of *Dear Miss Linfield.* This was not the steady and modest penmanship of the Duke.

She continued reading.

> *It is my sincerest hope that this missive finds you in good spirits. Please send word of your health—at the slightest hint of fever, cough or chill I shall send my physician.*
>
> *I myself am in excellent health. My brother has made a full recovery and will surely ask to see you posthaste.*
>
> *I believe we have found somewhat of an understanding, you and I, and I must admit I no longer balk at my compulsory chaperonage duties.*
>
> *Perhaps next time it will not take a storm to draw us into closer company.*
> *Tentatively yours,*
> *Lady Charlotte Rose Sterlington*

When Loretta was a child, her mother had taken her for peaceful strolls in the country. That was when fresh air and physical activity had been Lady Linfield's prescription—not bed rest and laudanum. Once, having wandered from the path in search of wildflowers, Loretta had nearly stepped on an adder just moments away from devouring a field mouse. She could still see in her mind's eye the tight coil of the snake, wound like a spring, its muscles tense with anticipation.

This was how Loretta felt upon reading Charlotte's letter.

Her limbs, her organs, her beating heart were not strung with the adrenaline of movement, but of the moment just before. She was coiled and vibrating—like a hungry snake, but without the venom.

She thought of Charlotte all through her morning cup of tea, her mustard bath, her lonely breakfast out on the veranda. It took her the whole day to understand this strange feeling of anticipation. It took her the whole day to name the hunger she felt, and the satisfaction that was about to come.

Charlotte and I are no longer acquaintances. Loretta smiled to herself. *The next time I see her we shall be friends.*

Chapter Seven

The last thing Charlotte wanted to be was Loretta's friend. Friendship, Charlotte had learned, was dangerous. Kept at a safe distance, an acquaintance could never cause true harm. The end of a one-night dalliance might bruise Charlotte's ego, but it could never break her heart. That was why she'd never spoken to Imogen Barlow before the sun set, and why she couldn't recall the name of that shapely opera singer in whose bed she'd once spent a blissful winter weekend.

So when Mrs Grant announced that a package had arrived from Charlotte's *'friend'* Loretta Linfield, Charlotte bristled.

'She's not my friend,' Charlotte said as she rose from her seat in the parlour.

'She could be your sister, soon.' Mrs Grant handed over two parcels, one shaped like a pillow and the other clearly a book. 'I imagine life would be easier if she wasn't your enemy.'

'She's not my *enemy*,' Charlotte whined, feeling like a child.

Mrs Grant had that effect on her—reminding Charlotte of all the times in her youth when she'd been reprimanded for playing pranks on other children, chief among them her older brother.

'She's…an acquaintance.'

It was true. Charlotte *knew* it was true. So why did the words feel so clumsy rolling off her tongue?

'You spent quite a bit of time together caught in the rain the other day.' Mrs Grant raised an eyebrow. 'You didn't bond with her at all?'

Charlotte sank into the chaise longue behind her and hugged the larger of the two packages. She *had* bonded with Loretta, and she was genuinely looking forward to seeing her again. But Charlotte's *favourite* way to 'bond' with women was strictly off limits when the woman in question was courting her brother. Friendship itself was off-limits, too. Friends always left, and loss hurt.

'I suppose I enjoy her company,' Charlotte finally admitted.

Mrs Grant offered a soft smile. 'You should let yourself enjoy her company more often.'

She left Charlotte to sit alone with her thoughts, Loretta's packages and the quiet *tick, tick, tick* of the grandfather clock. Charlotte didn't want to hear her own thoughts, and the clock was increasingly annoying, so she ripped open the package in her arms as loudly as she could.

The torn paper fell open like flower petals, to reveal her borrowed dress and stockings folded neatly within. She imagined Loretta wearing them home, her shiny brown hair blending sweetly with the gown's amber fabric. There was no use pretending Loretta wasn't lovely to look at, so Charlotte reluctantly gave herself over to the memory of their time in the greenhouse—the captivating shine of Loretta's green eyes, the way her lips had curled into a bashful smile, the way her soaked gown had clung to her slender figure…

If Loretta couldn't be a friend, and couldn't be a lover, what *could* she be?

Charlotte slid her fingers into the knot of the bow that was wrapped around the smaller parcel, then jumped at the sound of four sharp knocks from behind the door.

Arthur let himself in and smiled widely. Charlotte stuffed

the book behind a cushion in a flash of panic, even though there was nothing suspicious about receiving a gift from an acquaintance.

'Today, I resume my place in society,' Arthur said with a comically pretentious flourish.

Charlotte laughed and relaxed in her seat, burying her fingers in the folds of her skirt to hide her paint-stained cuticles. The two of them were always like this after a bout of illness—as jovial and playful as siblings should be, and as they had been in their childhood. But the familial warmth never lasted long.

'I take it you're in good spirits, then?' Charlotte asked.

'Yes, yes.' Arthur cleared his throat and tugged on his cravat. He stood straight and confident now, like a man who had never known a day of sickness or grief. 'And I offer my sincerest gratitude for arranging our entertainment this evening, dearest Charlotte. Tell me, what are we to see tonight?'

'A theatrical performance.' Charlotte grinned and glanced at the long-case clock in the corner. 'One you'll like.'

'I see…' He nodded hesitantly. 'Which one in particular?'

'The *one*,' she said, in mock imitation of his voice, 'currently at the Theatre Royal.'

Charlotte strode to the door, then turned to see Arthur's face when she delivered the blow.

'As You Like It.'

Arthur groaned. 'A *comedy*?'

'A *romantic* comedy,' corrected Charlotte. 'You do want to marry the girl, don't you?'

'Loretta Linfield is a *lady*, Charlotte, not a *girl*!'

But Charlotte was already through the door.

On her way out she caught her reflection in the tall Palladian windows: she wore a long cherry-red dress with a column of white beadwork down the centre, rings of pearl on the hem and a white shawl draped at her elbows. Her hair was combed up in the old Grecian style, with dainty ringlets poking out over her ears and the rest piled into a simple low bun. She felt the weight of her mother's thick pearl necklaces, the weight of Arthur's analytical gaze—and the weight of the unwrapped book she'd left behind.

Arthur rushed to catch up with Charlotte's quick pace as she stepped outside, and positioned himself between her and the carriage.

'Charlotte,' he said solemnly. 'Can I depend on you to behave as a proper, marriageable lady tonight?'

'Hmm…' She put her hands together in mock consideration. 'Can your backside depend on a one-legged chair to stay upright beneath it?'

Arthur's face turned red, and all humour drained from his eyes. He lowered his voice to almost a whisper. 'We are the last of the Sterlingtons. I clearly can't prevent you from making a fool of yourself, but I must insist you do not make a fool of our family name.'

'I don't see how I can do one without doing the oth—'

'That is *exactly* what I mean.' He glared coldly at Charlotte. 'You will *not* ruin this for me.'

Lord Arthur Sterlington, Duke of Colchester, was not a callous man. He was not vile or vicious, as so many men could be. At his core he was sensitive and generous, patient and kind. Watching him lock those traits away in the deepest drawers of his heart had been worse for Charlotte than watching someone who didn't have them at all.

He plastered a calm smile over his face and said, in the cheeriest of voices, 'What is a night at the theatre if not the perfect opportunity to see and be seen?'

He gestured her into the carriage and there was that weight

again—the pearls, the gaze, the unwrapped book—pulling at her like three round moons competing for control of the tides.

The grand marble steps of the Theatre Royal greeted them after a silent carriage ride, and the crowd that stood upon them was the very cream of the London social scene. Hopeful young women curtsied and swooned at the season's most uncatchable gentlemen, tall-hatted dandies with theatrical dreams recited their poems to all who would listen, and there, between the towering columns at the top of the stairs, hawk-eyed mothers murmured and meddled behind their fans and feathers.

Charlotte surveyed the scene from a distance, viewing this nineteenth-century *School of Athens* as though she were visiting a museum. In his massive fresco Raphael had given pride of place to Plato, Aristotle and Archimedes—the greatest thinkers of human civilisation. Or so he'd thought.

Charlotte couldn't help but notice how the mothers of the *ton* today would fit very neatly on Raphael's steps, debating and scheming over all the matches they would make. How many unwitting bachelors would soon arrive at their wedding ceremonies like chess pieces at the other end of the board? She wondered if Raphael had entirely misidentified the habitat of genius.

Arthur marched ahead the moment he spotted Loretta and called to her. She turned at the sound of his voice and the warm candlelight bounced off the gold netting of her milky white gown. She pinched the sides of her skirt and bent gracefully, her dress twinkling as if it were made of a thousand glowworms.

Charlotte was entranced.

But before she could take a step in their direction she was intercepted by a familiar voice. 'Are you staying after the show?'

Nathaniel Fletcher seemed to appear out of nowhere. Charlotte spun to face him, but not before Nathaniel could follow her gaze.

'Already?' he asked.

'What are you talking about?'

'Arthur's been courting her two weeks and you've already taken her to bed?'

'*Nathaniel!*' Charlotte looked around to make sure no one had heard him. 'It's not like that—not at all.'

'Not *yet*,' he said with a mischievous smile.

Charlotte cut him a glance. 'She is to be my brother's *wife*.'

'Like that would stop you!'

Heat flashed through Charlotte's torso.

'She's one of us,' he continued. 'Maybe she doesn't know it yet, but I can tell.'

Charlotte rolled her eyes. 'You always say that.'

'And I'm always right.'

'Even if she *is* like us, she's—she's kind, Nathaniel. She's *whole*.' She turned her eyes towards Loretta, who stood as pleasant and polished as ever as she listened to Arthur rattle on about something probably not worth listening to. 'She's not like *me*.'

'Not this again.' Nathaniel sighed. 'You aren't *broken*, Charlotte. You need to stop thinking of yourself as an ill-fated heroine in a Greek tragedy.'

'Oh, it's far worse than that, Nathaniel. I'm a consort of Satan himself.'

Nathaniel was getting exasperated now. They've had some version or another of this same conversation too many times.

'So you let yourself have trysts in the night,' he said, 'and you treasure them as vices, but you never let yourself have true love because…? What? Because you're damaged? Corrupted?'

'There's nothing *wrong* with the company I keep—'

'You're right. There isn't!' Nathaniel spoke a little louder and received a few glances from those passing by. He lowered his voice and continued, 'There's nothing wrong with you, or with us, or with what people like us do behind closed doors. But letting yourself *love* someone isn't wrong either...'

His voice trailed off as Amaryllis Evans emerged from a shiny black carriage, her sumptuous silver gown trailing behind her.

'No.' Nathaniel shook his head.

Charlotte didn't even try to hide the way she stared.

'That was years ago. Her words can't hurt you any more,' he told her.

But, oh, how they did.

Charlotte had spent more time with Amaryllis than with any woman before or any woman after. They'd been friends for years before their first stolen kiss on Brighton beach, with the moon half-full, the water lapping at their feet. Their relationship had been almost too easy to pull off—their fathers had been the best of friends, eating, travelling and holidaying together every season. Charlotte and Amaryllis had spent a sultry summer tangled up in sweaty limbs and crumpled sheets, and then the summer had ended, and the air had become cool, and the sermon in church their first Sunday back had been about resisting the unnatural urges that Satan himself had put in your heart.

Charlotte's hair had still been gritty with dried salt water when Amaryllis had said, *'It's not right, Charlotte. It goes against God.'*

'How do I know something like that won't happen again?' she asked Nathaniel now.

'You don't,' he said softly. 'But you try again anyway.'

'That's easy for you to say. You've got *Ru-u-u-pert*,' she sang in a teasing voice, poking Nathaniel's chest.

'And I courted *plenty* of reprehensible men before him.'

'Remember—oh, what was his name? *Chauncey!*'

Nathaniel groaned. 'I try not to.'

'He was a wet goose if ever there was one.'

'We're talking about *you*, Charlotte. Tell me in all honesty that you aren't even *a little* interested in Loretta Linfield.'

Charlotte crossed her arms. 'She's pretty, I suppose.'

Nathaniel raised his eyebrows. 'That's always been enough for you. Why don't you bring her tonight?'

'To the *party*? You must be joking.'

'Nothing says romance like an underground molly house in the basement of the Theatre Royal.'

'And what if she's not…like us?'

'Sinful,' as Amaryllis had said.

'If a woman *that* beautiful hasn't settled for a husband yet, there's a decent chance she's—'

'That doesn't mean anything.' Charlotte rolled her eyes.

'Then just talk to her, Charlotte.' Nathaniel sighed. 'Get to know her. And if that doesn't work out, you can marry me.' He winked.

'Oh, enough with that,' Charlotte huffed.

She turned to join her brother and his frustratingly gorgeous bride-to-be while Nathaniel clutched at his chest in mock heartbreak. Marrying Nathaniel would be a convenient cover for both of them, she knew, but any husband—even a fake one—felt like a threat to Charlotte's freedom.

Inside the theatre, Charlotte was met with a wide smile on Loretta's face. 'So lovely to see you this evening, Lady Charlotte.' Loretta curtsied.

'Please,' said Charlotte with a wave of her hand. 'You've gone home in one of my dresses. I think we're beyond such formalities.'

Loretta blushed. Her pale face turned pink so easily.

'All right, then. I rescind my curtsy.'

The lobby was clearing as well-dressed patrons found their seats. Charlotte looked around at its grandeur. A life-sized painting of the Greek muses covered the back wall, and potted plants of all kinds and colours lined the stairs. An enormous crystal candelabra sat on a marble shelf. Six of its nine candles were lit.

The trio made their way to the Sterlington box in the theatre's second tier. Its view of the stage was unenviable, but Arthur cared more about being seen by the audience than actually seeing the play.

'I cannot overstate how beautiful you look tonight, Miss Linfield,' the Duke said as they strolled to their seats.

'You are too kind, Your G—' Loretta replied.

'Beautiful in what way?' interrupted Charlotte.

Arthur was taken aback. 'I—I…' he spluttered. 'In all ways!'

'Oh, that seems rather lazy, don't you think? Doesn't your companion deserve specificity?'

Charlotte opened her fan innocently and winked at Loretta.

'Well…er…' Arthur did not enjoy being caught off guard. 'If I am to be specific, Miss Linfield, your choice of dress is quite angelic. Your fair skin, your modest hair and your gentle countenance are all admirable qualities.'

Loretta smiled the meek smile of someone who did not accept compliments easily.

Arthur straightened his jacket and marched forward to their seats.

The theatre was full and warmly lit. Charlotte loved the grandness of it all—the towering gold columns, the sparkling chandeliers, the luxurious velvet seats. She ungracefully moved her chair from the second row of the box to the first, squashing herself beside Loretta.

'A good chaperone must be as close as possible to her charge,' Charlotte said to Arthur.

Loretta leaned over and whispered, 'Were all those questions necessary?'

Charlotte whispered back, 'I'm simply trying to make sure he's here for the right reasons.'

'I can handle myself, Lady Charlotte.'

I'd like to handle you, Charlotte thought.

If she'd been more confident in Loretta's romantic preferences, she might have even said it out loud.

Oh, God.

She scanned the audience to find Nathaniel, then stared daggers at him when she did. *You've got into my head.*

It was too late now. She might as well discover if he was right.

'Just call me Charlotte,' she said, and winked.

She saw Loretta try and fail to bury a smile, then lifted her chin. 'Very well.'

The curtains parted and the play began. Charlotte had always adored *As You Like It*: the whimsical set, the strong-willed heroines, the witty dialogue. She skimmed the playbill she'd been handed on her way in and scanned the cast for names she might recognise.

She found a spelling mistake halfway down the second page: *Silvius, the young shepard.*

Her eyes drifted from the playbill, to the stage, to Loretta Linfield. She mostly paid attention to the stage, but every now and then she would stare at the woman next to her. She was beautiful indeed. She had all the qualities of a perfect bride, but no husband to show for it.

Loretta peeked back at Charlotte and caught her staring. Charlotte averted her eyes in embarrassment—only to catch

Nathaniel staring at *her*. He raised his eyebrows and nodded approvingly. She stuck out her tongue.

A few scenes later, Loretta leaned over and whispered, 'I'm glad women were eventually permitted on the stage, but it must have been delightful to watch a man play Rosalind as she pretends to be a man.'

'And then later,' replied Charlotte, 'watching a man play Rosalind as she pretends to be a man who pretends to be a woman.'

Loretta bit her lip, as if she was deciding if she should say whatever it was she clearly wanted to say. Without thinking, Charlotte found Loretta's hand and gave it an encouraging squeeze.

'It may be embarrassing to admit,' Loretta began, 'but I don't know much about having a friend.'

Charlotte nodded slowly. She wasn't sure what to do with this information.

'So please tell me if this is too private a confession,' Loretta continued, 'but I sometimes wonder what it would feel like to wear trousers.'

Charlotte couldn't help but hear again Nathaniel's words. *'I'm always right.'*
Damn.

She pretended to be shocked, and Loretta stifled a smile as her cheeks erupted with pink. On stage, Rosalind told poor lovesick Phoebe, *'I pray you, do not fall in love with me, for I am falser than vows made in wine.'*

'Would it scandalise you to know,' Charlotte asked, leaning in close, 'that I *have* worn trousers?'

Loretta's eyes widened. She was so earnest in everything she said and did, thought Charlotte. Just like Rosalind. Charlotte felt a falseness within herself, a coldness entirely undeserving of Loretta's warmth. But what a lovely warmth it was.

'*When?*' Loretta said, just a little too loudly.

Arthur flashed a look of disapproval in Charlotte's direction—as if *everyone* in the audience wasn't whispering about something.

'All the time,' said Charlotte.

She looked to Nathaniel for some sort of guidance, but he was now fully absorbed in the performance on stage. She followed his gaze.

Of course. Charlotte rolled her eyes. *Rupert's back.*

Rupert Wynn, the devilishly handsome actor playing Orlando tonight, was approaching the scene where he would trade marital vows with Rosalind, who was still dressed in her masculine shepherd clothes.

If the church's warnings were correct, and Charlotte was indeed headed to hell for her sexual preferences, at least—according to more than a few historians—she'd be going for the same reasons as Shakespeare. Maybe he'd even ask her to dance.

'I'm not sure I'd be brave enough to wear trousers,' whispered Loretta.

'You're brave enough to court a duke. And braver still,' continued Charlotte with a sly smile, 'for daring to spend time with me.'

'But I…' Loretta's voice dropped even lower. 'I *want* to spend time with you.'

Her eyes, verdant and shining, were fixed on Charlotte's.

Delicately, deliberately, Charlotte placed her hand on Loretta's shoulder. 'I can make that happen.'

Chapter Eight

Loretta had four minutes and thirty seconds to decide if she was going to alter the course of her life for ever. Well, *probably* alter the course of her life for ever. It was possible that a secret midnight party with a mysterious guest list would be utterly unremarkable, but as Loretta watched the hands of her old mantel clock *tick-tick-tick* in a circle, she became increasingly certain that this was a threshold she could not uncross.

The candle by her bed was nearly burnt out. The trees cast shadows on her wall. Her fingers began to slowly, quietly, stealthily peel back her navy-blue covers. A sliver of moonlight shone in through the window and illuminated the pile of books on her writing desk, carrying with it a question from the heavens.

Do you want to read about adventurers, or do you want to be one?

Loretta stepped out of bed, tingling with nerves. The night was cool. She slid into a simple long-sleeved day dress, a pair of stockings and a dark green travelling cloak. Balancing her candle and shoes in one hand, she reached for the ornate doorknob with the other. She bit her lip and prayed the hinges would keep her secret.

Like water through a cracked stone, Loretta slipped gracefully out of her bedchamber. Charlotte would be waiting for her by the back door, and had promised—*promised*—that Loretta would have an opportunity to change her clothes at the venue. Though she crept through the halls in three layers of clothing, she felt entirely naked without her corset, her face powder, her gloves… Her hair was pinned and plaited beneath an ivory nightcap, and her earlobes hung lightly without the weight of jewels.

Loretta imagined the stairs before her were made of thin, frail ice, and she tiptoed down each step accordingly. At the first landing, her portrait glowed orange and gold in the light of her candle, and she froze.

The judgement radiating from the painted Loretta was blazing hot.

The Miss Linfield of flesh and blood suddenly felt like a fool.

In this moment she could not look any *less* like the woman in the frame. The freckles and splotches on her skin were unpowdered, the slopes of her waist and hips were untied, and her behaviour was uncharacteristically unruly. This whole night was starting to feel like a mistake.

But surely Charlotte was outside by now, in a cloak of her own, waiting for Loretta in the brisk night air.

When Loretta had fallen into bed after the play, she'd brought with her a book of Shakespeare's sonnets to keep her occupied until midnight and distract her from her impending decision. But Charlotte's voice—Charlotte's enticing, bewitching voice—had rung in her head and would not be ignored.

'There's a party later tonight,' she had whispered as they'd filed out of the theatre, *'and I'd like to take you as my guest.'*

At first Loretta had assumed the invitation was made in jest. Who would host a party this deep into the night?

'It's not a party, exactly,' Charlotte had explained. *'It's a… a*

gathering. And a performance. There's dancing, and you can find a dress to wear at the venue.'

Charlotte hadn't said much more, but when she'd whispered into Loretta's ear, *'Say you'll come,'* a bolt of lightning had surged down Loretta's spine in a way she'd never experienced before.

'I shall consider the invitation...'

That had been the most Loretta would commit to.

Not long after, she'd been curled up in bed, reading some of her favourite lines of poetry. One of them found her now, on the landing at midnight, with a candle just moments from being snuffed out.

It is my love that keeps mine eye awake,
Mine own true love that doth my rest defeat.

Loretta knew that a poem such as this was meant to convey the love a gentleman had for a lady. The long-suffering heroes in the books she read were often kept awake by the passion aflame in their hearts, driven to cross oceans for their one true love. She had never felt that way about a man, but it was more than that—she couldn't even *imagine* feeling that way about a man. The company of a male suitor had never left her wanting more, but with Charlotte...

With Charlotte, all she wanted was more.

Loretta felt as if she was finally starting to understand what it felt like to have someone worth losing sleep over.

She didn't have to cross an ocean for Charlotte, but she could certainly cross the landing.

With a slow and steady breath, she inched her way down the stairs, over carpet and wood and tile, and through the dark corridor at the back of the house. Her candle blinked out into a trail of smoke just as she stepped into the night.

Charlotte greeted her with one finger over her lips, which were curled into a mischievous smile. She gestured for Loretta to follow her beneath a cloudless sky, the moon so bright they didn't need a lantern to see their steps.

Loretta wanted to ask where they were going, who they would see and what kind of party host provided outfits for his guests, but she was overwhelmed by the feeling that even the slightest whisper would reveal them. Someone would hear her, and find her, and march her home with irrefutable evidence that she was not the perfect daughter everyone imagined her to be.

But following close behind Charlotte, downwind from the scent of peonies and oil paint and something uniquely Charlotte that rolled off her swiftly moving body, Loretta wondered why she had ever wanted to be the perfect daughter in the first place. The perfect wife, the perfect mother, the perfect society lady—none of those personas had anything to do with Charlotte, which made Loretta want nothing to do with them.

She wasn't used to being so entranced. She didn't have the experience to know that her eyes, fixed as they were on Charlotte, needed a reminder to scan the cobblestones beneath her feet. Her toes caught on a bump in the ground and she stumbled, instinctively reaching out as she stifled a surprised squeal.

Charlotte caught her hand, steady and firm. And even though they'd touched like this before, Loretta's heart still fluttered as Charlotte's fingers settled into her own. They were inches apart, breath mingling between them, moonlight glittering in their eyes.

'Are you all right?' whispered Charlotte.

Loretta only nodded. She didn't have the words to describe just how much *more* than 'all right' she really was.

They continued on into the night, their hands still together.

It wasn't long before they were back where they'd started the evening: the Theatre Royal, its candles all snuffed, tall and haunting in the ghostly glow of the moon.

Charlotte paused in front of a narrow door at the side of the building.

'Are you ready?' she asked in the thick darkness of the theatre's shadow.

'*This* is where we're going?' Loretta looked around to see if she was missing something.

'This,' Charlotte said, before knocking on the wooden door six times, 'is one of the most *exclusive* clubs in all of London.'

A small rectangle just above eye level slid open.

'Shepherd,' she whispered at the door.

The rectangle slid shut and Loretta heard the sound of several locks and latches being undone. The door opened into a small, musty room lit by a single candle, and she saw a short old man with round spectacles and an impressively large silver moustache. The door closed behind them, and the man reset the locks.

'How goes the night, Hawkins?'

Charlotte had already made herself comfortable in the room. When she lowered the hood of her cloak, her shiny blonde curls burst forth like fireworks.

'It's *all the crack*, as you young people like to say,' said the man, smiling as he unlocked a door on the other side of the room.

Charlotte reached over and lowered Loretta's hood, then giggled at the sight of her nightcap.

'It's *fashionable*!' said Loretta, suddenly flustered. She covered her cheeks with her hands.

'It *is*,' agreed Charlotte as she tousled her own golden hair.

Loretta had never seen anything so…so wild. Come to think of it, she couldn't think of a time before now when she'd seen another woman's hair so blatantly and intentionally undone.

Charlotte pivoted on her heel and strode through the door with an easy confidence—like a lion ready to show off its mane.

'I don't believe I've seen you before,' said the man called Hawkins as he settled into an overstuffed armchair and lit his pipe.

Loretta knew how out of place she must seem, and furthermore how unacceptable this kind of behaviour was for a lady of her stature.

Sneaking around... Conversing with strange men... Wearing her nightcap out in public...

This was all wrong. Very, *very* wrong.

As if sensing Loretta was overwhelmed, Charlotte leaned in and wrapped an arm around her waist.

Loretta's body tensed. She wasn't used to any of this—the closeness, the affection, the exhilaration of skin against skin. The only physical touch she regularly received was when she was being helped into and out of her clothing, or when her hair was being pinned up and taken down. Charlotte's touch was something else entirely...unfamiliar, but not unwelcome.

Loretta lowered her shoulders and gave herself permission to lean back into Charlotte's embrace.

'A new friend,' Charlotte said affably. 'Trust me, she belongs.'

But Loretta wasn't so sure. She'd never been the type of person to belong in a place that needed a password just to enter.

Then again, she'd never felt she belonged anywhere else, either.

As Charlotte guided her through the next door and down a rickety staircase, Loretta stared down at her feet and mumbled to Charlotte, 'What would my father think?'

'Mmm…and what would Arthur think?' Charlotte chided playfully.

'And what would any other eligible bachelor think?'

'And what would the entire *ton* think?'

'And the gossip columns—'

'Loretta.'

Loretta looked up. And what she saw, she would never forget.

The basement of the Theatre Royal was regal, spacious, and full of life. They could see the whole room from where they stood, on a small raised platform crowded with racks of stage costumes. Beeswax candles were clustered in front of ornately framed mirrors, flooding the whole space with warm, pulsing light. Ruby-red stage curtains and lengths of colourful fabric—all slightly tattered, but no less majestic— were draped around the room in artful waves. The walls were painted a deep, inviting maroon, and the floor was scuffed from years of dancing.

And the dancing—*oh, the dancing.*

Men and women and people somewhat in between were whirling, waltzing and dipping each other in ways Loretta had never seen. They wore mermaid tails and powdered wigs, Grecian robes and jester tights, royal gowns and medieval crowns. They were smiling, and laughing, and…*kissing*!

Charlotte leaned in close. 'I could probably tell you what your father would think. I know what he wants for you. And I know what Arthur wants for you, and what the *ton* wants for you, and what every governess you've ever had wants for you—because they want the same for me.'

The performer on stage concluded a song, and the whole crowd erupted in cheers and whistles. People threw flowers onto the stage.

When the next song started, Charlotte continued, 'But this

is a place where only one question matters. Can you guess what it is?'

Loretta felt nauseous for a moment, because she knew what Charlotte was about to say. And it terrified her. But when she pressed her hands to her stomach, to calm the tempest inside, she was caught off guard by the soft give of her own body, corsetless and free.

She faced Charlotte and nodded.

'What do you want?' Charlotte asked.

Loretta knew she would probably regret this tomorrow. She knew her life was not a storybook adventure, and she knew that pretending it was would only get her into trouble.

But she also knew that her life would now be measured in halves: before and after Charlotte Sterlington. There was no going back to *before*, even if she didn't know how to articulate this new and wondrous *after*.

Loretta reached into the rack of costumes that stood next to her and flicked through clothing of every kind. Charlotte joined her. Loretta recognised some of the pieces from previous performances she'd seen upstairs. She could be an angel from *Faustus*, a knight from *Tancredi* or a brightly colourful harlequin from the pantomimes of her youth.

Loretta gasped when she saw tufts of cerulean tulle bursting from the rack. She pulled forth a magnificent gown made of everything—taffeta, satin, silk chiffon—in iridescent shades of blue. She'd seen this dress before, in *A Midsummer's Night Dream*. It twinkled with tiny silver jewels and culminated in a pair of gauzy turquoise fairy wings.

'This,' she said breathlessly. 'This is what I want.'

The two women rushed into the makeshift dressing rooms—canvas drop cloths tied to poles—and were transformed. Loretta released her strands of copper hair and combed the tangles out with her fingers until it spilled over the shimmering puffed sleeves. Her dress fanned out at the hips in layers of wide fabric. She gathered her skirts and entered the party.

Charlotte was already waiting for her, nonchalantly leaning against a chest of drawers with a rakish glint in her eye. She wore broad linen trousers with a thick black belt, pointed boots, a ruffled shirt, and a bright red jacket with large golden buttons. Loretta hadn't realised that trousers were an option—that Charlotte's claim earlier, about wearing them all the time, might *actually* be true. For a moment she thought about changing, but the allure of being a fairy queen for the night was too great to pass up.

'Captain Charlie,' Charlotte said as she removed her three-pointed hat and bowed low. 'Pirate King. At your service.' A sizeable white feather skimmed the floor as she dramatically scooped the hat back onto her bouncy hair.

'Titania…' Loretta curtsied. 'Queen of the Fairies.'

She extended her arm so Charlotte could lead her towards the dance floor.

'Do you know how many tiers of seating this theatre has?' Charlotte asked.

Loretta envisaged the theatre—the orchestra, the front and rear mezzanines. 'Three, I believe.'

'Welcome to the Fourth.'

A lively English folk tune filled the room, courtesy of a sprightly young pianist dressed as a member of the royal guard. The guests—none of whom she recognised in their costumes and make-up and Venetian masks—were dancing with such vigour, such joy, that she wasn't sure she would know how to join them.

'Who is here, exactly?' Loretta enquired as they reached the edge of the dance floor.

'People who don't…fit in with the rest. They don't have a

ball or a club to call their own. That's what the Fourth Tier is. A club for the clubless,' Charlotte answered.

'But we have balls…'

'Do you *enjoy* the balls you attend?'

Loretta paused. She grabbed Charlotte's hand, unable to hear her own thoughts over the passionate playing of the pianist, the shuffling feet of the dancers.

'All I ask is one dance,' Charlotte continued. 'If you loathe it here after one dance, you have my word that I'll escort you home without delay.' She placed a hand earnestly over her heart. 'Pirate's honour.'

'I'm not sure a pirate's honour is worth much,' Loretta teased. 'But, yes, one dance. Do you have any particular gentlemen in mind?'

She scanned the crowd to consider her options. Some couples glided to the music, while others stood near an old polished bar, ordering and sipping drinks. Furniture and set pieces from previous stage productions lined the walls and provided generous seating for anyone whose feet had tired.

A charming pair whirled past them, almost bumping into Loretta. The gentleman wore a dazzling white coat with long coat-tails, a silk waistcoat and heeled shoes, as if dressed for the court of Versailles a hundred years ago. And his dance partner…

No, that couldn't be.

Loretta blinked. Then blinked again.

In the gentleman's arms was another gentleman, being led around the room as though he were a lady. He was dressed in Petruchio's gaudy wedding garb from *The Taming of the Shrew*.

The heavy heartbeat in her ears competed with the music. 'Charlotte, I—' She turned back to her friend, who was holding a delicate silver tiara. 'I'm not sure if you've noticed,' she continued, 'but just over there are two gentlemen who are...'

Charlotte was nodding slowly.

'Oh...*oh*!' Loretta was feeling dizzy with the twists and turns of the night. 'When you said *"don't fit in with the rest"* you meant—'

She stopped. Charlotte still had that glint of mischief, but just beneath was something else. Vulnerability and hope.

'Do women dance with women, here?' Loretta asked.

That wasn't the part that bothered her—that part was *marvellous*, actually. What overwhelmed her in this moment was the newness of it all. The sudden knowledge that dancing didn't have to be a chore, that her lack of interest in men wasn't some rare flaw that singled her out from the rest of society.

That and the raucous noise of this strange and colourful room.

'This is a place where women dance with each other all the time.'

'And you thought...?' People were singing now, and Loretta raised her voice. 'You thought I might be the kind of woman who...would dance with women?'

'Are you?'

Loretta turned to face the dance floor again. She spotted a glittering mermaid with a crown made of seashells waltzing close to a shepherdess. They waved at some friends seated on a large royal throne—a convincing Marie Antoinette with a court jester on her lap.

'I'd never considered it an option.' Loretta shrugged. She lowered her head and leaned forward. 'You may crown me, Captain Charlie, and tonight I shall only be Titania—who dances with whomever she likes.'

'Queen Titania,' Charlotte said as she slid the tiara into place. 'May I have this dance?'

Loretta took Charlotte's elbow and let herself have, just this once, a night worth reading about. She placed her left hand on Charlotte's shoulder, the way she would if she were dancing with a gentleman, though she wasn't sure if there were different rules for dancing with a lady. Charlotte settled her hand into the curve of Loretta's waist, and they were off.

For once, Loretta didn't have to strain her neck upward to see the face of her dancing partner. The aureate glow of a hundred candles flickered light and shadow across the dancers, the floor, the champagne glasses in hands that were gloved and ungloved, callused and dainty, slender and wide, and bejewelled and tangled tight in someone's hair.

Loretta could feel more tangible joy in this room—and in herself—than at any formal ball she'd attended before.

The pianist dived into a festive country dance that had the whole crowd on their feet. Loretta didn't know the steps, but with Charlotte's guidance she caught on quickly, and soon she was prancing around like everyone else, switching partners, holding hands, twirling with strangers in their breathtakingly beautiful outfits. She was panting by the time she skipped past Charlotte again, whose pirate hat had flown off her head and released her buoyant curls. Their palms met and they spun around each other before parting ways to meet a dozen more palms.

In the beautiful chaos of it all, Loretta tripped on her skirt and fell into the arms of a woman wearing a moss-green medieval dress and an airy white veil. This medieval maiden saved Loretta from any embarrassment by gracefully turning her fall into a dip, as if the whole thing had been planned.

'Thank you!' Loretta said giddily when she was returned to her feet.

'Don't mention it!' The woman said, in a voice far deeper than Loretta had been expecting. The dance went on until the music slowed. Loretta found Charlotte, and they all but collapsed onto a bar stool to catch their breath.

'Captain Charlie!' shouted Nathaniel Fletcher, who had appeared from the crowd and slapped a hand on Charlotte's shoulder. 'I see you've brought a stowaway from your ship tonight.'

Mr Fletcher didn't appear to be in costume. He wore a casual linen shirt that showed the top of his dark chest hair, and he carried himself with a certain ease…a looseness that Loretta hadn't seen in him earlier. His smile was natural and kind.

Loretta extended her hand. 'Queen Titania,' she said as her breath slowly returned to normal.

Mr Fletcher kissed her hand, and Charlotte stepped away to order drinks.

'I'm delighted you're here. I had a feeling about you,' he said with a wink.

'It seems I'm the last one to discover that I…that I enjoy dancing with women,' said Loretta.

She wasn't ready to admit there might be more she'd like to do with women than dance. She didn't even know what there *was* to do, exactly. She only knew that wanted to find out.

And that she wanted Charlotte to be the one to show her.

'That's usually how it goes.' Nathaniel chuckled. 'Charlotte knew about me long before I did. And by the way she talks about you…' He paused for a moment. 'Well, I know she was really hoping you'd come here tonight.'

'Is that so?' Loretta's chest felt light. Charlotte had been thinking about her—*speaking* about her, even.

'Yes, kind of…' Nathaniel sighed, and there was a hint of exasperation in his voice. 'Charlotte hides what she feels under several layers of cynicism, but when you've known her as long as I have you learn to read the subtext.'

Loretta nodded. She didn't need to know the full details

of what Charlotte had said—her heart was full just to know that Charlotte thought of her at all.

'Do you come here often?' she asked Nathaniel.

'I do,' he said. 'I'm not particularly fond of dancing, or drinking, or dressing in fancy clothes—'

'But *I'm* here!' boomed a cheerful voice from behind Nathaniel. 'And that's all he needs.'

A tall man wrapped his muscular arms around Nathaniel's shoulders and planted a kiss on his cheek. His dark orange hair was thickly gelled, and his face was painted in stage make-up. Loretta recognised him as Orlando from the play this evening.

'There are good people here, Queen Titania,' Nathaniel said as his hands reached up to hold the actor's arms. 'Rupert being one of them.'

'Lovely to meet you, Your Majesty!' Rupert extended an arm and shook Loretta's hand as if she were a fellow gentleman.

'It's an honour!' she said. 'And I suppose I can call you Rupert?'

'You may.' His smile faltered ever so slightly. 'Some people don't use their names here, just in case. Most of us know each other by now, but still… There's a lot to lose if the wrong person gets in here.'

'How do you keep the wrong person out?' Loretta asked.

'The password,' Charlotte chimed in. 'The knock is the number of candles lit in the theatre's lobby, and the password is whichever word is misspelled in the programme. It changes every time there's a party—which is most nights these days.'

'Most nights?' Loretta gasped as the barman handed her a drink. 'I'm exhausted after just one.'

The group laughed, deep and hearty—the kind of laugh that would get you removed from a society luncheon.

'Sometimes I worry that we're pushing our luck,' said Nathaniel.

'Oh, don't cut up the peace of the night, Nathaniel.' Rupert tousled his hair affectionately. 'Dance with me, won't you?'

Nathaniel rolled his eyes. 'Don't mind him. He's always like this after a show.'

'I was magnificent!' shouted Rupert as he stood and spun Nathaniel into his arms.

They pressed their faces together and kissed, hard and passionate. It was like seeing every kiss Loretta had ever read about come to life in front of her. She had seen her parents share a kiss like this once or twice, when she was very young, but the kisses from those very foggy memories hadn't been replicated since. The married ladies of the *ton* often griped about their husbands, complaining that they were dull and ugly and had breath too foul for them to enjoy their kissing. Loretta had been starting to wonder if the kisses in romantic novels were largely imaginary, but here was indisputable proof that they belonged to reality as well.

The realisation sent a shiver through Loretta's entire body. Hours ago, Charlotte had asked her, *'What do you want?'*

You couldn't want something you'd never really seen. You could dream about it, wish for it, hope that it might come. But to really *want it*—well, that was something else entirely. And now that Loretta had seen it, every bone in her body trembled with want.

They spent another hour dancing and laughing and mingling with the patrons of the Fourth Tier, some of whom went by covert names, all of whom spoke freely with each other in lavish praise and cutting jests. Their honesty was shocking, and refreshing, and Loretta noticed herself blushing more than once.

I want to show you something, Charlotte mouthed.

Loretta lost herself for a moment, watching Charlotte's lips, the way they turned up when she laughed and gathered when she finished a sentence. And then they were holding hands, tight, as Charlotte led her through a dark corridor and up a wobbly ladder.

Charlotte pushed open a hatch in the ceiling and lifted herself into the space above. She helped Loretta through the square opening and said, with quiet reverence, 'This is the stage.'

They stood in complete darkness, but Loretta could feel the enormity of the room.

Charlotte took a step forward and Loretta followed, their steps echoing in the empty theatre. Loretta couldn't see Charlotte, but she didn't need to. In the velvety dark every other sense was intensified: the smooth heat of their hands finding each other, the heady fragrance of a night spent dancing, the sound of hitched breath as they moved even closer.

'Have you enjoyed yourself tonight?' Charlotte asked.

'I have,' Loretta replied.

There was no one to hear them, but still they whispered.

'And do you enjoy me?' Charlotte breathed.

'I do.'

'Fair Titania, benevolent monarch of the forest, may I kiss you?'

'Please.'

Loretta didn't wait. She moved her hand through the blackness until she found Charlotte's cheek, until Charlotte turned and kissed her hand, then her wrist, her forearm, her elbow, the thin crease of fabric where sleeve met shoulder. Her neck.

Charlotte paused, leaned forward, lifted her face.

Their lips came together. The pirate king and the fairy queen. And it wasn't at all like the kisses Loretta had read about in her books.

It was better.

Chapter Nine

'**S**top moving.'

'I'm not moving!'

'You're moving now,' said Charlotte.

'I'm only *moving*,' countered Nathaniel, 'because you're *talking* to me, and I'm talking *back*. My lips must *move* in response to—'

'Yes, I'm quite aware of how talking works,' quipped Charlotte without looking up from her canvas.

The great Nathaniel Fletcher had yet to release a self-portrait, and while Charlotte preferred painting women—'*Anyone can paint a man*' she liked to say—the ruse was more believable when the people got what they wanted. A self-portrait of the London art scene's boyishly handsome rising star would be a conversation topic at all the fashionable parties, and the profit from its sale would buy Charlotte the new brushes she so desperately needed now Arthur had made her pin money contingent on finding a husband.

She stood and stretched, her body sore from hunching over this way and that on her old wooden stool, her arms heavy from painting the smooth slopes of Nathaniel's face, her feet aching from a night of dancing.

Her lips tingling with the remnant of a kiss…

'Can I see?' asked Nathaniel eagerly.

Charlotte nodded and they traded places. She believed that a great portrait was a truthful portrait—one that stripped away all pretence and captured the subjects as they really were. She examined Nathaniel's face as he examined her work, searching his outward reaction for his inner being.

Nathaniel's easy smile told her everything she needed to know.

'Since I'm *in* this painting,' he began, 'instead of just pretending to paint it, I was wondering if I might negotiate a higher percentage of the profits.'

Charlotte smirked, amused. 'Are you unhappy with our arrangement, Mr Fletcher?'

'No, no, that's not it.' He left the painting and paced around the studio. 'A seventy-thirty split is more than fair. And the whole thing keeps my family from asking what I do with all my free time, or why I haven't taken a wife, or why I keep such strange hours…'

Charlotte tilted her head. Nathaniel wasn't sharing any new information, which meant he was stalling.

'Nathaniel,' she said firmly. 'What are you getting at?'

'Well…er…we don't have to pay a model for this painting, so…' He looked at his feet and spoke quickly now, but couldn't stifle a grin. 'With the extra money, perhaps I could buy some jewellery.'

Charlotte didn't understand at first. The Fletchers had plenty of jewellery—and plenty of cash—and even though second sons were expected to make it on their own, his parents had always been generous.

But when he looked up at her and she saw the bare, vulnerable expression of longing and hope and fear across his face, she knew what he meant. This was for Rupert, and it was meant to be for ever.

'Oh!' Charlotte exclaimed. 'Oh, Nathaniel.'

She wrapped her arms around him tightly, her head sinking into his chest. They stood like that for a long while.

'I know I could ask my father for money, but if he ever found out what it was for—'

'Of course,' said Charlotte. 'What's mine is yours. We can even go to the jeweller together, if you like.'

'I don't even know what I would choose. There's no custom for a man's betrothal.'

'I hear rings are all the crack these days,' suggested Charlotte, still holding on to him as if he'd break if she let go. 'Or maybe a locket that holds a snippet of your hair?'

'I never understood that tradition.' Nathaniel chuckled.

'*Everyone* does it,' she said with a hint of sarcasm.

'Well, not *everyone* asks a gentleman to marry him.'

'You've been smitten with Rupert since the day you met him.' Charlotte let go and nodded seriously. 'I really am so glad for you.'

Nathaniel leaned back and roared with laughter.

Charlotte furrowed her eyebrows. 'What, may I ask, is so funny?'

He placed a hand on Charlotte's shoulder. 'You are being quite sincere, dear Charlotte. It's a rare day when you choose such sincerity over mockery, or pride, or jest…'

'All right, all right.' Charlotte rolled her eyes and smothered a laugh of her own.

'Perhaps there has been a more virtuous influence in your life of late?'

'I am immune to such influences.' She waved dismissively. 'I always have been.'

'You mean to say spending time with the famously chaste and infamously gorgeous Miss Linfield isn't straightening your path?'

'Is she *famously* chaste? What an odd thing to be known for.'

Charlotte marched back to her easel and sat, arms crossed, facing her canvas but looking off into the distance.

And I was doing so well, she thought, *at avoiding all mention of last night.*

'I haven't heard one rumour about her,' he said. 'And I hear *everything* from Rupert. If he doesn't have any dirt on her, no one does.'

Charlotte suddenly became very interested in the dust motes floating in the rays of sunlight streaming through the ivy-covered glass.

'Unless…' Nathaniel inched forward. 'Unless *you* do.'

Charlotte knew that if Loretta had been the one sitting on the stool being interrogated by Nathaniel Fletcher, the red in her cheeks would have given her away immediately. Loretta was like a lighthouse that way, shining her emotions into the fog without even trying.

'I'd hardly call a single kiss *dirt*, Nathaniel,' Charlotte mumbled.

'I knew it!' Nathaniel leapt with excitement and spun on his toes—an uncharacteristic burst of energy from such a gentle-natured man. 'I could tell from that day at the gallery. She's the one for you.'

'Just because you have *"the one for you"* doesn't mean the rest of us ever will.'

'And just because half the ladies of London have been in your bed, it doesn't mean you'll never find *"the one for you."*'

'Half!' Charlotte laughed. She stood again, her hands on her hips. 'Is that what Rupert says about me? I'm offended.' Nathaniel raised an eyebrow, and she continued. 'It's easily three-fourths.'

They giggled and sighed and then cleaned up for the day. There had been a time when Charlotte had counted her lovers—the titled ladies, the married matrons, the opera singers, the foreign nobles. She'd lost track long ago and, while it certainly wasn't half the women of the city, it was more than the average clergyman might think.

Some women stayed only for a night. Charlotte would flirt with them at a ball, and they'd join her later for any number of reasons—curiosity, liberation, spite against their husbands. Sometimes they'd learn something about themselves they would never acknowledge again; sometimes they couldn't stay away.

'I can tell you like her,' said Nathaniel, interrupting her train of thought. 'But what are you going to do about it?'

Charlotte shrugged. 'I'll see what happens.'

'You'll see what *happens*?'

'She bewilders me, Nathaniel!' Charlotte said evasively. 'She's just so…*herself*. But she doesn't even know who that is exactly! And I can't seem to work her out either. Which is entirely unlike me.' She was talking quickly now. 'I know she's kind. Perhaps too kind. I can't imagine her ever raising her voice.' She laughed—the image was too unimaginable. 'And she's clever. And surprising! I'm never quite certain what she'll say until—'

'Yes, but what are you going to *do* about it?'

'I…' Charlotte looked down at her hands. 'I'm not sure I'm capable of really *being* with anyone…'

Nathaniel groaned. 'You know that isn't true!'

'And it's not like we could ever be together—not in any real way.'

'What about Rupert and I? What about all the spinsters who live with their *"lady friends"*?' He threw his arms up, exasperated.

'What if I don't deserve a lady friend? What if there's just something wrong with me?'

Nathaniel considered her for a moment. 'You vex me. You vex me indeed.'

There were very few things that could rile Nathaniel Fletcher, but he resented it—*abhorred* it, even—when Charlotte spoke unkindly about herself. Nathaniel saw the best in people, and Charlotte loved him for that, but Nathaniel could go home at the end of the day. It was easy to see the best in people you didn't have to see all the time—and Charlotte had to see herself all the time. She was sick of herself. And she had always assumed a life partner would get sick of her too.

Especially someone as sweet, as chaste, as purely *good* as Loretta Linfield.

The morning after her night at the theatre, Loretta sat at her dressing table, folded her hands in her lap and stared in the mirror until she recognised herself again.

It took longer than she'd thought it would.

Her bedchamber was silent and empty around her and there she sat, a slight smile frozen above her dainty chin, wide enough to indicate a pleasant disposition but not so wide that it crinkled the skin around her eyes and lips. Her lips, which still tingled with the memory of Charlotte's warm, soft mouth…

No.

She focused her attention back on the mirror. She studied the lines of her thick hair, held in place by pins and pomade, two sleek coils framing her lightly powdered face. She'd spent years learning which hairstyles, which necklines, which shades of rouge were most likely to attract a husband, but now she wondered if Charlotte's preferences had anything to do with the advice she found in ladies' magazines. Was there a different dress she should wear? Or maybe she should try a different perfume…?

No.

Loretta furrowed her eyebrows at the disobedient woman in the mirror. Last night had been lovely—*more* than lovely, so much more—but it had also been a dream, a fairytale. She could not live in a storybook, much as she would like to.

She stood up from the dressing table, abrupt and determined. *Of course* she would dwell on the beautiful, scandalous, impossible events of last night if she just sat there. She needed to distract herself. She needed to wake up.

Downstairs, the drawing room was empty, and a note was folded beside a half-empty platter of honey cakes and strawberries.

My dear Loretta,
I'm off to a business meeting this morning. Something about volcanoes in the Amazon. But do find me later! I must hear everything about your courtship with the Duke of Colchester, which appears to be going remarkably well. I shall remain in excellent spirits unless you give me cause to believe otherwise.
Your Father

She sipped her tea alone and wondered how many notes just like this her mother had read. How many silent rooms she'd sat within, how much loneliness her marriage had taken before it fell apart.

There had been happiness early on. Loretta's birth had brought much joy to the household, and her parents really had tried to find friendship in a union that had more to do with business than love. But there had been no babies after Loretta—more to the point, no sons. Her father had become a successful patron and travelled the world. Her mother had grown bored with her life at home, restless for what might have been if she hadn't become a wife, a mother.

After breakfast Loretta went to the library, as she usually did when there were no gentlemen competing for her time. She ran her fingers along the books' spines and took in their threadbare scent—what some might call stale, but Loretta called cosy. Some of these books had been her mother's.

Had Elaine read adventure tales and dreamt of something more? Had she let herself get swept up in romance and poetry until the difference between her monotonous marriage and the life she wanted had become so sharp it had broken her?

'A lady's mind is fragile,' she'd overheard a physician say as she'd crouched at her mother's door frame, out of the nursery past her bedtime. *'Too much thinking can weaken the nerves.'*

'You must learn to be happy where you are,' her aunt had said when she'd visited just after the first breakdown. *'You have a good life. You'll be miserable if you keep wanting more.'*

Loretta's hand dropped to her side. She wanted to be happy with Arthur Sterlington. She wanted to be grateful for the good life he would give her…for the chance to escape a future with Cecil Wrottesley. And maybe that was what had driven her mother mad in the end—the shame that came when you couldn't make yourself feel grateful for a life that by all accounts was good enough.

Loretta resolved then to be grateful for a good enough husband, and to be happy right where she was. She was already getting more than she'd been born for. The daughter of a baron could become the wife of a duke, but she could not become queen of the fairies.

Instead of reading, Loretta returned to her bedchamber and placed her hands firmly on the dressing table. She composed herself and stared forcefully into her own eyes. She would read less, think less, and most importantly—so importantly, in fact, that she would say this out loud:

'I will not see Lady Charlotte Sterlington alone again.'

* * *

'I *must* see Miss Loretta Linfield again,' Arthur said as he burst into the parlour.

Charlotte was lounging on a comfy chaise, peacefully enjoying a small bowl of candied lemon peels—her favourite—an activity her brother no doubt deemed worthy of interruption.

'She is everything a gentleman wants,' he continued, pacing the room excitedly. 'She is slender, but not sickly…educated, but not pretentious…polite, but not dull. She was born and raised to be a duchess.'

He strode over to Charlotte and snatched the candied lemon out of her hands, mumbling something about unladylike behaviour. Charlotte closed her eyes and pinched the bridge of her nose. She was just as eager to see Loretta again—probably more so—but she wasn't making such a show of it.

'Is there a ball tonight?' he asked urgently. 'Or perhaps another play. Maybe an opera? What is the social schedule of the *ton* and how quickly can we make arrangements?'

'You're making an absolute cake of yourself,' Charlotte said, her eyes still closed.

'You wouldn't understand, Charlotte,' he scoffed. 'You've never been in love.'

Charlotte's eyes flew open. Now he had her attention.

'You're not in *love*.' She sat up. 'You've known her for all of a *month*.'

'How long do you suppose it takes?' Arthur chuckled. 'Love is far less complicated than you make it out to be. If only you would allow yourself the company of London's fine gentlemen, you would know how easy it is to find a proper match.'

'What is it that you love about Loretta?'

Charlotte wanted to stand, but gripped the seat cushion instead. Loretta deserved to be *truly* loved. She deserved to be cherished and held and revered—nothing a Suffering Sterlington could do for her.

'Is it that hard for you to understand?' He shook his head. His arms were folded over his chest, and he stood over her as if she was a child. 'Last night you asked why I found her beautiful. Honestly, Charlotte, how do you not know any of this by now? Love is the most basic of human emotions, and you can't continue to act like you're above it.'

Her face burned as if she'd been slapped. She clenched her jaw and willed her rising tears to settle. 'I have loved more than you could ever know,' she said through her teeth.

'Don't tell me you mean *Thomas*,' he spat.

And Charlotte could stay seated no longer.

'Yes, I loved Thomas! Despite what your behaviour towards me suggests, it is not impossible for a brother and a sister to be the closest of friends.'

'That is far less important than the love shared between a man and his wife.'

'Do you really believe that?' Charlotte's voice was rising now, strained and piercing. 'Just because *you* have no one who loves you, it doesn't mean the rest of us are lonely and miserable.'

'And who loves you now, Charlotte?' Arthur was boiling with anger, each word louder and heavier than the last. 'Is there one living person on this earth who loves you? Or have all of them died?'

After a volcano had erupted, everything in its wake was covered in ash. Charlotte stood there, limp and grey, her eyes and throat stinging as though they were filled with smoke.

Arthur's outrage suddenly disappeared from his face, and he too stood in silence, extinguished by his own words.

'Charlotte…' he started.

But Charlotte was already rushing towards the door. She would not let him see her cry.

She barely made it to the garden before she fell to her knees, gasping in fast, ragged breaths. Her trembling hands were splayed out on the stone path, framing the tears that spilled from her face. She allowed herself one wail—one loud and desperate cry from deep within her heaving chest. Grief had awakened with a vengeance and it clawed at her from the inside. If she couldn't get it under control, it would consume her entirely.

She sat up, whimpering now, forcing herself to take deep, slow breaths. She blinked into the sun and saw some of the gardeners staring at her, still as statues, confusion plain on their faces. They immediately went back to work, as if they hadn't noticed a thing.

Charlotte pressed her skirt against her face until it had absorbed all the wetness. She looked to her right, through the trees, to the Fletcher estate. Nathaniel was her friend, and he loved her. She had her people at the Fourth Tier, and she had her art. And she had Loretta, who had followed her into the night, danced in her arms, kissed her on the empty stage.

Even though their moments together would likely end with the season, she had Loretta for now. Charlotte might not be any better than Arthur, but Arthur was no better than she.

He was no more deserving of Loretta Linfield.

And he was no match for the pirate king.

Chapter Ten

For a brief few weeks in the 1822 season every lady of status had worn the most hideous shade of muddy green. Their dresses had looked as if they'd been dyed in a puddle, and the hats and reticules made to match had launched the world of fashion into a level of dullness and drabness that had previously only existed in the nightmares of French modistes.

The first such dress had sat unpurchased for weeks in a crowded shop window. Most ladies had walked by without giving it a second thought, but for reasons that no one to this day quite understood, Lady Lavinia Radcliffe had the dress tailored to her figure and had worn it to her very next ball. Lady Radcliffe was known and respected for her fine taste, and almost overnight that putrid colour had been transformed from just another swatch of fabric to a desirable—and expensive—fashion.

Now, on this foggy spring afternoon in 1824, Loretta felt a kinship with that dress as gentleman after gentleman visited the Linfield townhouse. Now that she'd been spotted at the theatre with a *duke*, she was suddenly in fashion.

It was widely known that when it came to women no one had better taste than a high-ranking member of the peerage, so every newly titled earl or viscount or baron's brother looking to establish a lady in his house had followed the gaze of Arthur Sterlington right to Loretta's front door.

This was different from the ten suitors who'd brought bouquets a month ago. Loretta was used to such polite gestures and how they started each season. This was genuine interest, weeks after she should have disappeared from their minds. Men who'd never courted her before were now positioning themselves to catch Loretta if the Duke ever dropped her from his marriage prospects.

'Did you enjoy your visit to the theatre a few nights ago?' asked Mr Berkshire, a tall, lean man with a gaunt face and floppy brown hair.

'I did indeed,' Loretta responded, and lifted her teacup to her lips.

'How are you enjoying the weather this year?' asked Lord Putney, a widowed viscount with generous sideburns, an hour later.

'Quite nicely,' Loretta responded, and lifted a second cup of tea to her lips.

'The air up north is far better for my lungs,' said Mr Mitchell, who had just finished telling Loretta that he'd become an earl if his second cousin died without an heir.

Bridget embroidered beside her as the men rotated on a regal armchair, bringing flowers until the drawing room was practically a garden.

Mr Berkshire had brought a bouquet of puffy red-and white flowers—Sweet William, Charlotte had called them just before the rainstorm, along with a Latin name Loret couldn't remember.

The memory of Charlotte's voice transported Loretta of the drawing room into the theatre, back to the stage wh she'd let herself be so reckless. Try as she might to pay at tion to her gentlemen visitors, so often her mind wand instead to Arthur Sterlington's sister, to her round fac mischievous smile. No person had ever laid such claim

thoughts before. She was like a stone thrown into the calm waters of Loretta's soul, and Loretta wasn't entirely sure how she felt about that. She liked calm waters. She enjoyed the stillness and simplicity of a life moored to routine, to etiquette, to society's expectations. By all accounts this sudden ripple should be avoided, but the harder she tried to avoid it—the harder she tried to force thoughts of Charlotte out of her brain—the larger the ripple grew.

Bridget nudged Loretta softly. Mr Mitchell must have asked a question, and sure enough he was looking at her now with an expectant gaze.

'I do agree,' Loretta stated. This was usually the response a man was looking for.

Mr Mitchell looked pleased, and then continued discussing the humidity in Greece.

Loretta wasn't used to being restless when entertaining company. But now that she knew what it was like to have a real friend, a true confidante, these shallow drawing room conversations left her feeling unfulfilled.

But we can't be friends, Loretta reminded herself.

If just one kiss from Charlotte could throw her this far off her usual course, imagine what a second might do.

Just as she was imagining that second kiss, the butler arrived with an invitation from the Duke of Colchester, requesting the honour of a dance with her at Almack's tonight.

Loretta received vouchers to the exclusive dance halls of Almack's every season from Maria Molyneux, Countess of Sefton, an old friend of her mother's. The Lady Patronesses of Almack's were notorious for denying access to anyone who fell beneath their extraordinarily high standards for etiquette, dress, personality, heritage and reputation.

This is perfect, Loretta thought. *Charlotte is far too undignified to receive a voucher.*

'Do you attend Almack's, Mr Mitchell?' Loretta asked as she glanced at the mantel clock.

'I haven't had the privilege…' He lowered his head.

Well, that just would not do. Loretta and her final suitor of the day exchanged a wordless acknowledgement that perhaps Loretta was too high a reach for a man of his standing. Mr Mitchell appeared to be a perfectly nice gentleman, but the Patronesses of Almack's must know something she didn't.

He offered a courteous goodbye, and all that remained of him were the daffodils he'd left behind.

'Have you enjoyed today's company?' Bridget asked unconvincingly.

Loretta glared, and Bridget laughed.

'You seemed much less tolerant of boring gentlemen than usual.'

Loretta tensed. 'Is that so?'

'I only mean your responses were rather short—almost as if you were hoping *someone else* would walk through the door.' Bridget leaned forward and smiled.

Loretta *did* want someone else to walk through the door. Especially now that she'd realised how unbearable life felt without her…

But bear it I must, she thought, trying her best to clear her head.

Loretta forced a smile. 'I do look forward to dancing with the Duke tonight…and it would be quite poetic, I think, to wear the shimmering blue dress I wore the night I met him.'

'Quite poetic indeed…'

Bridget had outdone herself with Loretta's winding Grecian hairdo, her subtle make-up, her well-paired jewels. As Loretta passed her portrait on the stairs it was as if she was walking by a mirror. She was ready to take her place among London's best…to finally make her father proud.

As she stepped outside and climbed into the waiting carriage, Loretta tried her very best to wring from the fabric of her heart every last drop of the desire she had for the Duke's sister.

But Loretta had somehow failed to learn that Charlotte was a deluge one could only avoid for so long.

At first Loretta thought she was imagining things when she stepped into Almack's and saw Charlotte, dressed in the same lavender gown from the night they'd met. And then Loretta *knew* she was imagining things—because Charlotte was not standing by the refreshments, sniggering from afar. She was on the dance floor—and she was on the dance floor with a *man*.

'Miss Linfield.' The Duke greeted Loretta at the door. 'Such a pleasure to see you tonight.'

Loretta couldn't take her eyes off Charlotte.

'Ah, yes…' The Duke nodded. 'It appears your company has had a corrective influence on Charlotte's behaviour. She has finally embraced her role in society.'

So Loretta wasn't imagining Charlotte's presence. She was here, and she was dancing, and she was as gorgeous as ever. In that moment Loretta knew that the dam she'd built to keep her feelings for Charlotte at bay didn't stand a chance. Charlotte Sterlington, human tidal wave, had burst into Loretta's life once and for all.

And Loretta could deny it no longer—she wanted nothing more than to be drenched.

Everyone in London knew there was only one fate worse than failing to receive an Almack's voucher: receiving one, and then having it revoked.

Years ago Charlotte had debuted at Almack's, and her first

ball had been a whirlwind of suitors hand-selected by the Lady Patronesses themselves. She'd been seventeen, Arthur had been off seeing the world and Thomas had still been alive, waiting at home for Charlotte to return and regale him with the details of each handsome gentleman who had called her to the floor. He would sneak into her room and they'd gossip for hours. On some Wednesdays she would feign illness to get out of the weekly ball, then stay at home with Thomas and play the piano as he danced in one of her dresses.

A year later her heart had broken, and it had broken again every single Wednesday.

When the months set aside to mourn Thomas had finished, Arthur scolded her for continuing to ignore her societal obligations. Grief and whisky had devoured the details of what had happened next, but Charlotte had a vague memory of bursting into Almack's wearing trousers and a tailcoat and receiving a lifetime ban from London's most exclusive venue.

Her father had paid every newspaper in the city to keep the story off their pages. He had convinced every eyewitness that it had been a simple moment of mourning run amok. *'We all know how fragile women can be when overcome with such emotion.'*

Charlotte had not given Almack's a second thought since the unfortunate events of 1817, but now, after kissing Loretta Linfield on the quiet stage of the Theatre Royal, a second thought was warranted. Charlotte loved a good chase, and Arthur was inadvertently ensuring that this would be a challenging one. If she wanted to charm Loretta, she would have to enter the spaces Loretta inhabited—even if those spaces were as repulsive as Almack's.

It had been far easier to earn back her vouchers than she had expected. Lady Castlereagh had just returned from two years of mourning her husband in the countryside, and after her own intimate dance with grief could no longer fault Charlotte for her outburst.

Loss had a way of making what had once seemed important of no importance at all.

This was how Charlotte found herself back among the gilded columns and pilasters of Almack's, in the arms of a marquess who kept stepping on her toes. The music was as light and unexciting as ever, the company as dull and pretentious as could be expected. This would be tolerable, in the best of circumstances, but Almack's was not the best of circumstances. Everyone in attendance kept glancing at Charlotte and whispering, pointing, raising their eyebrows at the audacity it must have taken for her to show her face here. There would be no newspaper pay-off tomorrow.

Even worse, there was nothing to drink besides flavourless tea and sour lemonade.

Loretta had arrived not a moment too soon.

Arthur led Loretta onto the floor as the balcony orchestra leapt into a reel that was likely too rousing for his mild sensibilities but still far too tame for Charlotte's taste. With her arms limp at her sides, Charlotte skipped in loops around her fellow dancers, smiling politely at the gentlemen and ladies who hopped by her in the flickering gas light of elaborate cut-glass lustres.

There were few friends Charlotte could pass a knowing wink to in Almack's. But what Almack's did have was plenty of people with whom Charlotte would prefer to avoid eye contact altogether. From across the room she saw the caramel-brown hair of Arabella Beaumont, standing near the refreshments and listening to her soon-to-be husband rattle on about whatever it was men rattled on about. She was sipping a very full glass of lemonade that Charlotte hoped, for Arabella's sake, was spiked.

But soon Charlotte was swept back into the cyclical flow

of the dance, and she met Loretta the way two rivers might converge at the sea. They lifted their skirts for a moment of delicate footwork, facing each other as the dancers swayed around them for another four bars, before gliding away to their next partners.

That was when Charlotte spotted James Baxter, an old acquaintance of her brother and occasional patron of the Fourth Tier.

She tugged on his sleeve as the dance ended. 'Mr Baxter, I require a favour.'

'I haven't seen you here in ages,' he said, with amusement plain on his face.

'There's a flask of brandy in my garter that's yours if you can be overcome with nostalgia for your time in France with my brother.'

'Colchester!' Mr Baxter exclaimed with raised arms. 'Is that you?'

As Mr Baxter lured Arthur into conversation Charlotte grabbed Loretta's wrist and led her to the cloakroom. She slipped the attending maid five shillings for privacy, then waited *one, two, three* seconds for safety after the door had closed before filling her hands with Loretta's waist and pressing their bodies into a corner, hidden by shadows and cloaks and shawls of all colours.

She rose to meet Loretta's lips, but stopped with barely room for a hairpin between them. It was an offer, or maybe a challenge, or maybe both.

Your move, Loretta Linfield. What will you do now?

Loretta didn't hesitate. She cupped Charlotte's face in her hands and closed the gap between their lips. She filled Charlotte with warmth and bliss and blazing desire. And then she pulled away.

'What if someone finds us?' Loretta asked, her eyes suddenly wide.

'That's half the fun,' Charlotte teased.

'I shouldn't be looking for *fun*,' Loretta sighed. She laced her fingers behind Charlotte's neck and leaned forward until their foreheads rested against each other. She closed her eyes. 'I should be looking for a *husband*.'

Charlotte rested her hand on Loretta's face. 'Do you enjoy spending time with me?'

'Yes.'

'Do you enjoy kissing me?'

'Yes.'

'Do you want to do more than kiss me?'

A blush shot up Loretta's neck and across her cheeks. First pink, like carnations, then red, like crushed berries. It struck Charlotte then that Loretta might not know what else there was to do besides kissing, sheltered as she was.

'Does your heart beat faster when you see me across the room?' Charlotte tried.

Loretta bit her lip and nodded.

Every detail of her face was a marvel. Charlotte wanted to kiss her, then paint her, then kiss her again. She needed to stand in Loretta's presence the way a candle needs to stand in the presence of oxygen.

Loretta grabbed her shoulders and pulled her close for a hungry kiss. They were soon fully submerged in the scent of each other, in the sound of hitched breathing and shuffling skirts. Charlotte's lips were on Loretta's neck when she noticed the door handle begin to turn. Quickly, without time for explanation, she spun Loretta around and began fiddling with the silk bow at her lower back.

'What are you—?' Loretta started.

The doors flew open and in marched a young lady with a torn hem and her worried but determined mother.

'Ribbon adjustment.' Charlotte smiled at the pair. 'You?'

'Some gentlemen have never learned how to dance without stepping on a lady's skirts,' the mother grumbled.

Loretta's face had almost returned to its usual paleness by the time they left the cloakroom. They walked slowly down the corridor to the ballroom. The sound of a steady country dance grew louder and louder with each step. Charlotte didn't want to leave the corridor, didn't want Loretta to leave so soon. But when she tried to do anything about it, the fear of getting too close got in the way.

'You're quite brave,' Mrs Grant had said a few hours ago, while rolling Charlotte's long white gloves over her arms. *'Returning to Almack's after all this time…quite brave indeed.'*

'Is it that obvious?' Charlotte had responded. *'Does my face show how terrified I am?'*

'The only thing your face shows,' Mrs Grant had said as she placed her hands on Charlotte's shoulders, *'is that you recognise tonight for what it is. A turning point. You are finally trying, and of course that's terrifying. But you are brave, Charlotte Sterlington. You are brave.'*

Charlotte didn't feel so brave now, as she walked next to Loretta, silent and unsure of what to say. Mrs Grant was right—Charlotte *was* trying—but she wasn't trying in the way Mrs Grant had meant. She wasn't finally trying to find a husband, and she wasn't trying to win her way back into society's good graces. She was trying to spend more time with Loretta, and that was the part of tonight that terrified her the most.

But Charlotte, as Mrs Grant had said, was indeed brave. So she grabbed Loretta's hand just before they reached the line where the corridor's shadows ended and the ballroom's lights began.

'I wish we had more time,' Charlotte whispered.

She knew this would end. It had to. It always did. She just wished it didn't always have to end so *soon*.

'Me too,' Loretta confessed, her voice low. 'I wish I had more time to work out what all this means. To work out who I *am*.'

Charlotte wanted to work that out, too.

'What have you read lately?' she asked suddenly, without thinking. She was overcome with the overwhelming urge to learn everything she could about the woman before her.

Loretta's eyes brightened, as if she'd been waiting all night for someone to ask her that question.

'"*See the mountains kiss high heaven, and the waves clasp one another,*"' she said with a proud smile. '"*And the sunlight clasps the earth, and the moonbeams kiss the sea: what is all this sweet work worth, if thou kiss not me?*"'

Charlotte had never cared much for poetry—and she cared even less for *romantic* poetry—but hearing it now, in Loretta's voice, was like discovering poetry for the first time. The way each word danced off Loretta's lips, the way her lilting voice drew Charlotte in like a siren's song…

'Percy Shelley,' Loretta continued. 'Mary Shelley is the true genius of the two, of course, but I've been working through Percy's poems lately, and they're just so enchanting.'

'What does it mean?' Charlotte asked. 'The poem?'

'I've been thinking about that…' Loretta started, then bit her lip. She shook her head.

'No, tell me,' Charlotte nudged. 'I want to know.'

Be careful, Charlotte thought to herself. *You're letting yourself get too close.*

'Well…' Loretta's mouth spilled into a smile despite herself. 'I was wondering what the mountains know that I don't. Why can't I feel for a gentleman what the mountains feel for heaven, or what the moonbeams feel for the sea? The poem is saying that the whole planet is filled with love, even *made* of love, governed by it.' She squeezed Charlotte's hand. 'But the shape that love takes is different each time. There is no one *right* way. So *this*—how I feel about women, about you— it must be natural. It *must* be.'

Charlotte looked up into Loretta's sparkling eyes. 'As natural as the sunlight as it clasps the earth.'

'Exactly.' Loretta nodded. *"What is all this sweet work worth, if thou kiss not me?"'*

Charlotte almost forgot where they were. The music seemed so distant now, the swirling dancers miles away. All that existed was this dim corridor, Loretta's pale face and pink lips, the subtle rise and fall of their chests.

A group of giggling ladies stepped into the corridor, and the spell was broken.

'I *wish*,' one of them exclaimed loudly to her friends, 'that this *fine establishment* served something better than *dry cakes* with no *icing*!'

Loretta sighed. 'I suppose your brother will be looking for us… I'll head out first.'

And with that, she stepped into the hall, and Charlotte was alone.

She watched Loretta twirl across the dance floor—Charlotte still hidden in the dark of the corridor, Loretta illuminated by the bright light of the ballroom. Charlotte knew they could only ever be with each other as the waves were with the shore: for one glorious moment and nothing more. They would be like the leaves of a tree…green for a season. When autumn came, they wouldn't fall in love—they'd just fall, making room on their branches for whatever came next.

At least Loretta knew what would come next for her: Arthur, marriage, life as a duchess.

As for Charlotte?

She reached under her skirts and untied the flask of brandy from her garter, then took a long swig. She needed it more than Mr Baxter did. He would understand.

Chapter Eleven

For perhaps the first time in her entire life, Loretta didn't know what might come next. All morning questions she'd never considered before flooded her brain. How could Charlotte make her feel what a handsome duke and a hundred suitors couldn't? Why did her laugh and her mischievous smile and her bouncing blonde curls consume all of Loretta's thoughts? What if she didn't marry the Duke? What if she ran away with his sister instead? Was she going mad?

And so Loretta Linfield did what she always did when she was confronted with questions.

She researched.

The Baron had long been a collector of stories, and although many of those stories dealt exclusively with the natural sciences, he had no shortage of biographies, memoirs and published diaries. The history books and the gossip columns alike confirmed it: love and marriage were far more complicated and far less synonymous than she'd learned in etiquette lessons.

It was only a decade ago that Lady Caroline Lamb had an affair with Lord Byron. Lady Georgiana Cavendish had openly shared her husband with Lady Elizabeth Foster. Her own parents had stopped relying on marriage for love years ago.

As Loretta read, and thought, and read again, it seemed everyone was bound to have an affair with someone.

But Charlotte wasn't just *someone*. And Loretta didn't want to kiss her for a season then part ways for ever, as seemed to be the case with so many of the romances she researched. Loretta wanted her company, her warmth, her presence. And she wanted it every day. She wanted it even now.

All this was easy enough in cloakrooms and clubs, but at some point she would have to make some difficult decisions. Loretta couldn't imagine casting aside everything she'd prepared for—not to mention every expectation her father and the rest of high society had heaped upon her—just to run away with Charlotte.

But it wasn't any easier to imagine a future with someone else—even someone as decent and pleasant as the Duke. A life without Charlotte Sterlington was growing increasingly inconceivable.

But, she supposed with a frustrated sigh, *all of these are future concerns.*

For now, Loretta allowed herself to sink into her affection for Charlotte, to submerge her heart in the tender memory of Charlotte's mouth on hers. She went about the rest of her day with a newfound vivacity. She smiled, spoke and sipped her tea just as she always had, but with lips that were utterly transformed.

Loretta had always preferred the company of books to people, and now that she had a *person* whose company she preferred she wasn't sure what to do with herself. Charlotte didn't live in the library, ready and waiting for Loretta to pluck her off the shelf whenever she wanted.

She settled for writing a letter.

Loretta left the library for her writing desk, but a boisterous laugh from behind the doors of her father's study froze her feet in place. A chill ran up her spine as she heard the unmistakable voice of Cecil Wrottesley.

'If fossils are what you want, you can't do better than the land my second cousin owns in Bavaria.'

Loretta moved towards the door, her footsteps light as a falling leaf.

'I'm glad you see things as I do, Cecil,' came her father's voice in reply. 'There are those who scoff at the budding science of paleontology, but I say there's a fortune to be made in these excavations.'

'We could be successful partners, you and I.'

Loretta leaned in closer, the hair on her skin standing straight up.

'We could name a whole *species* after you,' Cecil continued. 'Your name, enshrined in history!'

The offer, informal as it was, must be intoxicating for the Baron. Loretta knew he was right about the bones, and about the ancient creatures engraved in rock—when discoveries like this were made, fame and fortune always followed.

'That *is* the goal,' Bertram said. Loretta detected some suspicion in his voice. 'But you know as well as anyone that I have the funds to manage this myself. If you have another motive, I'd prefer to hear it now.'

Loretta strained to hear over the rapid pounding of her heart.

'I'm wondering about your daughter...'

Her stomach twisted. She clenched her teeth to stifle a gasp. She hated how easily he could bring her up in a conversation about fossils—as if she were just another thing to discover, take home and put on display.

'You've been gone for three years,' her father said. 'I'm surprised you didn't find a wife on the Continent.'

'There are none to be found as beautiful as Loretta.'

She wanted to bang on the door and scream at them both. But she couldn't move, couldn't speak. Her throat closed as she realised that no matter how free she felt when she was with Charlotte, her life would always return to this: decisions made about her on the other side of a closed door.

'I'll admit, Cecil, I always hoped you'd clean yourself up and return—just as you have,' her father said after a pause. 'But I wasn't waiting around. I've pursued other options, and a duke is an impossible option to beat.'

It should have made Loretta feel better to hear this from her father. To know he still didn't consider Cecil an acceptable suitor...to know her marriage to the Duke was all but confirmed.

But the nausea persisted, her heart didn't slow, and relief never came.

'I don't deny that life as a duchess is everything Loretta deserves,' Cecil replied. 'But what do you really *know* about the Sterlington household? The Duke *may* be an upstanding gentleman, but his sister is practically feral.'

Loretta's hands balled into fists.

'Surely you've heard the stories?' Cecil went on. 'The dinner parties she's disrupted with her rude comments, the balls where she's refused to dance with anyone, and of course that one night at Almack's—'

'That's enough, Cecil.'

'We both know how vulnerable women can be when presented with the wrong role models. They need firm, virtuous leadership to guide them. You should know more than anyone how easy it is for a woman to—'

'I said, that's *enough*.'

Loretta heard a loud thud—her father slamming something onto his desk.

'You overstep, Cecil. You can see yourself out.'

Loretta ran to her room as quickly and quietly as she could

manage. She closed her creaky bedroom door behind her and sat at her writing desk, head buried in her hands.

Her instinct had been right. Cecil's wealth and status might be restored, but his pride demanded one last thing.

He won't have me, Loretta thought. Her father had dismissed his offer outright. *I'm safe.*

But she didn't feel safe.

Cecil would not be deterred so easily.

She imagined her life with him…her life with someone who would never ask what she was reading, who would never care. He would praise her beauty, and show her off to his friends the way he would a newly acquired sculpture, and over the years she would become cold and silent as marble.

Loretta reached for a smooth sheet of paper and uncorked a fresh bottle of ink.

Tell Arthur to send for me!

She penned the note in tall, thin lines with her crow quill. She scattered a dash of pounce to dry the ink, folded the missive and sealed it with the Linfield crest.

Loretta wasn't certain what she wanted from the future, but she certainly did not want to spend it with Lord Wrottesley.

An invitation arrived from the Duke the next morning: tea in the parlour, early afternoon. Loretta fretted about what to wear more than she ever had before. Dresses she'd never thought twice about were now all wrong—the cream-coloured gown was too old-fashioned, the sage-green too baggy, the pink embroidery on this one had begun to fray…

'Bridget,' she asked as her lady's maid entered the room, 'which gown says—?'

Says what? she thought. *Kiss me? More than kiss me? Con-*

*vince me to return to the life I've always expected? Convince
me to run away?*

'Oh, just choose one!' she said, throwing up her arms.

After some deliberation, Bridget paired a simple ivory
dress with an emerald-green bodice to match Loretta's eyes,
then spun her hair with gold ribbons. Loretta stood in front
of her full-length mirror and wondered what Charlotte would
think. She was familiar enough with Charlotte's paintings—
masquerading as Mr Fletcher's, of course—to know that Charlotte was used to looking at beautiful women. She sketched
them, painted them and danced with them in secret rooms.

Loretta began to sweat, wondering how she would com-
pare.

The carriage ride over was nerve-racking. Every bump in
the cobblestone felt like an earthquake. Loretta, of course,
had never experienced an earthquake herself, but she'd read
about one in Mansfield eight years prior—about stones falling from the church as the ground beneath its foundation vi-
brated. It seemed in many ways an apt analogy for her life
at the moment.

Her hand trembled as she knocked on the door, but when
Charlotte answered all Loretta could feel was a warm and
easy stillness.

Everything else—everything that wasn't those storm cloud
eyes, that amber gown, those gilded curls that flourished like
the filigree of a master jeweller—faded away. Cecil was gone,
her father was gone, the institution of marriage was gone.

To curtsy and smile was painful when all she wanted to
do was leap into Charlotte's arms, to feel the warmth of her
skin without layers of fabric in between them, to know and be
known by the most scandalous lover in all of London.

This is what the poets write about, Loretta thought. *This
is what drives them mad.*

'I have something planned,' Charlotte whispered as they entered the parlour.

The Duke rose from his seat with a warm grin. A feast of tea and treats lay before them—far more than would be manageable for three people. A tower of *macarons* in dainty pastels, plates of biscuits and small cakes of all kinds crowded the glossy round table in the centre of the room. A second table held the tea set—crisp white porcelain with shining gold flowers.

The room itself was magnificent: lightly patterned mint-green wallpaper, long curtains just a shade darker, with a heavy gold fringe, an ornamental rug with pink roses and swirling vines. It was like her father's parlour, but larger and grander, with more light streaming through the wall-length windows. But there was no artwork on the walls, no marble busts on the mantel. Perhaps she could do something about that when she was the Duchess of this house...

Charlotte sat at a distance with an embroidery hoop, stitching with unusually perfect posture. Loretta wanted to giggle at the act, but diverted her attention to the Duke.

'Such a lovely tea set,' she commented.

But His Grace barely had time to get a word out before the butler was informing him of a most urgent matter that needed his attention, and even though Loretta couldn't hear the details that were whispered into his ear, the Duke's face revealed that it could not wait. He apologised profusely on his way out.

'Finally!' Charlotte exclaimed the moment the door clicked behind him. 'That took *ages.*'

She tossed her embroidery onto the couch and reached for a frosted honey cake.

'I've been here all of five minutes!' Loretta laughed.

'Five minutes during which I'm not allowed to touch you,'

Charlotte said through generous, joyful bites of cake, 'is an eternity. Have you *been* in a room with yourself?'

Loretta felt heat flare on her cheeks before it spread to the rest of her body. Charlotte moved towards her, glanced out of the window, then kissed Loretta's neck as if the cake she'd just finished had only been an appetiser.

'I want…' Charlotte whispered just under Loretta's ear.

What? Loretta thought eagerly. *To hold me? To kiss me?*

'I want…' Charlotte continued, teasing Loretta with her lips.

Loretta didn't know exactly what people did during secret love affairs, but she wanted to find out. Every inch of her wanted to find out.

Charlotte leaned back, red-hot mischief in her cool blue eyes.

'I want to paint you.'

Charlotte had painted many women over the last few years, and Loretta was nothing special.

At least, that was how Charlotte *should have* felt. That would have been the easy thing to feel as she glanced back and forth between the Loretta on her canvas and the Loretta perched comfortably upon a stool.

Instead, Charlotte felt inconveniently, inconceivably, inappropriately attracted to the woman who sat across from her. How could oil and canvas capture the sweet mix of kindness and curiosity in her rich green eyes? Could the finest brush in Charlotte's collection do justice to the constellation of freckles that lit the sky of Loretta's face?

Charlotte had often wondered if being an artist made her vulnerable to swift and powerful bouts of lust. Her job was to notice people, to study the details of their faces, their bodies, their very souls, with such depth and specificity that she couldn't help but fall in love with each subject, if only for a moment. No painter of any real talent could escape a subject unscathed.

Even so, Charlotte knew in her gut that this was different. She hadn't just noticed Loretta, and she wasn't just painting her now. She was captivated, fascinated, utterly caught up. She knew she was in too deep, but part of her didn't seem to care.

This was dangerous territory. When cruel Cupid weighs the scales of love, he always leaves the Suffering Sterlingtons wanting.

'My father seems to think your brother will propose soon. Do you suppose he's right?' Loretta said.

At least it will all be over soon, thought Charlotte.

By the end of the season Loretta would be a duchess, and Charlotte would go back to much more straightforward flings at the Fourth Tier.

'Arthur, as I'm sure you've noticed, is as scrutable as he is competent at art criticism.'

The sound that escaped Loretta was a cross between a gasp and a laugh. Now, *that* was a facial expression Charlotte wanted to paint.

'He doesn't share much with me,' Charlotte continued. 'But I know he is quite fond of you, and it truly shouldn't be long now.'

'Hmm…' Loretta lowered eyes, her fingers twisting the fabric of her skirt.

Oh! thought Charlotte with surprise. *She thinks that Arthur's dilly-dallying has something to do with her.*

Charlotte changed her tone from jest to sincerity—a leap she did not often make. 'Do you want to see the painting so far?'

Loretta lit up, arched her eyebrows, and nodded with a sharp breath of excitement. She hurried to Charlotte and put her hands on her shoulders. The small canvas was all line and colour, hurried brush strokes that spelled out the shape of Loretta's torso, her arms, her neck. The face was closer to being done, but the hair faded into the backdrop. It looked as though she were emerging from a mist.

Charlotte watched Loretta as she scanned this rough and wild portrait of herself. There had been no patience in Charlotte's hand as she'd sketched the contours of Loretta's figure with all the same longing she would have while painting a bowl of fruit during a famine.

'You have to understand,' Charlotte said carefully, 'that everyone Arthur has ever loved has died.'

'You're quite alive,' Loretta countered.

'I know what I said.' Guilt filled the heavy silence that followed. 'But I shouldn't have said that. Arthur and I have never been close, but he does love me in his own way. In the past he was always travelling somewhere, and I was always too odd, and now we just happen to be the only Sterlingtons left.' She stood and cupped her hand around Loretta's cheek. 'He'd never admit this, but he must annul his marriage to grief before he can open himself up to any real relationship. We've just…we've lost so much.'

Loretta placed her own hands over Charlotte's and whispered, 'I can't imagine…'

'Then let's not.' Charlotte shivered, as if shaking off unhappy memories. 'When I'm here, in my studio, I sometimes pretend that everything outside these walls doesn't exist.'

She looked up into Loretta's sparkling eyes, a few inches higher than her own.

'I'm glad that I'm inside these walls.' Loretta dropped her hands to Charlotte's waist.

'As am I,' answered Charlotte, resting her face on Loretta's chest.

They stood there, quietly embracing.

Loretta broke the silence. 'I—I've been thinking about you.'

Charlotte pulled away to look into Loretta's face, which was rapidly turning red, and cracked a teasing smile. 'What have you been thinking?'

'About…our conversations. And your artwork. And dancing with you at the Fourth Tier.' Loretta swallowed. 'And… the cloakroom.'

'Oh, yes, your *ribbon adjustment*.' Charlotte ran her fingers up the back of Charlotte's neck and into her soft hair. She felt Loretta's rigid posture relax.

'I feel…unwound,' whispered Loretta. 'I suppose that's normal?'

'I stopped caring about *normal* a long time ago.' Charlotte gently dragged her free hand up Loretta's cheek. 'Do you like the feeling?'

Loretta nodded eagerly.

There were any number of beasts always fighting for attention in Charlotte's chest—grief, shame, recklessness. But whatever was beating against her ribcage now felt entirely different, light and life-giving.

And it was hungry.

Charlotte lifted Loretta onto the edge of the table behind her and leaned into her warm, inviting body. She relished the feeling of her lips on Loretta's, the blazing heat of their tongues together. Every pore of Charlotte's skin seemed to vibrate with pleasure as she melted into the scent, the taste, the sight, the feel of the woman before her. She traced her lips down the slope of Loretta's neck to her collarbone, eliciting a slow, heavy exhalation from Loretta. Charlotte would follow that sound to the ends of the earth.

Her lips slid down to the neckline of Loretta's dress like ice melting in the late winter sun. Loretta buried a hand in

Charlotte's thick curls, sending hairpins falling to the floor, and Charlotte sent her own hands to the back of Loretta's dress, where a row of buttons was begging to be unfastened.

'How about we take this off?' Charlotte muttered into the rise and fall of Loretta's chest as her fingers set the first button free.

'Yes…' she breathed, eyes closed and head tilted back, as if she had just stepped into a warm bath.

At the third button, Loretta snapped to attention. 'Wait.'

Charlotte froze.

'Why, exactly?' Loretta asked.

Charlotte scanned her face for any sign of regret, shame, embarrassment, worry… But all she found was genuine pragmatic enquiry.

'Well…' Charlotte started.

How did one explain sexual intimacy to someone as innocent as Loretta Linfield?

She likely doesn't even know where babies come from, Charlotte thought as she bit her lip. *At least she won't have to learn this on her wedding night.*

'When two people are attracted to each other,' Charlotte began, 'they…touch each other. Er…specifically the parts that are…usually hidden by clothes.'

Charlotte had never felt more inarticulate in her entire life. She held Loretta's chastity in her hands and was fumbling through every word of her clumsy explanation.

'Are you referring to sexual intercourse?' asked Loretta, matter-of-factly.

For a moment Charlotte was too shocked to speak. 'You know what that is?'

'Of course.' Loretta nodded. 'There are several scientific texts in my father's library that explain the mechanisms of reproductive anatomy.'

'Oh!' Now Charlotte really didn't know what to say. She was suddenly aware of all the painted eyes that were staring at them as they stood in the flickering candlelight.

'What does sexual intercourse have to do with us?' Loretta asked, leaning back against the cabinet. 'Neither of us have a penis.'

Charlotte burst into such unreserved laughter that she had to gasp for breath.

'What's so funny?' Loretta crossed her arms.

'Loretta, what on *earth* have you read?'

'I know exactly how it works, Charlotte. I'm not *naive*. I know how mammals reproduce, and I know all the necessary components, so I don't see a reason to go any further than this as we're clearly missing—'

'Yes!' Charlotte continued to giggle. 'A penis.' She wondered how many different shades of red pigment she'd have to mix in order to paint the indescribable colour Loretta's face was now turning. 'And you are right. I shouldn't have assumed you know nothing of reproductive anatomy.'

Loretta huffed in righteous indignation, but she couldn't keep a smile from cracking open her otherwise serious face. 'Shall we continue kissing, then?'

'Let me ask you one more question,' Charlotte said into Loretta's ear. 'Did you know that there is plenty of fun to be had with the parts that we *do* have?'

'Fun?' Loretta blinked. 'What does ensuring the survival of one's genetic line have to do with *fun*?'

'Surely you know it feels good?' Charlotte's eyes scanned Loretta's body like a bird deciding where to land. 'That sometimes people have sex just for pleasure.'

'Charlotte,' Loretta said doubtfully, 'I am certain the books would have mentioned if sex included *pleasure*.'

Charlotte rested her hands on Loretta's knees. Loretta,

who could say the word *penis* with a straight face but couldn't imagine what could be done without one. Loretta, who trusted in books so much that she'd never thought to question if something vital was missing.

'You think that *science* books…' Charlotte gripped Loretta's knees and slowly slid them apart '…which I assume were written by *men*…' she snaked her hands up to Loretta's hips '…men who don't have *vulvas*…' she squeezed '…would have told you about *this*?'

In one swift motion she tugged Loretta forward and moved her own body closer, until they were nearer to each other than they'd ever been, Charlotte's abdomen now tantalisingly warm from the damp heat of Loretta's thighs. She was weak with the thought of how much warmer she would be without the four layers of fabric that lay between them.

Loretta moaned, her eyes wide.

'Tell me you feel nothing,' challenged Charlotte, her fingers gently tugging at Loretta's skirts.

'That,' Loretta responded breathlessly, 'would be a lie.'

'Because I can always stop—'

Loretta shook her head fervently and squeezed her thighs into Charlotte's waist. 'I just don't understand.' She laced her fingers at the back of Charlotte's neck. 'It's like…being hungry. But when I'm hungry I know what to eat. Or when I'm thirsty I can have a cup of tea. I don't know what to do with—' she glanced down at the place where their bodies met '—with *this*.'

Charlotte bent at the waist until their noses touched. 'I can be your cup of tea,' she said, as her lips slowly curved up.

'But the books…' Loretta whispered, struggling to let go of everything she'd thought was true even as her body softened like butter at Charlotte's touch.

'How do scientists set out to prove or disprove a hypothesis?' asked Charlotte.

'They…experiment,' Loretta said, slowly catching on.

Charlotte bunched the rest of Loretta's skirts up to the very top of her thighs, until only a single layer of muslin hung between them. The hair on her legs shot straight up.

'Shall we experiment…for science?' Charlotte asked, her own desire reaching a fever-pitch.

'For science,' Loretta agreed with breathy hunger.

Charlotte didn't have long to study this new glint in Loretta's eyes before she felt ankles locking behind her back, fingers making a mess of her hair and the most passionate kiss she'd ever received.

And then Loretta lifted the final fold of fabric.

Chapter Twelve

Loretta often stayed up late to finish a good book, her bedside candle burning down to a stub. But tonight her room was pitch-black, and no book was open on her bed. The memory of the last few hours was all it took to keep her wide awake, tossing and turning, too hot to stay under her blankets and too excited to doze off.

Charlotte's unrivalled beauty had once belonged only to Loretta's *eyes*, but now that her skin, her hands and her aching thighs were involved there was nothing else that could claim her attention. Not even sleep. Not even a very good book.

Once Loretta had wrapped her legs around Charlotte in that dim and dusty greenhouse, she'd known she was done for. She'd known that she wanted to sink into her desire, to disappear beneath the surface, to be consumed.

Even here, in her own bed, Loretta felt the warmth of Charlotte on her skin, the pressure of Charlotte's hands, the ravenous hunger of her mouth. She was glorious. She was incendiary. She was utterly insatiable.

Loretta's fingers craved the arch of Charlotte's neck, the softness of her breasts, the shaking of her thighs. She ached to hear again the sound of Charlotte's voice, the liquid murmur that had poured into the core of her being.

'Can I kiss you here? Do you want to keep going?'

'*Yes,*' Loretta had said. '*A thousand times yes.*'

And then—time freezing, or leaping forward, or unfolding all at once.

And then—the slow heat of Charlotte's hands drifting downward, the pleasure pooling between her legs, the bundle of nerves throbbing under Charlotte's expert touch.

And then—

Loretta couldn't fully describe what had happened next. *Eruption? Effervescence? Ecstasy?* She had convulsed until a box of paint brushes had flown off the table.

Loretta could still hear the brushes clattering to the floor. She could still hear the moans—Charlotte's or her own, she wasn't sure—the softening beat of Charlotte's heart as they lay beside each other afterwards. She ran the memory through her mind over and over again, turning each page the way a monk might study a sacred tome.

Loretta didn't see Charlotte for several days, even though their houses were just streets apart. The Duke was too busy in Parliament to send for her, and Loretta was too inexperienced at romance to know if she was supposed to send for Charlotte.

In her memory, those moments in the studio felt suspended in time, perfectly preserved like summer fruit in winter's cellar. If she found out that Charlotte had regrets, or didn't want to see her again, the memory would be spoiled and Loretta would be devastated.

She tried to distract herself in the library. It didn't work. Every page reminded Loretta of Charlotte's supple skin, every word of her tantalising whispers. She couldn't finish a paragraph without her mind wandering to the greenhouse, to Charlotte's firm hands holding her tight, their bodies pressed together. Every night she dreamt of Charlotte's mouth on her own. Loretta felt as if her body were on fire, and she wanted nothing more than to climb deeper into the flames.

On the fifth day, Loretta realised she'd go mad if she sat around any longer.

Her father was delighted when she asked to visit Lady Charlotte. 'Befriend the sister! Yes, yes, that's very clever!'

On her carriage ride to the Sterlington townhouse, Loretta pulled nervously at her powder-blue dress and rehearsed in her head what she would say to Charlotte. Her teeth chattered. She wasn't sure if it was afternoon chill or anxiety.

Loretta arrived in what felt like seconds. A stiff-looking footman met her at the door and led her through the labyrinthine corridors of the enormous home, turning this way and that until finally he came to a stop.

He pushed open a pair of simple wooden doors. With a deep, shaky breath, Loretta followed him inside. They were in a sunroom—three walls were made up entirely of ceiling-height windows, and much of the floor space was occupied by exotic potted plants. Just outside stretched the Sterlington gardens.

At the far end of the room, facing away from the door, Charlotte lay sprawled across an ornate purple daybed. The ample curves of her silhouette sent a shiver through Loretta. She wanted at once to run towards Charlotte and to run away.

'Miss Linfield,' the footman announced solemnly, with a half nod.

Charlotte lifted her head ever so slightly. The ruffles of her wine-dark dress shifted, and her golden curls cascaded magnificently down her shoulders.

'You may leave us.' Her voice was unreadable. She did not turn around.

Loretta clasped her trembling hands together.

The footman nodded again, retreated into the corridor and closed the doors with a resounding thud.

Loretta took a step forward.

'You've woken me from my nap.'

'Oh!' Loretta stopped. She could feel the blood rush to her face.

This is it, she thought miserably. *Whatever romance I've imagined between us—*

She clenched her fists to clear her mind. 'I haven't seen you in many days. Not since…' She stepped closer, took a deep breath and recited the lines she had practised in the carriage ride over. 'I've missed you terribly. I can't stop thinking of you. And I want to know if you feel the same.' She was only a few paces now from where Charlotte lay. 'I—I want you.'

Charlotte turned slowly to face her, eyes bright and mouth half turned in a roguish smile. 'What are you going to do about it?'

The desire building in Loretta burst forth. She ran the remaining distance to the daybed. Charlotte grabbed her by the waist, dragged her down beside her, pulled Loretta's head towards her own. Their lips crashed into each other, their legs wove together, their bodies became one.

Loretta imagined that every inch of her skin was blushing pink with the syrupy heat that spread from her lips all the way to her toes.

When they had finished and finished again, and they lay tired and entangled in each other's arms, and Loretta was certain that she had never been so happy in her whole life, Charlotte leaned forward and whispered, 'Meet me in my bedchamber.'

She slid gracefully off the bed and hurried out through the door. Loretta took a moment to catch her breath, her body bearing the sweet pressure of Charlotte's hands as if they were still there. She stood and straightened her skirts, then was startled when Charlotte reappeared in the doorway.

'Up the stairs, third door on your left!'

And again, she was gone.

As Loretta moved through the house she couldn't help being impressed—and perhaps intimidated—at the sheer size of the place. Each room she passed was grand and dignified and immaculate.

She felt a rush of warmth as she stepped into Charlotte's bedchamber, the only room in the house that actually felt lived-in. Rich mahogany panels stretched to an ornate gilded ceiling with a low-hanging chandelier. The decorations were opulent—marble busts, polished mirrors, a Jasperware vase overflowing with daisies. And in the centre was an unfathomably large four-poster bed, covered in decadent golden blankets, crowded with plump velvet pillows and draped in a shimmering canopy.

All around the room were paintings– probably 'gifts' from Mr Fletcher. Most of them were nudes: women bathing in forests and grottos, near waterfalls and willow trees. Many of them were wrapped in the flimsiest of wet, white linens.

Loretta wasn't sure why these weren't in a museum, or a private collection. They were stunning, and they would fit perfectly with the bathing nudes of any of Europe's finest painters.

No. Loretta changed her mind. *They wouldn't.*

Looking closer, Loretta could tell these were nothing like the nudes one might find in the Louvre, or the Uffizi, or in Somerset House. They were stranger, and better, and—this was how Loretta knew they were Charlotte's—they were truer.

The painting closest to the door was a wide rectangle elegantly framed over a chest of drawers. It featured three naked women lounging by a woodland lake in various stages of undress. Loretta furrowed her brow and called to mind the usual subjects of this genre: women with smooth, glowing, unblemished skin. Women with soft features and slender waists. Women with dainty pink nipples and dome-shaped breasts that defied the laws of gravity. Loretta had thought all women must look like that—or were *supposed* to look like that—beneath their gowns; otherwise, who were these gentlemen painting?

The first figure in Charlotte's scene sat on a grassy bank, dipping her feet into the calm water. Her thin ivory dress was pooled around her hips, revealing two pendulous breasts that sagged against her torso. She was tying up her curly orange hair, and all along her body were creases, folds and freckles. The figure on the other side of the painting stood on a small rock, her shoulders covered with a creamy shawl. She was wringing out her slick, wet hair, water dripping down her plump body. Her belly was not the flat plane Loretta was used to seeing, and her thighs were painted with ripples of texture. The hair on her shins and between her legs was dark.

In the centre of the painting was the most spellbinding woman of the three, half-submerged in the lake and staring right through the canvas into the gawping eyes of the viewer. Her face bore a frown and her eyes bore a challenge—*Look at me, just as I am.* Her sandy blonde hair fell unfashionably straight onto large, bumpy nipples. But what transfixed Loretta most about this woman was that one of her breasts hung lower than the other.

Loretta's hands trailed up her body to her own asymmetrical breasts. With the naked women of men's paintings and men's anatomical diagrams as her only reference, she had spent her life assuming that something was odd about her body, that something was wrong. Beauty was found in symmetry, she had been told, which meant breasts of different sizes were unnatural—perhaps even ugly.

Loretta jumped at the sound of the door behind her. Charlotte stepped in carrying a basket of glass jars. She glanced between Loretta and the painting and grinned.

'It's one of my favourites,' Charlotte said as she climbed onto her tall, regal bed and patted the spot next to her.

Loretta walked over. 'Why do they look...?'

'Real?' Charlotte finished her sentence. 'Why do they look like actual women?'

She hiked up her skirts and stretched out her thighs, bending her knees slightly and enticing Loretta with the sudden sight of bare skin. Loretta soaked in this luxurious closeness, the rich sight and sound and scent of Charlotte Sterlington.

She joined her on the bed and nestled into Charlotte's shoulder, tracing her fingers along Charlotte's thighs. She noticed the pale ridges that spread across her legs, like streaks of lightning across the sky. The tips of her fingers followed the subtle dips and dimples all the way up to the black lace hem that rested at Charlotte's hips.

'Somehow,' Charlotte sighed, 'the gentlemen painters always leave this detail out.'

'How did you get these?' Loretta asked as she leaned down to kiss the marks.

'It just happens. You'll get them too, if you haven't already—' The end of Charlotte's sentence was broken by a gasp. Loretta's lips were getting dangerously close to that lacy hem.

'And the breasts?' Loretta looked up at Charlotte. 'I've seen as many paintings of naked women as anyone else, but I've never seen breasts that look so—'

'Heavy? Long? Asymmetrical?' Charlotte was playing with Loretta's hair.

'I was going to say, breasts that look so much like mine.'

Loretta rested her head on Charlotte's abdomen to feel the soft rise and fall of her body. She could drift into sleep like this and let the whole world disappear around them.

'Most women don't look like the portraits and sculptures in art galleries,' Charlotte said with purpose. 'Which means most women never see themselves as worthy of art.'

'Have you tried to sell them?' Loretta asked.

Charlotte reached across the bed for the basket and motioned for Loretta to sit next to her. She opened a glass jar and let a floral aroma waft into the room.

'I try to talk myself into selling them or exhibiting them every day,' Charlotte muttered as she dipped two fingers into the jar. 'There's a basin of water next to the armoire where you can rinse your face. We're going to relax today.'

Charlotte slathered a sweet-smelling mixture onto her face and sank back into a pile of pillows, and Loretta hopped off the bed and found the basin.

'What is it made of?' she asked, as she washed the rice powder off her face. She'd grown up with oatmeal and onion juice face lotions, but Charlotte's smelled far more enjoyable.

'Egg whites, honey, breadcrumbs and crushed flower petals from the garden. My mother wrote in her journal that she used to put *lavandula pedunculata*—French lavender—in all her beauty products, so I've added it to my recipe.'

When Loretta returned, Charlotte had spread the lotion across her forehead, cheeks, nose and chin. She passed the jar to Loretta and opened a second one, which contained candied lemon peels.

'My favourite snack.' Charlotte stifled a smile to keep the concoction from falling off her face.

'Why don't you exhibit the paintings?' Loretta asked.

Charlotte was more than just the master artist behind the

name of Mr Nathaniel Fletcher. She was a true genius, a visionary, a talent for the ages...

And, Loretta thought, *for a little while she is mine.*

'No one will want them,' Charlotte said, chewing on her candied peel. 'And that will be the end of Nathaniel's "career," and his family will think him disturbed for painting something so indecent.'

Loretta felt Charlotte's hand reach for hers, and soon their fingers were wrapped together, warm and tight and comforting.

Loretta finished coating her face in the lotion, wiped her hand on a napkin and reached for a lemon peel.

'Why do you paint as Mr Fletcher?' She took a bite and tried to remember which pieces at home were painted by women. 'My father has a Gérard in his library and a Villers in his study.'

'We don't live in France,' Charlotte said flatly.

Loretta could feel the tension radiating from Charlotte's body. The last thing she wanted was to be a source of stress, but she wanted to *know* Charlotte—fully and completely—and this felt like an essential part of who she was.

'I read in our library that two women were among the founders of the Royal Academy,' Loretta offered.

'That's *technically* true,' Charlotte huffed, 'but they weren't even allowed at the committee meetings. And— Wait... Did you just say you *read* about the Royal Academy?'

Loretta suddenly felt sheepish. This was a way of confessing love—or something close to love, at least. 'I've been reading about painting, just a bit. So I can know more about... about you.'

'Loretta!' Charlotte giggled. 'That's almost *too* endearing.'

'I'm sorry, I can—'

'No, no, I *am* quite fascinating.' Charlotte smiled. She bit into another lemon peel and continued, 'I think it's sweet. What else do you want to know?'

Loretta hesitated. 'Have you ever thought of running away?' she asked. She was posing the question to Charlotte, but if she was being honest the question was just as much for herself.

'To where?'

'To France, maybe. Somewhere in the country. You could paint as yourself, and there might be more…privacy.'

Charlotte considered for a moment. 'Sometimes I think of it. But I have a life here. Nathaniel and the Fourth Tier and you. Not to mention that Arthur would be even more insufferable without me.'

Loretta giggled. 'But if you *did* run away, what would it be like?'

'Hmm…' Charlotte smiled. 'I suppose I *would* paint as myself.'

'You could open your own art gallery and fill it with paintings just like these.'

'Paintings that would scandalise the Continent.'

'Paintings that would make women feel seen and known.'

Charlotte pulled Loretta close. 'We would need a garden. It's not a daydream without a garden.'

'You could teach me how to name all the flowers.'

Loretta understood now why people became poets. Surely this—what she and Charlotte shared between them—was what all great writers of romance spent their lives trying to narrate. And she understood their words now, too. When poets wrote about *falling* in love, or *following* their hearts, it was because love did not stand still. Loretta felt moved, transported, carried away. The place she was now was nothing like the place she had been.

They lay together until the sky began to darken and Loretta's stomach began to grumble.

'I suppose I ought to go home soon,' she said, with a groan.

'Yes, I suppose…'

Charlotte sounded disappointed, and this made Loretta's heart soar. Charlotte didn't want her to leave. And maybe, if they were brave enough, they could make a life for themselves where she didn't have to.

They rinsed their faces and pinned back their hair, and then moved through the maze of corridors back to the grand hall she'd so nervously stepped into several hours earlier.

All the fear and doubt she'd brought with her had faded long ago. Loretta could imagine a future with Charlotte—a real future filled with genuine love and companionship. She'd never had reason before to imagine a future different from the one she was supposed to want. But now that she understood how rich, how full, how wonderful a life of love could be, the only thing she *couldn't* imagine was going back to the way things had been before.

They were alone when they reached the front door. Charlotte looked around, just to be safe, then gripped Loretta's waist and stretched up to kiss her nose.

'What would you do, if you could run away?'

'I'd go with you.' Loretta didn't hesitate.

Charlotte laughed. 'You'd get tired of me eventually.'

'I would never.'

'Well…' Charlotte shrugged. 'We'll never have to find out. That's what daydreams are for.'

She tilted her head back with a wide, dreamy grin and closed her eyes.

'But what if it doesn't have to be a daydream?'

'What do you mean, exactly?'

'What if we *could* have our garden? And spend our days talking of art and books and botany? What if we could sleep in each other's arms every night?'

Charlotte opened her eyes and studied Loretta's face. 'You're being serious?'

'Of course I'm being serious. If you were a man, you would expect me to cut off my courtship with Arthur and marry you instead. So I don't see why—'

'But I'm *not* a man.'

'Yes, but—'

'Loretta.' A shadow passed across Charlotte's face and her shoulders sagged. 'I don't think you understand how this works.'

Loretta bit her bottom lip.

How else *could* it work? So many people didn't find love until *after* they married, and then they had to split their life in half to accommodate a spouse and a lover. But Loretta had found Charlotte *now*, before any other future had been finalised.

Surely there's still time to build a life that can be whole?

'How *does* this work?' she asked cautiously.

'We have fun together.'

'And then?'

Charlotte exhaled slowly. She looked suddenly very tired. 'And then it gets complicated. And then it ends.'

Loretta winced. All the colour drained from the imaginary future in her mind. 'That's it? *"And then it ends"*? There must be some way for us to stay together—'

'You aren't hearing me,' Charlotte interrupted. 'There are no happily-ever-afters for people like us. There is only right now.' Her face softened into a small and bashful smile. She spoke softly. 'And I like right now. I really, really do.'

The realisation felt like a plunge into the ice-cold ocean: this was all she was going to get from Charlotte Sterlington. It wasn't nothing—the vulnerable look on Charlotte's face communicated as much—but it wasn't what Loretta had hoped for.

She pulled Charlotte into a tight hug, so she could hide the sadness on her face when she said, 'I like right now, too.'

It was all Loretta could do to make it into the carriage before the tears in her eyes spilled over. She let them drip down her cheeks as she travelled home. But she didn't give herself over to the heavy cry building in her chest—not entirely.

Charlotte felt something for her—something strong and powerful and meaningful. All Loretta had to do was convince Charlotte that this *something* was worth holding on to.

Chapter Thirteen

Charlotte gave herself over to the heavy laugh building in her chest. She was trying to tell a story—of how Renée had feigned illness to come with them tonight, how Charlotte had helped and how they had both almost been caught by Mrs Grant at the eleventh hour—but the details were just too ridiculous to get through without laughing.

Loretta leaned in to kiss Charlotte's cheek. Their rented carriage, full by now with the warmth and mirth of good company, bounced along towards the Fourth Tier. Charlotte often sneaked out on her own, but every now and then she and Nathaniel made it an event.

'I'm always amazed the Duke still falls for your antics,' Nathaniel said.

'If there is one benefit to living in the Suffering Sterlington household,' Charlotte replied, 'it must be how *easy* it is to gain sympathy just by feigning sickness. Arthur will simply *not* have our staff up and about when they're ill, lest it bring even more misfortune upon our family.'

Renée showcased her impressively convincing sneeze again, and everyone laughed once more.

'I see we didn't scare Loretta away last time,' Nathaniel said with a wink, nudging Loretta's knee with his own.

'Quite the opposite.' Loretta lifted her chin and rolled back her shoulders. 'I plan to become a regular patron.'

There was a confident edge to her voice that Charlotte hadn't heard before. *Charlotte* was used to being the bold one, but the sly and playful smile on Loretta's lips told her she'd be sharing that boldness tonight.

Nathaniel had the password when they arrived—four knocks, and the word *soprano*—and soon they were back in the familiar outer room, sharing greetings with Mr Hawkins, then moving off to rifle through the racks for costumes, then onto the dance floor as the pianist played an old Scottish folk tune.

Tonight, Charlotte wore the billowing blue sleeves of Mercutio from a performance of *Romeo and Juliet* she'd seen in her first season. The silver-paned Elizabethan sleeves were a bit frayed, and the skin-tight trousers beneath were long on Charlotte's short frame, but she felt regal and glamorous and, *oh, so alive.*

Loretta, of course, looked stunning as Romeo, in a nearly identical costume in green and gold. The masculine fit was baggy on her, and Charlotte's heart soared to watch Loretta twirl and kick her legs in trousers for the first time.

She spun into Charlotte, glee radiating from her face, and caught her breath. 'If society allowed it, would you always wear trousers?'

'Goodness, no!' Charlotte exclaimed. 'How on earth would I relieve myself?'

They laughed, and kissed, and revelled in the freedom of the night.

'Come on!' Loretta shouted over the joyful din, taking hold of Charlotte's hand and pulling her towards the dance floor. It was crowded tonight—even more so than usual. Brightly dressed bodies twisted and twirled and gyrated all around; strangers smiled and embraced; couples kissed openly, without shame.

It was *magnificent.*

She settled into a rhythm with Loretta and let the music move her. But Loretta didn't seem settled at all. Her eyes were darting around, her movements buzzing with nervous energy. Her smile was bold, as it had been in the carriage, but a little frenzied now.

'I *wa-a-nt*,' she sang over the lively tune coming from the piano, 'a *dri-i-i-nk*!' She spun in the direction of the bar, giddy and breathless.

'Then let's go and get one!' Charlotte said, but the enthusiasm in her voice was undercut by a note of concern. 'Where's all this energy coming from?'

But Loretta didn't answer—she turned to look at Charlotte and barrelled into Renée.

'*Oh!*' exclaimed Loretta. 'Terribly sorry. You look *gorgeous*!'

Charlotte agreed. Renée wore a dazzling Grecian gown, her hair adorned with a crown of gold leaves.

'Fair Romeo…' Renée regained her balance and curtsied. 'Might I introduce you to some of my friends?'

'Yes, please!' Loretta exclaimed, then turned back to Charlotte. 'Get me something fun!'

And she disappeared with Renée into the crush of people.

Charlotte nodded and wove her way through the crowd, eager to make it to the bar and back as quickly as possible.

The pianist played her final notes, and then the room erupted in applause as Aunt Nelly took the stage. Known outside the Fourth Tier as Mr Lloyd the cheesemonger—a shy, stocky man who mostly kept to himself—here, Aunt Nelly blessed the stage on select performance nights with her charismatic presence.

Charlotte lifted herself onto her toes and surveyed the dimly lit room. All these friends and strangers…hugging, kissing, laughing. This community that had to hide so much of itself and bury so much of its pain; this community that came together each night no matter how vicious the condemnation from society.

Charlotte let her heart be warmed by all the love and resilience in the room, then leaned against the bar and ordered two sherries.

'Ladies and gentlemen,' Aunt Nelly began, then twisted her face in dramatic disgust. The crowd laughed and whistled. 'I must be in the wrong dance hall, for I see no *ladies* and *gentlemen* here!'

She was dressed in an opulent white gown with silver brocade and a wide farthingale skirt, the kind French royalty would have worn before the Revolution. She wore a tall powdered wig adorned with ribbons, and her lips were painted a shiny pink with the rose oil and beeswax recipe she only gave to her closest friends.

'Mollies and Tommies…' she curtsied low '…sapphists and sodomites. In defiance of the law, we are gathered tonight to celebrate our way of life!'

A cheer rippled through the crowd.

'Please, be a dear, and raise your glass for our song mistress of the night,' Aunt Nelly continued as the entire hall stamped on the floor in anticipation. 'Sugar-Anne Stuart!'

The pianist scaled the keys to the cheers and whistles of the audience. Sugar-Anne was a successful confectioner with a thick Scottish accent, whose club persona shared a surname with Mary, Queen of Scots. Tonight she was dressed as a shepherdess, with an apron, a bonnet and a shepherd's crook that would definitely become a lewd prop before the night was over.

Sugar-Anne found her note and dived passionately into a classic English ballad:

A brisk young lass so brisk and gay
She went unto the mill one day.
There's a peck of corn all for to grind,
The devil of the miller could she find!

Everyone joined in after the first verse, singing and stamping, dancing and drinking.

Charlotte stood on her toes to look for her lover; she could imagine the red blooming across Loretta's face as she realised this song wasn't really about milling.

But Loretta wasn't paying attention to the song at all.

Charlotte watched as she danced with another woman—a tall brunette in an angel costume. They were noticeably close to each other. Charlotte squirmed at the sudden twist of her stomach.

But alas last the miller he did come in
And this fair maid she did begin:
'There's a peck of corn all for to grind;
I can but stay a little time.'

She clutched their drinks and cut through the crowd, eager to see Loretta's relieved face when she returned.

Then she sat down all on a sack,
They talked of this, and they talked of that,
They talked of love, of love proved kind,
She soon found out the mill would grind.

By the time Charlotte reached Loretta she had spun into the arms of another woman, her face flushed from dancing. She already had a drink in her hand—where had she got that?—but downed it as Charlotte approached with the sherry.

'This is Mary.' Loretta gestured to her dance partner, whose arm was wrapped around Loretta's waist.

Before Charlotte could respond, Loretta snatched the drink from Charlotte's hand and swayed into Mary for another round of dancing.

Then he got up the mill to grind
And left her down the stones to mind.
Then an easy up and down,
She scarce could tell when her corn was ground.

Charlotte stood awkwardly, her stomach twisting tighter. Her muscles began to ache from tension she hadn't realised she'd been holding.

'Then go you home, my sweet pretty dear,
The corn is ground and the mill is clear.'
She swore she'd been ground by a score or more
But never been ground so well before.

Charlotte was only halfway through her drink by the time Loretta finished hers. The song ended and Charlotte moved forward, her feet driving her body forth on their own. She wasn't thinking any more—her heart was beating far too loud for that—and all she could feel was an awkward, itchy, relentless heat that crawled beneath her skin.

Jealousy. The word pierced through Charlotte's mind and made her sick.

'Loretta,' she said firmly. 'What are you doing?'

'What do you mean?'

Loretta was louder than usual, and jarringly nonchalant. But Charlotte *knew* Loretta, and she knew that being like this didn't come easily to her.

'You aren't acting like yourself.'

Loretta giggled, and furrowed her brow in mock solemnity. 'We're here to have fun. *You're* the one who's not acting like yourself!'

'I—'

But she realised Loretta was right. They *were* here to have fun. Charlotte just hadn't expected Loretta to want that *fun* with someone else.

She raised her voice over the music, an even raunchier tune than the last. 'Dance with me?' she tried, but Loretta was avoiding her gaze, looking around the room as if for somewhere else to go. 'What is going on—?'

'I'm going to dance,' Loretta interrupted, but too loud and too determined.

'Loretta—'

'We're having fun!' she called over her shoulder, striding towards a curvy woman in red ruffles.

Oh. Recognition hit Charlotte like a bolt of lightning… like a crashing wave, a violent gust of wind. *'We have fun together.'* When Charlotte had spoken those words the other day, this wasn't at all what she had meant.

Jealousy turned into resentment—at Loretta, at herself, at the laws and customs that made their togetherness impossible.

I can have fun.

She searched for a lady—any lady at all.

The next half hour passed in a haze of hands and faces, each new dance partner blurring into the one before. When she saw a beautiful blonde woman lean into Loretta and whisper something in her ear, Charlotte found an even *more* beautiful blonde woman and bought her a drink. She flirted and twirled and laughed with anyone who would have her, and she watched bitterly as Loretta did the same.

Are you having fun now? she wanted to scream.

Loretta laughed wildly across the room. The woman she was dancing with—the *stranger* she was dancing with—wrapped her arms around Loretta's shoulders, her long medieval sleeves and sparkling headband obscuring Loretta entirely. She was wearing—of all things—the Juliet costume.

She spun Loretta around and pulled her into a ravenous kiss.

Enough.

Resentment snapped within Charlotte and gave way to throbbing pain. Her heart was sore with how this night had bruised her again and again. She broke through the crowd like shears through silk, as if everyone in her path should feel the sharpness of her pain.

'Come with me.'

She grabbed Loretta's wrist and left the dance floor in search of a private room in the back. They didn't speak as they marched through the narrow corridors, as they found an empty dressing room, or as Charlotte found a burning candle and used it to light three more. The scent of recent passion still hung in the air from whoever had used the room last.

'What,' said Charlotte through gritted teeth, 'is going *on*?'

'We're having f—'

'Don't.' She crossed her arms defensively. 'This isn't fun. I'm miserable—I'm not having any fun at all. Are you?'

Loretta nodded. 'I've danced with *so* many people.'

She opened her arms wide and spun on her toes, then stumbled onto the couch behind her. She laughed, but it sounded forced. She nestled into the cushions behind her, then peered up at Charlotte's face for the first time in what felt like years.

Charlotte unfolded her arms and let her shoulders drop. 'Loretta…' she said softly as she moved towards the couch. '*Are* you having fun?'

Loretta buried her face in a cushion and spoke, but the words were too muffled for Charlotte to make out.

'What was that?' Charlotte sank down onto the couch and ran her fingers lightly through Loretta's hair.

Loretta hugged the cushion to her chest. 'No,' she confessed.

'Then why—?'

'Because it's what you *wanted*.' Loretta sat up straight now and looked directly at Charlotte. Her face was ruddy and damp. 'You said we would *have fun* until life got *complicated* and then it would *end*. You said that!' Tears were dripping down her face. 'And I thought maybe if you saw me dancing with all those other women—' Her voice hitched on a sob, and she looked away.

'You thought I'd get jealous?' Charlotte sank deeper into the couch. 'That I'd decide this doesn't have to end?'

Loretta nodded and wiped her tears on her sleeve. 'That you'd decide you want to be with me.'

'But, Loretta, I *do* want to be with you.' Charlotte hadn't realised how true those words were until she said them out loud. 'I'm just…' Now she felt her own tears coming on. She stared at the ceiling and blinked until they disappeared. 'I'm just trying to be realistic.'

Charlotte felt the inadequacy of her own words, heard how they shrivelled beneath the heat of Loretta's overwhelming hope.

'Other couples have found ways to make it work,' Loretta said weakly. 'I was reading about these two women in Wales who live together in a cottage. They have a dog named Sappho, and…' She sighed.

'I met them once, a while ago.'

'*Really?*' Loretta turned back to Charlotte now, her eyebrows lifted.

'Eleanor Butler and Sarah Ponsonby. They've hosted much of the aristocracy, and I was on a trip with my father when a mutual friend invited him for tea. They have a *fabulous* library.'

Charlotte knew she shouldn't have said that last part. She knew it would only make Loretta yearn to run away that much more. But Charlotte just *had* to hear the romantic sigh she knew would fall from Loretta's lips—just *had* to see the dreamy look in her eyes.

Loretta exhaled, and Charlotte's heartbeat slowed to its softest pace of the evening so far.

'But their life isn't without struggle,' she clarified. 'They're in debt, and with no income they have to rely on their friends' generosity.'

'And people tolerate them? Their lifestyle?'

Charlotte shrugged. 'Most people think the two of them are just friends. And they say it so dismissively—*just* friends. Even if there's nothing romantic between them, I still think they have more love for each other than any of the married couples I've met.'

'Then why don't you want that for yourself? For us?'

Loretta shifted close and wrapped an arm around Charlotte's shoulder. They lay back into the couch, and Charlotte brought her knees up to her chest.

'Loretta—'

Charlotte hated to snuff out the radiant hope on Loretta's face.

But what choice do I have?

'One example of two women who've made a life for themselves isn't enough evidence for *us* to build a life on. I know plenty of couples who try to do the same, but they always get caught, or their families stop them, or they run out of money and have to get married to some *man* anyway.' She kissed

Loretta's forehead. 'You have an opportunity for a good life with Arthur. A life that's safe and secure and comfortable. Never tell him I said this, of course, but he will make a better husband than any other gentleman you could find.'

A weak laugh fell from Loretta's mouth, despite her sadness. 'And what about you?'

Charlotte shrugged. 'I'll be all right. I'll have you…for a while. Then you'll get busy being a duchess, and a mother, and I…'

I won't want to stay, she almost said. *I won't want to watch him being happy with you.*

'I'll get Nathaniel to rent me a flat somewhere. And I'll meet someone else. And you will too. And the heartbreak won't ever go away fully, but we'll find ways to be happy even so. You'll meet so many fascinating people as a duchess— maybe you'll have an affair with a *princess.*'

And maybe you'll even grow to love Arthur.

Loretta huffed quietly, but the fight had left her face.

She pulled Charlotte into her and kissed her cheek. 'And this is just the way it has to be?'

Charlotte nodded.

'But we can still care for each other? Until it ends?'

'I care about you immensely.' Another sentence Charlotte hadn't realised was true until she spoke it aloud. 'And it's because I care about you that I don't want the pressure of permanence to loom over all the fun we can have right *now.* Real fun—not whatever we were doing in there.' She gestured towards the main room.

'I'm so sorry.'

Loretta's fingers were lazily tracing the contours of Charlotte's body, brushing over her waist, her arms, her shoulders.

'I'm sorry too.'

They held each other tightly, and Charlotte gave herself

permission to love this moment as it was—to hold and be held without worrying that she was getting too close, that saying goodbye to Loretta someday would break her. If she wanted Loretta to focus on *now*, then she had to follow her own advice.

She leaned up and pressed her lips against Loretta's, the touch light and ticklish. 'Do we understand each other now?' she whispered.

Loretta closed the distance between them and flooded Charlotte's face with warmth. They kissed—slowly at first, then with urgency and purpose.

'Yes.' Loretta broke away to say it, her breath coming quickly. 'We understand each other.'

Charlotte smiled to see that joy—*real* joy—was back in Loretta's eyes.

The sound of roaring applause carried down the corridor, and Charlotte wondered what song had been sung, and what would be sung next.

And then she remembered.

'We've got to go!' Charlotte exclaimed, and lifted herself and Loretta out of their lounging embrace. 'Nathaniel's performing tonight. I completely forgot.'

'Nathaniel *performs*?' Loretta asked, an amused grin on her face.

'Not at all. And that's why I *must* be there.'

They stood and adjusted their clothes, stretched their limbs from all their stillness. The dissonance between their conversation and what Nathaniel was about to do was not lost on Charlotte.

'He's proposing to Rupert,' she said gently. 'But it's so much easier to be a bachelor than a spinster.'

'That makes sense,' Loretta said, as if to convince herself.

They left the room and travelled back through the dark corridors. Loretta paused at the open door of a room where two men were tearing off their costumes—Achilles and Patroclus—as they kissed passionately.

'Oh, my...' Loretta whispered, and walked away quickly. 'Do they not want privacy?'

'We spend our whole lives being private,' Charlotte said. 'Sometimes we just want to...' A sardonic smile tugged at her lips as she remembered Arthur's annoying catchphrase. 'See and be seen.'

Light and sound flooded the two women's senses as they stepped back into the party. They turned a corner to see a man with bright painted lips in a lacy nightgown lying on a bed that had been brought onstage. His knees were raised and he was groaning in pain.

Charlotte anticipated Loretta's question and said, 'This is one of our many rituals. We perform the lives we cannot have, and for a moment they become ours. The men like to perform birthing ceremonies.'

The pianist played a quick and dramatic tune as friends of the man in 'labour' doted on him, told him to push and cooled him with their fans. And then, with a mighty cry, he lifted a wooden baby doll from beneath his skirts and presented it to the crowd. Everyone whooped and whistled, and Charlotte studied Loretta's confused but delighted face.

The stage was cleared and there was Nathaniel, walking up the steps and mustering his courage. He straightened his shoulders and lifted his chin, then fiddled nervously with the buttons on his waistcoat. He was, as usual, not in costume.

Charlotte smiled widely at the sight of her old friend, his floppy dark hair and his gentle eyes. He cleared his throat and began. 'This is for Rupert,' he said quietly, and then again, louder, 'This is for Rupert.'

Charlotte scanned the crowd for Mr Wynn, and found him

near the front, surprise and amusement spread across his painted face. He wore the glittering crown and fancy garb of King Richard III, a thick red cape with spotted white fur flowing regally from his shoulders. The people around him patted his back and kissed his cheeks as he beamed up at the stage.

Then, with a tender voice, Nathaniel sang.

> *I'll weave my love a garland, it shall be dress'd so fine*
> *I'll set it round with roses, with lilies, pinks and thyme*
> *And I'll present it to my love when he comes home from sea.*
> *For I love my love, and I love my love, because my love loves me.*

Loretta wrapped her arms around Charlotte's waist and rested her chin on Charlotte's shoulder. They swayed to the familiar song and hummed along.

> *I wish I were an arrow that sped into the air*
> *To seek him as a sparrow, and if he were not there*
> *How quickly I'd become a fish to search the raging sea.*
> *For I love my love, and I love my love, because my love loves me.*
> *I would I were a reaper, I'd seek him in the corn,*
> *I would I were a keeper, I'd hunt him with my horn.*
> *I'd blow a blast when found at last beneath the greenwood tree*
> *For I love my love, and I love my love, because my love loves me.*

Nathaniel extended a hand and beckoned Rupert to the stage. He reached into his pocket as the piano picked up the tune and the gathered patrons restarted the song, then pulled out a gold pocket watch.

Charlotte had helped Nathaniel choose the time piece from a hundred others, had watched him order the inscription it held inside:

Because he loved him as he loved himself.
1 Samuel 20:17

Rupert was the wayward son of a country clergyman, and although he'd left the church years ago he still found comfort in the complicated love story of David and Jonathan. Charlotte had never cared much for the language of church, but as she looked around her now she knew this room was somehow *holy.* The songs were sometimes lewd, the drinks were often cheap and the hearts were almost always broken...

But people like us, Charlotte thought, *have got to claim sacredness every chance we get.*

Nathaniel placed the pocket watch in Rupert's hand and asked, 'Will you be mine?'

Rupert used his stage voice to say, 'I already am—and I always will be.'

They kissed and the room erupted in cheers. Charlotte clapped her hands and yelled, and felt Loretta kiss her neck. Rupert dipped Nathaniel dramatically as flowers were thrown onto the stage and Nathaniel blushed—and Charlotte let her guard slip just enough to imagine that she was the one on that stage, dipping Loretta, who would blush in just the same way.

She shook her head. *Nonsense. But what if...?*

The pianist jumped into another bawdy tune and the singing and dancing resumed. People rushed to Nathaniel and Rupert to offer their congratulations. A woman dressed as Macbeth kissed a handsome knight; Marie Antoinette swept a mermaid off her feet. Charlotte squeezed Loretta's hand

and looked into her eyes. This moment would not—*could not*—last for ever, but it deserved to be savoured nonetheless.

Everyone in this room had experienced the full depth of heartbreak, and Charlotte knew now she would not be spared. But she did take comfort in this simple truth:

We have always existed, she thought to herself. *And we always will.*

Chapter Fourteen

In the complicated politics of dinner party seating charts, it was common for the hostess to place two young people she considered a suitable match beside each other at the table. Had Lady Castlereagh any sense as to who the most infatuated pair at her dinner party was, she certainly wouldn't have placed Loretta and Charlotte at opposite ends of the table.

At this moment, as the fourteen guests dined on roast beef and Yorkshire pudding, Loretta wanted to raise her eyebrows at Charlotte and direct her attention to the large pineapple in the centre of the table. It had an unmistakable tear in one of its leaves and Loretta was *certain* it was the same pineapple from Mrs Drummond-Burrell's luncheon just two days earlier, which they had attended the day after their night at the Fourth Tier.

After that particular luncheon, the Duke had officially asked Loretta's father for her hand in marriage. Which meant that soon—tonight, even—he would ask her too.

And she would say yes.

But Loretta tried not to think about it. Her third glass of wine was helping her do exactly that.

Since Charlotte was several seats down on the same side of the table as her, Loretta had to either lean back or tilt forward to find her. This, of course, went against every table etiquette rule Loretta had ever learned, so she forced herself to sit still. The mystery of why Lady Castlereagh had the same pineapple as Mrs Drummond-Burrell would simply have to wait.

'This is the finest Yorkshire pudding I've had all season,' the Duke said to Loretta.

'I quite agree,' she replied, but she was only half paying attention.

Charlotte was seated next to a wealthy guest of Lady Castlereagh from Berlin. He had a strong jawline and round, amber eyes. Loretta allowed herself just the slightest inch forward to glance at them in their conversation, and from what she could tell they were getting along famously. He was nodding along to a story Charlotte was telling, and she was smiling.

Loretta felt the smallest fissure of heartbreak within her chest.

What are they talking about? Does Charlotte enjoy his company? Does she even enjoy the company of men, or is it only women? Is it possible to fancy both?

Loretta took a deep breath to clear her mind. Thinking this way wouldn't stop the future from coming, but it *would* spoil the present she already had.

Charlotte is mine for now, she reminded herself. *And that is enough.*

'Have you been to Woollett Hall?'

The voice of her future husband came as a much-needed distraction.

'I have indeed,' Loretta said. Her father adored the private zoo of the Castlereagh country home. 'It was the first and only time I've seen a kangaroo.'

'I don't have a taste for adventure myself, but I was there when Wellington's tiger arrived, and I must admit it was quite exciting.'

'I am also not much of an adventurer. Though we are travelling to Worthing in two weeks, to visit my uncle's new resort.'

She wanted to go on a journey right now—to escape with Charlotte and sail away and never have to walk down the church aisle. Loretta couldn't keep her thoughts straight—these thoughts she shouldn't be having at all. She had already made peace with marriage. She had *just* made peace with eventually saying goodbye to Charlotte.

She took a long gulp of wine.

The Duke beamed. 'If outings to the seashore are all the adventure you require, we shall get along quite well. Quite well indeed.'

Loretta tried to remind herself that this was what she had always wanted. Women were married off every day to men who were cruel and hideous, but Arthur Sterlington was as upstanding a gentleman as anyone might find. His steely grey eyes lingered on Loretta and she willed herself to feel something for him—anything at all. He was well-mannered, and polite and handsome. He wouldn't abandon her for months the way her father had done to her mother…the way her mother did now.

Marrying the Duke was the best possible outcome for Loretta's life. Even Charlotte knew that was true.

The visiting nobleman laughed loudly at something Charlotte said.

This is a good thing.

Maybe Charlotte was right now meeting a man worth tolerating, or even a man she could be happy with. Maybe she could have an agreeable marriage too, with someone who wouldn't try to control her.

Someone who would take her to Berlin.

Loretta's breath went shallow at the thought of being so far

from Charlotte. Six chairs away already felt like an ocean—
there was no way she could handle an *actual* ocean.

'Speaking of getting along quite well...' the Duke said with
a hint of nervousness in his voice.

He cleared his throat and pushed back his chair, then stood
with his hands folded behind his back. This was the moment
Loretta's entire life had been building towards.

'If I may briefly interrupt tonight's festivities...' he began.

But Loretta didn't hear what came next. Her heart banged
against her chest like a blacksmith's hammer. She was light-
headed and trembling. The room began to spin.

'Loretta?' she heard someone say, but the voice was distant.

She didn't know what was going on, but she knew she
needed to get to Charlotte. She tried to stand, vaguely aware
that her chair had toppled over.

Her vision was clouding at the corners.

And then, unable to stop herself, Loretta did the very thing
she had sworn she would never do. The thing other women did
that Loretta had never understood. The thing she had always
been too calm for, too steady. Such theatrics were supposed
to be beneath her—but this was no performance.

Loretta swooned.

Had this been any other lady of the *ton*, Charlotte would
have assumed the swoon was a ruse. While genuine fainting
spells were not unheard of, most swoons were a performance
of femininity—an opportunity to fall into the arms of a chivalrous suitor, or an excuse to get out of a boring or otherwise
undesirable task.

Charlotte knew women who had used swooning to spare
themselves from outings, dances, conversations, etiquette lessons, hosting obligations, sexual intercourse and confronta-
tions about their extramarital affairs.

Ladies of the previous century had often succumbed to their lung-choking corsets, but as the cotton stays of today's fashions were far gentler there was nothing left to blame but nerves—and Loretta Linfield was not the type to feign a nervous fit. She was genuinely anxious, Charlotte knew, genuinely overwhelmed.

The whole scene had happened impossibly fast. One moment Arthur was standing up from the table, and the next moment he was awkwardly propping up Loretta's limp form. Charlotte barely had time to acknowledge the stone-like feeling in her gut that had materialised as Arthur had begun his proposal—which was a true gift, because the *last* thing Charlotte wanted to do was process any new and dangerous feelings related to her brother's soon-to-be-bride.

She rushed to Loretta's side without considering the watchful eyes of the gathered company, and helped Arthur lower her to the floor and lean her against the wall.

Other people in the room were already talking, probably. There were most likely gasps and murmurs, women rustling through their reticules for smelling salts, but Charlotte didn't register any of it. All that mattered was Loretta, fragile and vulnerable, completely at the mercy of the people around her. Charlotte hated how helpless she felt, gazing down at her friend and unable to do anything but sit by her side.

'You're all right...' Charlotte murmured as she placed a hand on Loretta's forehead. Her face was pale, her lips slightly parted. 'You have to be all right.'

The sharp aroma of smelling salts pierced the air around them as a woman Charlotte didn't know waved her silver vinaigrette before Loretta's face. Lady Castlereagh was inviting her guests into the drawing room for a round of cards.

'Give her some room,' Charlotte said to Arthur. He looked shaken.

'Quite right,' he agreed awkwardly. 'She's best left in the care of another woman.'

Charlotte stifled a smile. *He has no idea how right he is.*

Loretta's eyes blinked open, wide and startled. She inhaled and gripped Charlotte's arm, silently pleading for help.

Charlotte improvised. 'You must be quite taken with the Duke,' she said, with raised eyebrows and a forced smile, 'to be so overcome with emotion at the thought of marrying him.' She turned to Arthur. 'Ladies can be quite delicate.'

'Yes,' Loretta agreed quietly. 'Quite delicate.'

'You have no reason to worry,' Arthur assured her, though he stood at a distance as if swooning might be contagious.

'I can handle things from here,' Charlotte said to the remaining guests.

Charlotte squeezed Loretta's hand as the guests cleared the room, then rose to Arthur's side and walked him to the door.

'Everything is all right,' she said in hushed tones, not entirely sure if Arthur was the one she was trying to convince.

'Is this…?' He glanced back at Loretta, who was slowly fanning herself. 'I mean…er…is this…normal?'

No, Charlotte wanted to say. *Not at all.* People like Loretta and Charlotte spent their whole lives on the margins of *'normal'.*

'Oh, it happens all the time.' Charlotte tried to keep the sarcasm out of her voice. 'We're just so easily overwhelmed by big emotions. That's why you men are in charge.'

'Fair point…fair point.' Arthur stepped through the doorway, then paused and turned around. 'Then why have I never seen *you* swoon?'

'Because I'm a cold-blooded harpy.'

Charlotte closed the doors before she could see her brother's facial expression, then hurried back to Loretta's side.

'I'm so embarrassed,' Loretta mumbled, her face falling into her hands.

Charlotte sank to the floor beside her friend, wrapped an arm around her and pulled her close. Loretta rested her head on Charlotte's shoulder.

'Embarrassed?' Charlotte asked. 'This is hardly the most embarrassing swoon I've ever seen.'

'Really?' Loretta looked sceptical.

'It doesn't even crack the top *ten*,' Charlotte continued, delighting in the soft staccato of Loretta's body as it laughed against her own. 'I once saw the Countess of Oxford swoon straight into a pond!'

Loretta looked up at Charlotte with merriment in her eyes. The way they giggled together was melodic—like two instruments that were built to be played in harmony. Charlotte wanted to rest in this moment for ever, to stay right here on the cold wooden floor with Loretta tucked into her arms. She felt stable and steady, moored to something that felt permanent even as it was destined to end.

Charlotte had fancied plenty of women before, and some she had even loved, yet somehow this was different. She *trusted* Loretta. But as Charlotte felt Loretta's body relax into her own she realised it was even worse than that—Loretta trusted her too. And that trust meant it was Charlotte's duty to have Loretta's best interest at heart.

Her best interest was currently in the drawing room, likely losing a game of cards. Arthur had never been an accomplished liar, and although it made him terrible at the low-stakes gambling he engaged in at dinner parties, it would make him a decent husband.

Perhaps this was what made Arthur and Loretta such a good match. They were both honest—if not always with themselves, then at least with those they cared about most.

'This changes nothing…' Charlotte sighed. 'Arthur still wants to marry you. He will ask at a time when you can be better prepared—perhaps in a more private setting.'

Loretta tilted her head to Charlotte, resting in her arms as if in the boughs of a mighty tree. 'Does he know about you? Does he know you fancy women?'

'Arthur and I aren't close enough for those kinds of secrets.' She ran her fingers through Loretta's hair softly, soothingly.

'Did anyone in your family know?'

Low in Charlotte's belly, grief blinked one sleepy eye open. She nodded. 'Thomas knew,' she said, her voice thin. 'We worked it out together, actually. We'd stay up late when we were children, until everyone else had gone to bed, then we'd sneak into each other's rooms. I would try on his trousers and he would try on my dresses. I taught him how to curtsy, and we would dance, and laugh, and have so much fun. We didn't know what it meant, exactly, but we knew it had to be a secret.'

'It sounds like he would have loved the Fourth Tier.' Loretta smiled, as if she were remembering Thomas too.

'Yes,' Charlotte agreed, and reached for Loretta's hand. 'He would have loved it.' Grief rumbled in her gut, but didn't rise.

'Did your father know?'

'I think he may have suspected. He never pressured me to marry, and he didn't chide me for my *unladylike* behaviour.' She cupped a hand around the side of Loretta's face and leaned in to kiss her forehead. 'Then again, he was so absent after Thomas died that it's hard to know what he even noticed.'

But it wasn't hard to know what Loretta was noticing. Her eyes were steady, and curious, and compassionate. Charlotte might have kept talking all night if there had not been a party to return to.

She was used to keeping her memories locked away, but

Loretta coaxed them forth without even trying, without even needing a key.

'We should let everyone know you're all right.' She placed a hand on Loretta's forehead. 'You *are* all right, yes?'

Loretta sighed. She looked resolved and uncertain all at once. 'How do I just…pretend?'

They were both quiet now, quiet enough to hear the gentle *whoosh* and *crack* of candlelight.

'How do I pretend,' Loretta continued, 'that you are not my favourite person in the entire world?'

Charlotte's heart beat fiercely against her chest, threatening to escape and leap right into Loretta's hand.

She pivoted safely to humour. 'Why would you have to pretend such a thing? I'm brilliant, beautiful, mysterious… no one could fault you for admiring me.'

But this time, Loretta didn't take the bait. 'Don't do that.'

'Do what?'

'That thing you do when everything becomes too serious—you make it funny instead.'

'All right…' Charlotte huffed. She let her head fall onto Loretta's. 'Pretending,' she started—and it was a much nicer word than *lying*— 'is really not that difficult. Or uncommon. When the Countess of Oxford swooned, it was to get the attention of a man who was not her husband. She had plenty of lovers, and she didn't hide it particularly well. One of those lovers was Lord Byron, who then had an affair of his own with one of their mutual friends.'

'I know that.' Loretta nodded. 'But at least the Countess pretended to like her husband's company, even if she didn't in actuality. It must be so much easier to pretend that way.'

'Do you not like gentlemen at all?' Charlotte asked.

Loretta thought for a moment. 'Most suitors bore me. Cecil *agitates* me.'

Charlotte laughed. 'Perhaps he's not a representative specimen of the entire male species.'

'I hope not.' Loretta laughed too. 'He's been quite persistent in visiting lately, and each time is more irritating than the last.'

'Does he not realise you are about to be engaged?'

Loretta shrugged. 'He sees what he wants to see. He had something of a falling-out with my father, but they've repaired the rift. He won't leave me alone until I'm someone else's wife.'

Charlotte clenched her hands into fists. She wanted to stand up right now, march to Cecil's house, and then… Then *what*? What could Charlotte do?

Only Arthur could protect Loretta—at least in this way.

'He should leave you alone *now*,' Charlotte said. 'But soon he won't have a choice.'

Loretta nodded. 'I've courted a few men who were far more pleasant than Cecil, but they just…didn't quite capture my attention. Not like you. And you're a woman, so that must be what I fancy. It can't be both, can it?'

'Oh, it can indeed.'

Loretta lifted her eyebrows, and there was that spark of curiosity and wonder that Charlotte had come to cherish.

'It can be *both*?'

Charlotte laughed. 'Rupert was quite the ladies' man before he and Nathaniel decided to be monogamous.'

'And what about *you*?' Loretta teased. 'Were you…*enjoying* the company of the nobleman from Berlin?'

'Oh, dear…' Charlotte shook her head. 'I am not like Rupert. Believe me, I have tried.'

'That sounds like a story,' Loretta said, clearly intrigued.

It was strange to see her acting this way, thought Charlotte. So accepting of their fate. They would both move on to new people soon enough, and Loretta was already joking about it. But this was what Charlotte had wanted. This was the relationship—the *right now*—that Charlotte had asked for.

'It didn't go very far,' Charlotte said, indulging her. 'One night at the Fourth Tier there was a masquerade ball, and Nathaniel made a joke about how I'm such a tommy that even in disguise I would balk at a man's touch. So I told him that I could fancy men if I wanted to.'

'And then…?' Loretta asked, obviously eager to hear the rest of the story.

Charlotte shrugged. 'And then I kissed the first man who would have me.'

Loretta waited, expectant. *'And then…?'*

'Well, then he kissed me back.'

'You are a *terrible* storyteller!' Loretta pushed playfully at Charlotte's shoulder. 'I want details.'

Charlotte leaned in close and whispered, 'Oh, I'll *give* you details…'

'I'm starting to think you're making this entire story up just to vex me.'

'Fine!' Charlotte relented, rolling her eyes sheepishly. 'We kissed quite vigorously in the corner of the room for about ten seconds. Then I felt the bulge in his trousers and I ran back to Nathaniel in defeat.'

'Thank you!' Loretta giggled. 'Perhaps I should kiss a man the next time we're out…'

'Or perhaps,' said Charlotte with an exasperated smile, 'you've already kissed enough other people for one week.'

Loretta looked up with bashful eyes. 'Have I kissed *you* enough for one week?'

'That,' Charlotte said, 'would be impossible.'

'Shall we find out?' Loretta lifted her lips to Charlotte's. 'For *science*?'

Time slowed. The din of voices in the other room disappeared. Loretta's words brought Charlotte right back to the greenhouse—right back to when their bodies had collided for the first time.

She leaned in. 'For science…'

Their lips met, and nothing else existed.

Nothing else existed for a very long time.

Loretta pulled away first. 'Shall we return to society?' She extended her hand to Charlotte.

'Oh, I suppose so.'

Loretta's slender fingers intertwined with her own. They kept their hands together, even as they entered the drawing room. Charlotte told herself it was to keep Loretta steady, to keep her upright. But she knew, deep down, that it was because she couldn't bear to let go.

Oh, God, Charlotte realised. *I don't want this to end.*

Chapter Fifteen

'Tell me what you've heard,' Loretta said the moment Bridget entered her room. She'd been pacing for nearly an hour, anxious to know what kind of gossip was circulating about last night.

'The story is certainly making the rounds,' Bridget confirmed. 'But you don't have anything to worry about. Everyone just thinks you were so overwhelmed by your love for the Duke of Colchester that you couldn't possibly stay conscious. Most people think it's romantic.'

'*Most?*'

'I've heard a few snide remarks about how your swoon had more to do with the sudden title and fortune you'd gain from the marriage, but it's not like half the people of your class don't marry for that reason anyway.'

Bridget cracked a smile, and Loretta laughed.

'Something more interesting will happen by this afternoon— it always does,' Bridget reassured her. 'But I *do* think I deserve an answer as fair recompense for my investigative work.'

'Thank you, really.' Loretta exhaled and lowered her shoulders. She was not an embarrassment after all. 'An answer for what, exactly?'

'Why *did* you collapse?'

Loretta stopped pacing. She twisted her fingers together and looked out of the window.

'If it really was love,' Bridget continued, 'I don't think you'd be worried about what everyone is saying.'

'I had too much to drink…' Loretta started.

It was true, but it wasn't the whole truth. She'd spent so much of her life dealing in half truths like this, and she knew it was unavoidable—she knew most women did the same, certainly Charlotte did—but sometimes she felt as if it was going to break her.

She thought of her mother.

'You don't have to tell me if you don't want to,' Bridget said and crossed her arms. 'But I want it known that I'm suspicious.'

'As you should be.' Loretta lowered her head. 'I'm not in love with Arthur Sterlington. And I know plenty of people get married without being in love, but…but there's someone else.'

'Oh?' Bridget raised her eyebrows.

Loretta looked up, and noticed there was a letter in Bridget's hand.

'There *was* someone else. Or there is now, but there won't be eventually… It's hard to explain… Is that letter for me?'

Bridget handed over the missive. 'Do you want to marry this *"someone else"*?'

'I did…' Loretta ran her thumb over the Sterlington wax seal. 'But this love is…a temporary arrangement. It's unrealistic to think otherwise.'

Last night had revealed to Loretta that there was still some hope inside her—some hope that she could run away with Charlotte. But if Charlotte wanted that too—*truly* wanted it, as badly as Loretta did—then she would at least *try* to make it work. Even if they couldn't do it in the end, even if Loretta still had to marry the Duke, surely Charlotte would at least *wonder* if something else was possible.

But Charlotte isn't wondering that at all, Loretta reminded herself.

Charlotte had made her decision before they'd even kissed.

Bridget nodded, then went to choose a dress from the armoire as Loretta read Lord Sterlington's note.

My dearest Miss Linfield,
I hope and trust that you are in good spirits today, following a night of rest. You certainly seemed much improved by the end of the evening, but I would nevertheless like to offer my sincerest apologies for causing such a stir and leading you into a frenzy.
You are a private, quiet and sensible lady, who of course would balk at such a showy engagement. You do not need an audience to be content—we are similar in that regard.

Loretta smiled and made a sound of appreciation. The Duke was, of course, oblivious to the real reason why she'd swooned, but Loretta *did* treasure her quiet privacy. Perhaps he knew her better than she'd thought.

Instead of waiting for the perfect occasion in front of the perfect people, I will simply ask you here and now.
Loretta Linfield, will you be my wife?
Perhaps we can lead a quiet life together.
A simple response via post will suffice,
Arthur Sterlington, Duke of Colchester

The words echoed off the page and floated around Loretta's head.

Perfect...wife...life together.

Right here in her trembling hands was everything she had once dreamed of. All those years of learning table manners, dancing with suitors, watching her figure, studying just enough Latin and literature and arithmetic to make her an interesting wife but not so much that she outshone her future husband... All those years had culminated in this crisply folded piece of paper.

Somewhere beyond her bedchamber walls, the portrait of Loretta that hung above the stairs was grinning smugly.

'Half the gossip I hear is about who's having an affair with whom,' Bridget said as she smoothed out a parchment-coloured day dress. 'Marriage doesn't have to mean the end of love.'

They both turned at the sound of the front door opening. Loretta wasn't expecting any morning callers...

Bridget dressed her swiftly and swirled her hair into a simple bun before they went downstairs.

'Loretta,' Cecil said as they entered the drawing room. He stood up with a worried expression fixed on his face.

Loretta curtsied. 'How nice of you to visit, Cecil.' She reluctantly took a seat across from him as tea was served.

'I wanted to see if you were all right,' he said.

Loretta noticed that Bridget had found a seat behind Cecil and was nodding in his direction pointedly. Her face looked like she was asking a question.

What? Loretta tried to ask through her own facial expression—a subtle head-tilt and a squint of the eyes.

She turned back to Cecil and said, 'I take it you heard about last night?'

'Of course I heard,' Cecil responded. 'It's not every day that a woman *faints* at a marriage proposal.'

Bridget nodded her head towards him again—more forcefully.

Oh! Loretta realised that Bridget was asking if Cecil was her *'someone else'*.

Loretta shook her head quickly while Cecil reached for his teacup, and Bridget mimed a sigh of relief.

'I was just so overwhelmed with joy…' Loretta repeated the story that Cecil had likely heard. 'It's such an honour to marry the Duke of Colchester.'

Cecil took a long sip of his tea, then sat back comfortably in his chair. 'Did you say yes?'

'Excuse me?'

'To the proposal. Did you say yes?'

'Not yet, but—'

'I knew it!' Cecil stood again, triumph sparkling in eyes. He turned to Bridget. 'Could you leave the room?'

'Cecil!' Loretta gasped.

'We've known each other our whole lives, Loretta. It's not as though we weren't alone all the time when we were children.'

'We are not children any more.' Her jaw was tight. She could feel a headache coming on. 'It wouldn't be proper for us to be in a room without a chaperone, and you know that.'

Cecil paused, nodded and took his seat. 'You're quite right. You always had better manners than I.' He smiled fondly. 'I know what people are saying, but I don't think it was joy that caused you to faint. I think it was nerves.' He leaned forward now, his hands on his knees, and spoke quietly. 'I think you don't want to marry Arthur Sterlington.'

Loretta reached for her teacup to buy herself some time. She had to be as convincing as possible in what she said next. And nothing was more convincing than the truth.

'I can't think of anything that would bring me more happiness than to join the Sterlington family.'

She smiled politely, but it wasn't enough to erase the tension boiling between them. They sat there in thick silence for a moment longer, then Cecil clinked his teacup onto the table and stood to leave.

'My sincerest congratulations,' he said, but his tone betrayed the lie.

Bridget stood as the door closed behind him. 'What was *that*?' she whispered loudly.

Loretta threw up her hands in exasperation. 'Cecil Wrottesley can't imagine a world in which someone is more handsome, more intelligent, more desirable than himself. He doesn't want to lose to Arthur Sterlington. He *can't* lose.'

'But he's already lost,' said Bridget.

She was right.

Loretta hurried to her writing desk, inked her quill, and wrote at the bottom of Arthur's card:

Yes.

Nathaniel Fletcher—in reality, Charlotte—was dangerously close to missing the submission deadline for the 1824 Summer Exhibition at Somerset House. This would be the event that secured Mr Fletcher's place in the London art scene—not just as a rising star, but as a venerable master in his own right. He might even be elected to the Royal Academy itself.

Charlotte knew the stakes, and yet she found it increasingly hard to focus on the deadline when there was so much *Loretta* in her life. They'd been inseparable for the week and a half since Lady Castlereagh's dinner, their days passing slowly and sweetly in the garden, the greenhouse, the sunroom, the bedchamber. They spent Loretta's outings with Arthur glancing and giggling at each other behind their fans, Charlotte making lewd gestures behind Arthur's back while Loretta tried and failed to keep a straight face.

The formal engagement came and went. Rather than being a blight on their romance, it only made it easier for them to see each other. Meetings between Arthur and Loretta's father to discuss the logistics of the wedding would give them time for quick secret trysts in the library. Tea in the garden would give way to steamy portrait sessions in the studio... which in turn gave way to tumbling and stroking and trying *so* hard not to scream.

They talked, as well. About botany, about poetry. About their secrets and memories. About their mothers.

They talked about everything, really. Charlotte told Loretta stories that made her sore with laughter, and Loretta recited poetry that brought tears to Charlotte's eyes.

Then they'd return to their separate beds, and Charlotte would be alone with her terrible thoughts.

You don't deserve this.

The words came in whispers, sneaking into her mind unbidden.

You don't deserve this happiness, and that's why this will end.

And then a different voice, calling out in strangled hope.

What if it doesn't have to end? What if you were wrong?

She'd sleep away these thoughts and find Loretta in the morning, focusing on the here and now and nothing else.

And that was how Charlotte had made it to the day before the Academy's deadline without selecting a painting.

She knew the cleverest submission would be a conventional piece—a portrait or historical scene in the style of the day, with that trademark 'Fletcher twist' that the critics could never quite describe.

A man had written about it in a newspaper once.

It's the bold colours. It's that bewitching look in his subjects' eyes. It's the way the painting stays with you, long after you've left the gallery.

It was all that and more. But Charlotte wanted the world to know what it truly was that set her apart from other painters—those whose work would hang on Somerset House's walls at the start of May. Charlotte wanted to submit something different…something risky.

She jumped at the sound of the door opening and closing behind her, and felt the chilly morning breeze wafting into the greenhouse. Nathaniel was exactly on time to help make their selection for the Summer Exhibition. Dressed in a casual blue waistcoat and beige trousers, with tousled hair and a bashful smile, he was effortlessly handsome. And this was how Charlotte knew for sure that she was only attracted to women—Nathaniel was the best you could find, and if he didn't do it for her then no man would.

'Are you ready to dazzle me with your latest—?'

He stopped suddenly, jarringly, as though he had walked into a wall. His eyes were fixed just over Charlotte's shoulder, to the painting propped up behind her—a stark and striking portrait of the goddess Venus rising from the sea.

'Charlotte…' Nathaniel sighed, a pained mix of empathy and disappointment spread across his face.

Charlotte stood defensively in front of her painting, anxiously twisting her fingers in the drab grey fabric of her charcoal-dusted dress. Then she stepped to one side.

'Just look at it,' she urged.

Nathaniel glanced at Charlotte, then softened his expression and took a step towards the painting.

In François Boucher's *Birth of Venus* the titular deity lounged peacefully in a blanket of gentle waves. Her eyelids drooped beneath carefully sculpted golden hair, a pearl brace-let draped over porcelain skin. In Jean-Honoré Fragonard's version the reclining goddess revealed the subtle slopes of her breasts and her penny-sized nipples. And at Sandro Bot-ticelli's hand a chaste Venus with toned muscles and a long neck covered herself with her own sunshine hair, as if em-barrassed by her beauty.

Charlotte's Venus was someone else entirely. She did not float gracefully in airy sea foam, nor did she lie in peaceful repose. This, after all, was a birth story—and what did Bot-ticelli know of that?

In Charlotte's painting the sky was dark and stormy, a vortex of heavy clouds looming in the distance. The shore-line was rough and muddy, all broken shell and violent ocean spray. Venus had hauled herself out of the water, shoulders hunched, her drenched black hair clinging to her body. There was pain on her face, but the pain was overtaken by fierce de-termination. She was marching forward, as if her very next step would take her off the canvas, leaving nothing behind but a trail of saltwater footprints.

Her skin was a canvas in itself, covered in freckles and folds. Her breasts sagged, their wide areolae partially covered by tendrils of dripping hair. Her arms swung in the movement of laboured walking, and she made no effort to hide the patch of wiry hair between her legs.

Nathaniel exhaled slowly, deliberately. 'It's your best work,' he said, barely louder than a whisper.

'I know it would be a bold choice—'

'It isn't a choice at all, Charlotte,' Nathaniel interrupted, gentle but firm. 'The committee would send this straight back. They would never hang it on the wall.'

'You are *impossible*.' She crossed her arms and fell back

onto the stool beside the painting. 'We'll never make a difference if we don't try.'

'What is the difference you're trying to make?'

'I want women to know that they're worthy of being painted even if they *don't* have perfect breasts, and perfect hair, and a perfect waist, and perfectly smooth skin, and—' She broke off to inhale. Nathaniel knew this already. She tried again. 'And I want *men* to know that they don't own the female figure— that we're allowed to represent ourselves.'

'But the painting would be under *my* name.'

'I *know*!' she snapped, her voice angrier than Nathaniel deserved. 'But you don't *understand*, Nathaniel. You can't imagine what it's like to run home from a museum as a child and look in the mirror, believing something is wrong with your body—wrong with *you*.'

Her voice was raspy now. She cursed the tears that rose too swiftly to be stopped. She glared at Nathaniel, her chest rising and falling with heavy breaths.

'We've talked about this before,' he said carefully.

Charlotte could see how hard he was trying to keep the pain off his face. She knew she should feel guilty, but in this moment she didn't care.

'And you know I agree with you. But you also know that a painting can't make a difference if it doesn't get shown. And this one will not get shown. You *know* this—so can you please tell me what's really going on?'

'I want to submit the painting in my own name,' she said quickly, forcefully. She didn't mean it—but she needed something to say…something other than the truth.

'Charlotte—'

'I want everyone to know that I'm the painter, and I want them to hate me for it, to ridicule me in the paper, to—'

'Charlotte…' Nathaniel was walking towards her now, slowly, opening his arms.

'I don't have anything left to lose, Nathaniel, so I might as well—'

She let him wrap his arms around her as she began to wail, to feel the deep and ragged cry she'd been suppressing rip through her. He rested a hand on the back of her head and they stayed like that for a long while, her tears soaking through his shirt.

When her breathing began to slow, he whispered, 'Why do you have nothing left to lose?'

'Don't make me say it,' she grumbled into his chest.

'I *am* going to make you say it.'

She could hear the smile in his voice. She looked up at him, her face puffy and damp. She didn't want to say it. She didn't want to say something that she could never *un*say.

But if Nathaniel had already worked it out, then she could no longer pretend it wasn't true.

'I love her,' she said, and she didn't look away. 'I love Loretta Linfield.'

Nathaniel nodded in the direction of her painting. 'It shows.'

Charlotte was confused. 'What is it about *that*—' she pointed at her painting, moody and defiant and nowhere near romantic '—that makes you think I am in *love*?'

Nathaniel hugged her closer. 'Because it is *brave*, Charlotte. Because it is brave.'

Charlotte just breathed.

Eventually they pulled apart, and settled on a striking but inoffensive landscape for the Summer Exhibition.

Charlotte was relieved that Nathaniel didn't ask what she was going to do with her love for Loretta. There was nothing *to* do. Not when wedding preparations were already under-

way. Not when Loretta was so close to the comfort and stability she deserved. Not when the marriage certificate was
all but signed.

It's not signed yet.

A sudden knock on the door startled her. She glanced at
Nathaniel. The knock came again.

'Charlotte?' Loretta said as she poked her head inside,
then smiled warmly against a blue afternoon sky. 'I'm sorry
if I'm interrupting.'

'Not at all,' Nathaniel said happily. 'We've just finished
packing up our submission.' He gestured to the crate in the corner of the room, then gave Charlotte a final hug before leaving.

Loretta crossed the floorboards between them and placed
her soft hands on Charlotte's cheeks. Her rich green eyes
were alive with purpose as she leaned in slowly, then crashed
into Charlotte for a kiss so deep and all-consuming that for
a moment there was no greenhouse, no Summer Exhibition,
no wedding.

There was only Loretta.

And the three words Charlotte couldn't bring herself to say.

Chapter Sixteen

When Loretta had posed for the portrait that hung in her father's house there had been no recourse from the chilly draught leaking through the window, for the itchy fabric taut around her ribcage, or the ache in her muscles from standing in the same position for so long.

The portraitist had been a serious old man who'd chastised her every movement. His stern, reproving voice was seared into her memory for ever: *'Great art requires perfect stillness.'*

But here in the greenhouse, lounging on a pile of plush cushions in front of Charlotte's easel, Loretta was anything but still.

'Oh, gorgeous!' Charlotte laughed as Loretta shifted from one dramatic pose to the next. 'The canvas loves you!'

Even with the door open, the sultry air of the greenhouse wrapped itself around Loretta's skin like a warm blanket. She ran her fingers along the delicate white linen draped over her body, thin and ethereal. She was nearly bare, but she didn't feel exposed. She felt free.

Giggling, Loretta pulled the fabric around her shoulders, across her chest, over her head. She was an angel, a witch, a ghost. Her long hair fell in auburn waves across her face, curling slightly in the humidity. She noticed that she was slouching, but felt no urge to sit up straight.

'Am I beautiful?'

The words escaped through her teeth before she could stop them. It was a selfish question, she was well aware of that, and a nonsensical one—everyone knew a lady was more beautiful the less aware she was of her own beauty. But Loretta also knew how much effort went into 'effortless' beauty. She wanted—*needed*—to know how Charlotte saw her in this moment, when she wasn't even trying.

'That's not quite what I mean—'

Charlotte leaned out from behind the canvas, a puzzled expression tugging at her eyebrows.

'I'm—I'm wondering,' stammered Loretta, 'if I'm beautiful like *this*?'

'Like what?' Charlotte returned briefly to her painting, then set her brush down.

'Like...' All Loretta could do was gesture towards herself.

A pang of insecurity twisted her gut, sudden and all the more noticeable in contrast with the calm of the rest of her body.

Charlotte stood back, a black paint-streaked apron tied over her pewter gown. In the dimness of the studio, her golden curls glowed like a cluster of stars.

'Of *course* you are beautiful. You are...' Her eyes moved slowly down Loretta's body, from her hair to her bare feet. 'You are marvellous and dazzling and handsome and alluring and angelic. A feast for the eyes. It is a shame Samuel Johnson did not live long enough to meet you, for if he had, his dictionary entry for *"beautiful"* would be nothing more than a sketch of your face.' Charlotte smirked. 'A face, I may add, that is as red as beetroot.'

Loretta's hands flew to her warm cheeks.

'You wonder if you are beautiful on your own terms? When you do not burden yourself with expectations and conventions?' Charlotte fixed her gaze on Loretta's. 'The answer is yes.'

Loretta had lived disconnected from her thoughts, her feelings and her opinions for so long that she hadn't stopped to consider how her body bore the weight of it all. The tension in her shoulders and the tightness of her jaw. The strain on her spine from relentlessly perfect posture. The way she instinctively sucked in her stomach when dance partners placed their hands on her waist. The way her legs shook with the tedium of domestic life, with the utter impossibility that she'd ever be allowed something *more*.

Becoming the woman in her father's portrait had come with a daily cost, and her body kept the ledger.

But here, under Charlotte's sheltering gaze, Loretta could shrug off the heavy armour she'd fashioned for herself. She could allow the soft fat of her abdomen to rise and fall without reining it in. She could relax.

For once, she wasn't afraid of being seen and known.

For once, she craved it.

'And in your painting?' Loretta stood up, holding the linen sheet around her like a cape. 'Am I beautiful?'

'Of course,' said Charlotte quickly, biting her bottom lip. 'But beauty isn't what I'm going for. Not in the way that men paint it, at least. Women are so much *more* than that. *You* are so much more than that. But that's all we ever see on exhibition walls. Something is lost between the subject herself and the object she becomes on the canvas.' Charlotte narrowed her eyes in agitation. 'Or it isn't *lost*, but intentionally *left out*.'

Loretta stepped closer. She could listen to Charlotte for hours, she thought. For a lifetime, perhaps.

She shook her head.

Not this lifetime.

In the week and a half since Lady Castlereagh's dinner

Loretta had got a glimpse into what life might be like with Charlotte. They saw each other nearly every day—they shared stories over tea, they read poetry, they spent long hours lying in each other's arms. But they had to be so secretive every time they met. Each meeting required a set-up—an excuse to get Arthur out of the room, an elaborate ruse to justify extended privacy. Sometimes their scheming failed, and they'd be stuck on a tedious outing with Arthur and her father for the whole day.

The moments she shared with Charlotte were wonderful, but arranging for those moments to happen was…exhausting.

She understood, finally, why any sort of permanent togetherness was impossible. She had torn her heart back from Charlotte's hands—a heart that Charlotte had never asked to hold in the first place—and it was now back where it belonged: safely tucked within Loretta's chest, never to stray so far again.

But she could still enjoy this afternoon in the greenhouse. It wasn't much. It wasn't enough. But she could enjoy *this*.

'Can I see?' she asked hopefully. 'The painting?'

Charlotte caught her in a playful embrace and said with theatrically downcast eyes, 'You wouldn't rather look at *me*?' She leaned up on her toes to kiss Loretta, and then pulled them both down onto the pile of cushions.

Loretta was wedged between an overstuffed velvet cushion and the warmth of Charlotte's body. Candlelight and shadow danced on the dusty windows. Loretta looked up into Charlotte's eyes, combed her fingers through Charlotte's hair and pulled her even closer. She set her lips on Charlotte's jaw, on her neck, on her bare collarbone. She freed her leg from the cushion and pressed it between Charlotte's thighs.

Charlotte gasped.

Loretta found the apron strings tied around her lover's waist and pulled. As Loretta lifted the apron over her head

Charlotte grabbed her hips and rolled on top of her and pinned her down. Loretta inhaled her sweet perfume. Orange blossom. Coriander. Sandalwood. *Charlotte*.

And then Charlotte's lips were on hers. Their bodies rocked together. She moaned—or perhaps Charlotte did—or perhaps they both did together. They were one.

Loretta was on top now, gently fingering the hem of Charlotte's skirts. The delicate sheet wrapped around her own body had fallen to her waist.

She leaned close to Charlotte's face, resting comfortably on a soft silk cushion, and whispered, 'What do you want, Charlotte Sterlington?'

She ran her hand up the soft skin of Charlotte's leg, the smoothness of her inner thigh, the thick tangle of hair where her legs came together.

Charlotte breathed out, low and melodic, and pulled Loretta's chest to hers. 'Take me,' she said. 'All of me. *Please*.'

Loretta inhaled a shaky breath and pressed down into the damp ruffles.

'Yes, Loretta,' Charlotte gasped. 'Just like that.'

She pressed her lips to Loretta's breast. Their bodies were sleek with sweat, undulating with passionate urgency. Charlotte's breath quickened and her chest heaved. She was wet and blazing hot under Loretta's fingers.

'Faster...' she begged.

Loretta's wrist ached, and her arms were exhausted. She relished the feeling. Charlotte began to twist and turn, to writhe. Her moans climbed an octave, and then another. Loretta felt her own body tremble.

And then they were still.

They lay breathing heavily on their jumble of cushions, the light of high noon casting shadows over their skin.

Loretta propped herself up with her elbows. 'How did I do?'

'You,' said Charlotte, arching her back in a slow, sleepy stretch, 'are magnificent.'

'I suppose that I am,' answered Loretta, glowing. 'And I suppose,' she said, leaning to kiss Charlotte's nose, 'that you are too.'

'Oh?' said Charlotte. She pushed herself upright. 'How would you know? I haven't even...' she leaned closer '...tasted you yet.'

Charlotte pounced on Loretta and straddled her hips. Their lips met again. Loretta realised it was her turn to be taken over the edge.

Charlotte wound a trail of kisses down the length of Loretta's body. Neck. Chest. Torso. Navel. She tugged the linen sheet from Loretta's waist and moved further still.

Hips—both sides.

The pale crease where body becomes leg.

The soft tuft of tangled hair.

And then suddenly she stopped. 'Don't move. Your body... the lighting...' She exhaled. 'It's perfect.'

She rushed to the easel and began to paint.

Charlotte's burst of creative energy made Loretta crave her even more. As if reading her thoughts, Charlotte peeked out from behind her work and said, with a tantalising grin, 'I'm not done with you yet.' She brushed a few swift marks onto the canvas, speaking again as she hurried to realise her vision. 'Just one...more...moment... *There.*'

And Charlotte was back on top of Loretta as quickly as she had left, invigorated by her own artistic genius and the muse who lay beneath her. Loretta parted her legs like the pages of a well-read book...the kind with no resistance left in its spine.

Charlotte held Loretta's knees, then slowly slid her hands down the tender expanse of Loretta's thighs. The touch ignited every inch of her skin.

'Yes...'

Charlotte trailed her tongue down the same path her hand had just taken. She looked up from between Loretta's legs. 'Are you ready?'

Loretta clutched the linen sheet in her fists. 'Devour me,' she begged.

Charlotte's face disappeared.

Loretta gasped. She reached down, ran her fingers through Charlotte's hair, pulled her deeper. Her back arched upward, taut as an archer's bow. Sweet tension swelled deep in her core. Pressure gathered, and pleasure followed. Her breathing became laboured. Each minute, each movement of Charlotte's tongue, brought her closer to release.

Loretta lost track of the sounds she was making. She lost track of everything but Charlotte. She desperately gripped the cushion behind her as the bowstring finally snapped... as the arrow flew higher and farther than it ever had before.

And then she melted into the damp cushions, panting and weak. Charlotte pulled a paint-covered sheet from beneath them, and burrowed into Loretta's side.

'What did you like?' Charlotte asked as their breathing slowed.

'Everything...' Loretta sighed, her eyelids drooping. 'I liked *everything*.'

'I only ask,' Charlotte clarified, her voice low and rumbling across Loretta's chest, 'so I can know what to repeat.'

Loretta offered a wordless hum, adrift in a calm euphoria she had no intention of coming back from any time soon.

She felt the shift of Charlotte's cheeks tugging into a smile, the delicate brush of her eyelashes fluttering shut. 'I'll ask again next time,' Charlotte whispered.

Loretta didn't know how many *next times* they had. But she was sleepy...and, oh, so cosy in the warmth of Charlotte's embrace. She closed her eyes, and didn't mind as time slipped away. She dreamt of an eternity sweeter than any that could ever be real. She dreamt of Charlotte.

Together, they were an hourglass with no sand, a sundial in the dead of night. They were endless. They were infinite.

They were free.

'It's done!'

Loretta felt a hand on her arm, gently nudging her awake. 'Loretta…'

Charlotte's whisper sounded distant as Loretta blinked away the haze of sleep. Distant, but excited. The space beside Loretta was cold and empty. The sheet had fallen to the floor and she was shivering.

Charlotte was kneeling over her, smiling expectantly. 'The portrait—it's done.'

Half-asleep, Loretta reached for the sheet and wrapped it around her shoulders. 'Why did Lady Castlereagh's dinner table have the same pineapple from Mrs Drummond-Burrell's luncheon?'

Charlotte eyebrows furrowed. 'What?'

'I think I dreamt of it just now. I meant to ask you, but I forgot.' Loretta sat up. 'Almost a fortnight ago—at the dinner. It was the same pineapple. I'm sure of it.'

'Yes! I remember.' Charlotte shifted to sit beside her. 'Pineapples are expensive. They're a sign of wealth and prestige. Sometimes a circle of friends will secretly share the cost of one, then pretend it's fresh and new for each event.'

'Very clever,' murmured Loretta. 'Very clever…'

'But they just end up rotten. By the time the pineapple has finished making the rounds, it's too spoiled to actually *enjoy*.'

Loretta tried to recall if she had ever tasted pineapple before, or if she'd only seen them as party centrepieces.

'Would you like to see the portrait?' The smile on Charlotte's face returned.

'Oh, yes!'

They rose from the floor. Loretta stretched, then followed Charlotte.

The light streaming through the windows was gold and red. The candles, new when she'd arrived, were half-burnt. The white dress she had worn to the greenhouse no longer lay crumpled on the ground—instead it hung neatly from an empty basket meant for flowers. Her stockings and undergarments were folded carefully on the cabinet.

Charlotte grabbed her hand and pulled her towards the easel.

'It's…' Loretta started, too amazed and too tired to find words worthy of the masterpiece before her. 'It's marvellous,' she tried—but even that was not enough.

It was, of course, technically marvellous. Charlotte had captured the physical likeness of Loretta's face and body with unparalleled expertise. But it was marvellous in a different way, too. A more important way.

The Loretta in this painting reclined comfortably, entirely unposed. Her body sank naturally into the peaks and valleys of the cushions; her hair spilled joyfully around her freckled face. A cloth of sky-blue silk rested over her hips and wrapped behind her back, leaving one full breast exposed. She was sensual and she was satisfied. She was Loretta.

'I look so…'

'Beautiful?' Charlotte suggested.

'Alive.'

They stood there in silence, the air thick with wonder.

'Perhaps…' Loretta said eventually. 'Perhaps you can take this portrait with you. Wherever you end up.'

The suggestion brought her genuine comfort. Maybe Charlotte would even paint a self-portrait for Loretta as a wedding gift.

But Charlotte did not look comforted. Her expression was hesitant, as if she was choosing her next words carefully. 'What if where I end up is…with you?'

Loretta laughed and looped her arms around Charlotte's shoulders. The sheet fell softly to the floor. 'I've only just awakened—don't drag me back into my dream.'

Charlotte laughed too—but nervously.

Loretta stroked a hand through Charlotte's hair to calm her. 'Are you worried about the painting? I know you hold yourself to a high standard, but trust me—this is perfect.'

It was getting harder to see Charlotte's face as the sun sank below the tops of the trees. Loretta was struck by anxiety. They'd been in the greenhouse for hours. Surely her father and Arthur would be looking for her soon.

'I should go,' she said, and walked towards her clothes. 'Hopefully we can see each other soon?'

She remembered then that she was leaving for Worthing tomorrow. The week away would be a return to normal life— it would ground her in herself again, in the *self* she had been before she'd met Charlotte.

She wondered briefly if Charlotte would find someone new in her absence. If they would even want to see each other again after a week apart.

'Help me with my dress?'

Loretta was wearing her undergarments now, her stockings tied at the knees.

Charlotte hugged her from behind and kissed the back of her neck, then leaned her head into Loretta's shoulder.

'I was wrong…' Charlotte whispered.

Loretta wasn't sure she'd heard correctly. 'Wrong about what?'

'About us.'

Loretta stood very still, her dress clutched in her hands. She had never known Charlotte's voice to be this quiet, this small.

Charlotte continued. 'I don't want... I don't want to lose you.'

'You don't mean that.'

Loretta squirmed at the uneasy feeling spreading across her body, and Charlotte dropped her arms. But when Loretta turned around, the broken look on Charlotte's face told her that she *did* mean it.

And that was unacceptable.

'Loretta.' Charlotte spoke again. 'I know what I said before, but—'

'I didn't want to lose *you*,' Loretta interrupted. 'But you told me to be realistic, so I *became* realistic.'

Her muscles were tense, her breathing shallow. If this was their last private moment together, she didn't want it to end in anger and tears.

She tried her best to speak evenly. 'We have fun, and then it ends. Isn't that right?'

'I know,' Charlotte said, her voice strained. 'I know.'

Loretta lifted her dress over her head and exhaled slowly as it fell over her body. Weeks ago Charlotte had unleashed something in her—something fierce and wild and lovely. And then Charlotte had forced that very part of her back into its cage.

'I only did what you wanted me to do.' Loretta shook her head, her dress still loose and undone around her frame. 'I was ready to marry Arthur, and then I was ready to run away with you, and now...' She paused to take a breath.

Do not get angry.

'Now I just want to be at peace with the life I've chosen.' *With the life you've chosen for me.*

'But I was wrong,' Charlotte pleaded, pain clear in her eyes. 'I didn't anticipate— I didn't want to *let* myself believe that we—that I—'

'You do not know what you are saying.'

'I *do* know—and I'm being more honest with myself *now* than I have been in my entire life.'

Their words were coming quickly now, tumbling over each other.

'I don't want to hear this…' Loretta's voice was losing its calm.

'I wish I'd worked it out sooner—'

'I'm leaving tomorrow—'

'Loretta, *I love you.*'

The words hung heavy in the air.

Charlotte dropped her head into her hands. Her shoulders sagged. 'I love you.'

Anger was tearing Loretta apart from the inside out, and she couldn't even move, couldn't even do anything to stop it. The humid air of the greenhouse crawled down her back and reminded her that she could not lace this dress up on her own.

'Do not speak to me of love,' she said through gritted teeth. 'Not now. Not after I've made myself give up on everything we could have been.'

'Everything we still could be—'

'I loved you!' The words launched themselves from her chest. Her voice wavered with oncoming tears. 'How dare you speak of love to me when it was I who loved you first?'

Loretta felt a sharp pain beneath her skull and pressed her fingers to her temples. Her breaths were quick and shallow.

She'd seen this before.

She thought of her mother.

This is how it starts.

'You cannot make me want more than I can have,' Loretta said, and forced her breathing to slow. Her headache was growing and her stomach was turning sour. 'You cannot make me mad with longing for another life.'

Charlotte lifted her head now, sympathy in her eyes. She knew Loretta well enough to know who she was talking about now. 'Loretta—'

'I must be content with what I have or I'll be miserable. Those are the only two options.'

'You know that isn't true.'

'And what happens when you decide that you don't want me any more? What happens when you decide it's too impractical or too dangerous? That it isn't *realistic*? That you're too *broken* to be loved?'

Charlotte flinched, but Loretta kept going.

'What will happen is that I'll be married off to Cecil Wrottesley, or someone worse. And I won't be able to bear it, Charlotte. I'll lose my mind every time I remember how good it was with you—' Her throat burned with a smothered cry.

Charlotte stepped forward, barely an inch. 'I know what I want. I'm not going to make the same mistake twice.'

Loretta's voice rang louder than it ever had before:

'I refuse to let you break my heart and put it back together every time you change your mind!'

A bird took flight from the greenhouse roof, its wings beating hard.

Loretta turned away from Charlotte and closed her eyes. 'Would you please fasten my dress?'

'Loretta—'

'Would you, *please*?' She kept her voice steady to hide her tears.

Charlotte approached slowly, then laced the back of Loretta's gown in silence. Her hands lingered on the final knot.

Tell me again, Loretta thought, despite herself. *Tell me again that you love me.*

She forced herself to the door before she could say it out loud.

She didn't pause at the threshold.

She didn't look back.

Chapter Seventeen

'You are the first being I've spoken to in days,' Charlotte said to the wide oxeye daisy in her hand. 'And I must say, you don't seem pleased about it.'

The bright white petals thrashed in the wind.

Five days had passed since she'd last seen Loretta. Five days since she'd confessed her love. Five days since her heart had collapsed in on itself.

'I read my mother's journal this morning,' Charlotte said, and sighed as she twirled the flower in her hands. She was nestled in the branches of her favourite walnut tree, hidden from sight by its long green leaves. 'And I don't just mean the botanical pages. I was thinking that maybe if she had any motherly advice in there now would be the time to read it…'

A cool spring breeze washed over her. The leaves of the tree fluttered and bounced.

'Anyway,' she continued. 'It turns out she was a bit more eccentric than my father let on. She wrote about you—the flowers, that is—and how she would speak to you when she was lonely, or distraught, or had a problem to sort out. *"Flowers are the best listeners,"* she wrote. *"And trees make a close second."'*

Charlotte patted the rough bark beneath her. The daisy's soft white petals lifted in the wind, urging her to continue.

'So I thought I would try telling you.' Charlotte sighed

again. 'The last time I felt anything *close* to what I'm feeling now was when Amaryllis Evans decided loving me was *sinful*.' Her voice caught on the last word, her throat suddenly thick with sadness. 'It shouldn't bother me any more.' She was angry at the tears forming in the corners of her eyes. 'I know she didn't mean *me*. She meant women in general. But *I* still feel like *I'm* the sin.'

She gave in to the raspy, desperate cry building in her chest.

The walnut tree held her steady as she shook and sobbed against its bark. She didn't know how much time had passed before her breathing was slow once more.

'My mother knew what she was talking about,' Charlotte said to the flower. 'You are a good listener.' She sniffed and dried her tears on her sleeve. 'I read a journal entry about me. I was two years old, and she was playing with me in the garden. We were near the raspberry bushes and she told me how tasty the fruit would be in a few weeks. But I grabbed one right away. I plucked a small green berry from the bush and put it in my mouth. The face I made was quite amusing, apparently. I was disgusted by the hard, bitter thing! She loved raspberries, and she was so worried that I would never want to try them again.'

She could imagine it in her head so clearly, as if she were remembering it herself.

'But the next time we were in the garden I ran straight back to that raspberry bush. I'd pick one each day as they slowly grew redder and softer. On one of those days I finally ate the perfect raspberry, round and ripe and juicy. Then I kept on eating, until my lips and fingers were stained red. I was a joyful, sticky mess, and my mother wrote…'

She paused for a long breath in, a slow breath out.

'My mother wrote, *"I hope she stays like this for ever. I*

hope she always goes back to the raspberry bush, no matter how sour its fruit was the day before.'"

Charlotte could see the garden in slivers through the walnut leaves. She knew in her heart that her feelings for Loretta were ripe and ready for harvest. But somewhere in the last two decades she had lost her willingness to love again when love had been so sour before.

'I suppose I've been—'

'Have you gone mad, Lady Charlotte?'

Charlotte jumped at the sound of a familiar Scottish accent.

'Or is your conversation partner even better at hiding in the branches than you are?'

'Mrs Grant!' Charlotte placed her free hand on her forehead. 'No, just me. Mad as ever. And I know I'm being unladylike. I'll come down.'

She didn't have a fight in her today.

'On the contrary. It's rather nice to see someone climbing the trees again,' said Mrs Grant. 'Lord knows it was never going to be Arthur.'

Charlotte blinked. Was *Mrs Grant* the one who had gone mad? She leaned over the bough on which she balanced to better see the housekeeper, pushing aside a curtain of leaves.

'Your mother used to do it.' Mrs Grant softened her tone. 'Before you and your brothers came along. I haven't spent much time in the garden since then.'

Sometimes Charlotte forgot that Mrs Grant had been Catherine Sterlington's lady's maid. And sometimes Charlotte forgot that Mrs Grant didn't just want Charlotte to be a proper lady—she wanted Charlotte to be happy, too.

'Would you like to join me?' Charlotte teased.

'Oh, dear, no. I'm more than happy with two feet planted safely on the ground.'

Maybe that was why Charlotte found such comfort in the

high limbs of trees. She'd never felt tethered to anything—not even the ground itself.

'The reason I came to find you,' said Mrs Grant, 'is to en-quire if you're quite finished moping about.'

'I mope,' replied Charlotte. 'It's what I do.'

'Indeed it is.' Mrs Grant began to pace. 'But you stopped. Two months ago, to be precise.'

'That's not—'

'Ah, save your breath,' Mrs Grant continued. 'I don't need to know the reason. I've just *noticed* that your spirits lift whenever Miss Linfield is around, and I *noticed* several days ago when she left rather quickly from this very garden. And I *notice* that you've been bringing down the entire household with your irritable mood ever since.'

'That's an awful lot of noticing,' Charlotte said as she tucked the daisy behind her ear and gingerly made her way down the trunk of the great walnut tree.

'There's an awful lot to notice by the time you reach my age.'

Charlotte leapt from the lowest branch and landed in front of Mrs Grant, who was holding a book.

'I found this tucked behind a cushion on one of the par-lour couches.'

She held out her hand, and Charlotte reached for the book that had escaped her memory weeks ago. Loretta had sent it, along with the dress she'd borrowed, after the rainstorm that had pushed them into the greenhouse. After they'd begun to see each other truly for the first time.

'Thank you.' Charlotte nodded, her throat tightening with the threat of oncoming tears.

Mrs Grant sighed and clasped her hands behind her back. 'You've never wanted the life that was expected of you, and I understand that. But it doesn't mean you have to be alone.'

'Mrs Grant, you have never married, and you've done all right for yourself.'

'Who said anything about marriage?' Mrs Grant said with a sly smile. 'You think in all this time I've never let myself have any fun?'

She winked, turned on her heel and marched back to the house.

Charlotte stood there, bewildered, eyebrows raised. 'How unladylike,' she said under her breath, and grinned.

A gentle breeze made the daisy petals dance against Charlotte's temple. She looked down at the book in her hands: *A Short Guide to British Wildflowers*. Inside the front cover was a note in Loretta's delicate, thin handwriting:

Flicking through these pages last night felt very much like walking beside you through the gardens. I hope to see you soon.

Her stomach turned. The garden felt suddenly empty, sapped of colour and life without Loretta there beside her.

Charlotte leaned in close, her lips hovering over the daisy's yellow face. She whispered, 'I still love her. I still love Loretta.' She closed her eyes and let the tears fall.

When Charlotte was twenty, she'd attended the wedding of a second cousin in Paris. After the ceremony, some of the women had pulled flowers from the decorative bouquets for a game of love: they'd plucked each petal, one by one, to determine if the object of their affection felt the same way in return. Charlotte wondered, now, if this daisy had something to say after all.

'Loretta loves me…' she said as she pinched a silky white petal '…*un peu*…a little.' She tugged the petal from its home and moved on to the next one. '*Beaucoup*…a lot… *Passi-*

onnément…passionately…*à la folie*…to madness…*pas du
tout*…not at all…'

She heard the quiet *snap* of each petal as she made her way
around the circle. *A little, a lot, passionately, to madness and
not at all.* But as the daisy grew increasingly bare Charlotte
grew increasingly restless. She did not want to stand here and
ask a flower a question that only Loretta could answer.

She tucked the nearly naked flower behind her ear and carried the book in her arms. She hurried indoors to her writing
desk, reached for a fresh sheet of paper and began to write:

Dear Loretta…

Loretta stood on the wide stone balcony of the hotel at her
uncle's seaside spa resort and let the vastness of the ocean
and the stars above make her feel small.

For five days she had carried a sorrow larger than herself.
It filled every chamber in her heart, and it grew with each
passing hour.

Somehow she had smiled at all the gleeful congratulations
offered to her. Somehow she had gone through the motions
of an eager bride-to-be. But inside all she could feel was the
crunch of her heart breaking and breaking again. All she knew
was an ever-present sorrow, and her ever-present family who
demanded she be anything but sorrowful.

If everyone were like the ocean, maybe she would have time
to think, to feel, to work out what she was supposed to do next.

The ocean demanded nothing from her. It didn't even notice she was there.

The sounds of mirth and merriment wafted out from somewhere behind her. Loretta stood alone, wrapped in a honey-
coloured shawl, filling her lungs with fresh ocean air. She'd

been out of the city for nearly a week, but the endless stream of congratulations from her father's family still felt suffocating.

By the time she and her father had arrived in Worthing, the rest of his many brothers and their families had already settled into the hotel. Most of them had near-identical personalities—they were charismatic, boisterous, self-aggrandizing. Each had a keen eye for business, or science, or marrying into a titled family. Her father pretended to feel guilty for overshadowing his youngest brother's accomplishments with his own—a brand new spa in Worthing paled in comparison to a Duchess for a daughter—but his glee was poorly hidden.

Loretta's days had passed in card games and charades, strolls along the beach and dips in the baths. Here in Worthing, Loretta was at once the centre of attention and entirely invisible; everyone wanted to talk about her, or at her, but no one really wanted to talk *with* her.

No one, that was, except Uncle Steven. He had always been her favourite family member—a kind soul, with a sharp eye for interior design. He was every bit as boisterous as his older brothers, but far humbler, and he had built a comfortable life for himself in this seaside town with his business partner, Donald.

The resort hotel was furnished with art from Italy, France, Spain and Greece. Every painting she saw inevitably led to an imaginary conversation with Charlotte. She would ask her about the brush strokes and the composition, what decisions Charlotte would have made differently if she had been the painter.

Loretta's chest tightened and she bit into a candied lemon peel and looked out at the clear, dark horizon.

Charlotte made her choice. She can't just take it back on a whim.

Loretta jumped at the sound of a knock on the door behind her.

'I didn't mean to startle you,' said Uncle Steven gently. He strolled across the wide balcony and joined her, their elbows leaning against the ledge. They stood like that for a while, lost in the rhythmic sound of crashing waves.

'Everyone in there is overjoyed for you.' Uncle Steven nodded inside, where his brothers and their wives were playing charades. 'Everyone, that is, except you.'

'It will be an honour to marry the Duke of Colchester,' Loretta replied dutifully.

'An honour indeed. But I've noticed you don't smile much when you talk about him.'

Uncle Steven had a lovely smile, wide and genuine. Maybe if Loretta saw it now, it would lift her spirits. 'What makes you smile?' she asked him.

'Oh, plenty of things!' He laughed. 'A nice cup of tea, the first snow of winter, watching seagulls pluck food from the hands of unsuspecting aristocrats on holiday.'

Loretta giggled at that. And then, his tone shifted ever so slightly.

'But mostly Donald. He makes me smile more than anyone or anything.'

Loretta nodded. 'My father tells me he's always been your closest friend.'

Steven didn't respond right away.

Oh, thought Loretta as her eyes widened. *Steven and Donald.*

They had been business partners and close friends since Loretta was a child, but she hadn't ever wondered if they were anything else to each other. She hadn't known it was something she *could* wonder about.

'I'm glad you have him,' she said quietly, meeting his eyes. She passed him a lemon peel.

'I've noticed, over the years, that you never talk of princes or knights the way other girls do. And it's none of my business, but…it *is* possible to find love—even if it's not in the way everyone expects.'

Love was hard to talk about in secret when you had no practice talking about it at all. To go from hiding in the shadows to sharing it in pure daylight was an impossible task. Perhaps that was why they were talking here, now, on a balcony lit only by an almost full moon.

'It is possible, yes…' Loretta sighed.

Charlotte had kept herself hidden for so long, in so many ways. She hid her talent, her desire, her grief, her love. And maybe she did want to share herself with Loretta—maybe she had *always* wanted to, since their very first kiss—but maybe she just didn't know how.

'But wouldn't it be easier to never find out?' she asked her uncle. 'To never know there was another way? A better one?'

'It sounds like you already *do* know.' Steven gazed at the horizon, where dark sea met darker sky.

They were both quiet.

'You can say anything to the ocean,' he said as he stepped away from the railing. 'She's an excellent listener, you know. She won't tell anyone.'

He offered a gentle smile, then went back inside.

Loretta leaned forward and closed her eyes, felt the salty breeze on her skin.

Then, she stared into the sea. 'I still love her,' she whispered. 'I really do.'

The sea washed over the rocky shore, then returned again into herself. She told no one what she had heard.

* * *

'Are you absolutely sure you don't want to join me?' Nathaniel said to Charlotte as she rifled through his drawer of cravats.

'And watch all of London praise you for *my* work? I think not.'

Charlotte held three cravats up to Nathaniel's neck—classic white, delicate ivory and daring red—and avoided eye contact. She felt jittery and nervous, not fully present, and she knew Nathaniel was catching on. She wondered, for a moment, if she could blame it on the fear of getting caught in his Albany flat—women were strictly prohibited on the property—but Nathaniel knew Charlotte had stopped worrying about that years ago.

'Never in my life have I seen you pass up an opportunity to poke fun at your own artwork in front of unsuspecting strangers. You do remember this is *the* opening day of the Summer Exhibition, right? May the third?' He shrugged on his waistcoat and fastened the buttons.

'I don't even remember which painting you submitted,' Charlotte tossed the white fabric back in the drawer and poked around for something else.

'Which painting *we* submitted,' Nathaniel corrected. 'You helped me choose it!'

He reached for the ivory neckband, but Charlotte snatched it away and held out the red.

'I'll make you a deal, Charlotte. I will wear what you want if you tell me what's really going on with you.'

He crossed his arms, and Charlotte sighed.

He continued, sympathy practically dripping from his face. 'It's about Loretta, isn't it?'

'It might be,' Charlotte mumbled.

The cool nonchalance that had once come so naturally to

her felt false and clumsy—like trying to walk in shoes that no longer fitted.

She changed course reluctantly. 'I told her that I love her.'

Nathaniel started to smile, but stopped himself. 'And what happened?'

He took the red cravat and turned towards his mirror.

'She said it's too late. And then she ran out of the greenhouse. And then she left the city.'

Charlotte began to pace.

Nathaniel grimaced in the mirror. 'Not what you were hoping for?'

'Why would that possibly be—?' Charlotte sighed. 'I'm sorry. I just feel so—'

'Heartbroken?' He turned to face her.

'Yes, heartbroken. But I've written her a letter,' Charlotte said, with the faintest trace of hope in her eyes. 'I've apologised, and I'm… I'm going to fix this. I'm going to get her back.' She paused, and said, 'You would be proud of me.'

Nathaniel put his hands on Charlotte's shoulders. 'I am.'

He turned back to the mirror and finished tying his cravat, then checked his pocket watch. 'Oh, dear, I'm running quite late.'

'You're late on purpose,' Charlotte reminded him. 'It's part of your character.'

'Yes, but this is *late*. The exhibition's been open all morning.'

They walked towards the door just in time for it to burst open, slamming against the wall with such force it knocked a nearby still-life to the floor.

'Nathaniel Fletcher,' Arthur growled as he stormed into the room. 'What have you *done*?'

And then he punched Nathaniel squarely in the face.

Chapter Eighteen

The residents of Albany were known for their discretion. They valued privacy and decorum above all else, and they could always be depended upon to maintain an air of peace and quiet. Nathaniel was pleased to count himself among them—though now he was beginning to worry his days here might be numbered.

He, Charlotte and Arthur were brazenly violating Albany's strict *no noise* policy as they each shouted over one another, hurling accusations and explanations without stopping to listen.

'I don't know *what* kind of fool you take me for—' yelled Arthur as a lock of bronze hair bounced over his forehead.

'It's not just *you*—we've fooled all of England!' Charlotte gesticulated widely, knocking over a flower vase that Nathaniel caught with his free hand. The other was clutching a warm cloth soaked in water and vinegar to his bruised face.

'Would you *please* hear her out?' Nathaniel begged Arthur. But on and on they fought.

After ten or so more minutes of this, the trio eventually tired themselves out. Nathaniel slouched in an armchair, his legs stretched out. Arthur sat on the floor, head in hands. And Charlotte paced, slowly and thoughtfully.

'The sooner you believe us, the sooner we can work out what has actually happened,' she said to Arthur.

Anger and confusion and panic had been boiling inside her since the moment her brother had burst into the room and accused Nathaniel of stealing his bride.

'How *dare* you?' he had yelled, after throwing the first punch Charlotte had ever seen him thrown. 'She'll be ruined for this, and you know it.'

Loretta would indeed be ruined if Arthur's news was true. Somehow, some way, by some means beyond her comprehension, the portrait she had painted of Loretta now hung in Somerset House.

The portrait of Loretta with loose hair…with just a sheet to cover her body.

The portrait that all of London would now see.

Charlotte could almost hear the rumours now—Loretta had been wooed by the great Mr Fletcher and had become a wanton woman along the way.

Before Charlotte could work out how this terrible mistake had occurred, she had to get Arthur on the same page as her—and currently he wasn't even in the same *book*.

'I think I would have noticed, Charlotte, if you'd spent the past three years in a secret art studio. There would be paint beneath your fingernails, or—'

Charlotte ripped a glove off and held her hand up to his face. '*When*, in the last three years, have you spoken to me long enough to notice the paint beneath my fingernails?'

The room fell silent.

Charlotte took a deep breath. 'You believed our ruse for the same reason everyone else did—because it's *believable*. Everyone knows a second son with a lucrative hobby. And no one is going to wonder why the mad Sterlington girl spends all her time hiding in the garden.'

Arthur turned to Nathaniel. 'Why would you agree to this?'

'Because Charlotte's my friend. And because it affords me

a level of privacy I could previously only dream of. No one wants to bother a genius at work.'

'If it's really been you this whole time...' Arthur looked at his sister with tired sincerity, his eyes rimmed with red. 'Then why did you paint Loretta like that? And why would you submit—?'

'I've told you already,' Charlotte interrupted. 'I *didn't* submit the painting. We chose a landscape, and Nathaniel made sure it was delivered. Isn't that right, Nathaniel?'

Nathaniel's face was exasperated, and bewildered, and increasingly purple. *'Yes!'*

'So let's go! Let's go to Somerset House and fix this.'

'We need to go to the studio first,' said Nathaniel. 'To work out what happened.'

Charlotte nodded and strode towards the door, but Arthur stood and blocked her.

'Perhaps you are telling the truth,' he said. 'I'm not saying you are. But *if* you are telling the truth, then you still haven't answered my question.'

'Which *is*?' Charlotte struggled to keep a lid on the bubbling frustration that grew closer to boiling over each minute they remained in Nathaniel's flat.

'Why did you paint her,' Arthur said slowly, 'like *that*?'

Charlotte scanned her brother's face for judgement but found none. There was no blame in his eyes, no disgust in his worried frown. Just concern. He wanted to know what was happening to his future wife. He *needed* to know. And Charlotte bitterly admitted to herself that he *deserved* to know, too.

'Please don't be cross,' she whispered, and then turned to look at Nathaniel for support.

He stood and nodded his head.

Charlotte took a deep breath and faced her brother. 'I am in love with Loretta Linfield.' She let the truth hang between them for only a moment before she continued. 'She has my entire heart. And you might think it unusual, or perverted, or sinful, but we don't have time for any of that right now. If you care for her, you will put aside your questions and help us fix this bloody mess.'

Arthur stood very still, his brow furrowed, his shoulders raised.

'Arthur,' Charlotte said with as much patience as she could muster. 'You can hate me later. We need to go *now*.'

'I can't believe I never found you out here,' Arthur grumbled for the hundredth time on their journey to the greenhouse. 'Right under my nose…'

'You always were the worst at hide and seek.'

Charlotte and Arthur trudged down the muddy garden hill. She squinted at the greenhouse door, looking for any sign that the lock had been tampered with. But as she stepped closer, nothing seemed to be amiss.

The dread that had settled in her stomach over an hour ago swelled once more—a broken lock would have at least given them something new to analyse, and perhaps brought them closer to solving this dreadful mystery.

But if all went well, they would have their answer in a matter of minutes, then collect Nathaniel from inside the house— where he sat receiving parsley butter on his face from Mrs Grant, who swore by its bruise-healing qualities—and run to the Academy to explain the mistake and have the painting removed.

'I haven't been here in ages,' Arthur said as they approached the door.

Charlotte retrieved the key from her reticule and propped the door open for light. She considered warning Arthur about her paintings—telling him that some of them were strange, or dark, or honest—but the thought passed as quickly as it came. Anything that didn't bring them directly to the source of this mayhem would have to wait.

Charlotte scanned the cluttered room for anything out of place. Right away she noticed the empty easel where her painting of Loretta had once sat—but that was to be expected. She was looking for… Well, she didn't know exactly what she was looking for.

'All of this…' Arthur gaped '…is you? This is your work?'

'What did you really think I've been up to all these years?' Charlotte snapped. She wasn't angry with Arthur—not really. But she *was* angry, and he was there. 'I'm sorry…' She sighed. 'I didn't mean…'

'No, you're right,' Arthur said. 'That's the problem. I didn't think at all. I never wondered what you were doing when you weren't in the same room as me. How…how terribly selfish.'

Charlotte paused her searching to take in the sight of her brother and the pained expression that covered his face. 'We have much to catch up on,' she said gently.

He nodded—then gasped at something just over Charlotte's shoulder. He looked as if he'd seen a ghost, and when Charlotte turned she realised he had. The watercolour eyes of Thomas stared back at them.

'Did he know?' Arthur asked, his voice strained.

'About my art?' Charlotte felt the creep of panic rising through her body. She did not have time for a heart-to-heart with Arthur, but she didn't want to rush past this moment either. 'Yes, he knew. I wasn't nearly this good back then, when he—' Grief stirred within her. She felt the heaviness of oncoming tears and pushed them down. 'I mean, I wasn't this good until long after he died. But he knew. And he knew about me—how I never wanted a husband.'

And he never wanted a wife, she almost said—but that wasn't her secret to tell.

'Now, Arthur,' she continued, 'I don't mean to be impatient, but right now we must—'

Her eyes were suddenly drawn to a barely perceptible movement behind where Arthur stood—a subtle flicker hidden behind her easel. She walked over and moved it aside, revealing a stack of unstretched canvases that fluttered slightly, caught in a breeze. It was too far from the door to catch its draught, which meant...

'Oh...oh, no,' was all Charlotte could say as she pushed aside the canvases and found a gaping hole where a window had once been. 'I never doubted Nathaniel,' she said. 'I knew he wouldn't have mixed up the paintings. But... I didn't want to believe it was a thief, either.' Cool air rushed into the room. She turned to look at Arthur, and asked, as if he'd have any idea, 'Why would someone do this?'

He stepped close to examine the jagged edges of the hole. 'First we have to discover who *"someone"* could be. Who else knows about this place?'

'No one.' Charlotte shook her head. 'A handful of women know about me from when I painted them, but that was always at the theatre. I only finish my work here, I don't start it.'

'The theatre?'

'As I said—we have much to catch up on...'

Their next stop was the Royal Academy itself. As Arthur told it, Somerset House was buzzing with activity as anyone who was anyone arrived for the Summer Exhibition's opening day. And Loretta's scandalous modelling debut was naturally *the* topic of interest for a crowd who loved to see a chaste woman taken down.

'Did you speak to anyone?' Charlotte asked her brother, cutting through the tense silence of the carriage.

They were only a few streets away, and her legs were bouncing with nervous energy.

'Not…not anyone specifically…' Arthur averted his gaze.

'It's important that we know what we're walking into,' Nathaniel said.

'I was…' Arthur sighed. 'I was quite distressed…'

'Just tell us what happened.' Charlotte tried hard to keep her voice calm.

'I was trying to find Nathaniel, but people kept gawking at me, and whispering, and then someone said in such a sneering voice, *"Isn't that your bride-to-be, Your Grace?"* And I said, *"Not any more."* Of course I would call the engagement off. I thought she was… Well, *you know*…with Nathaniel! And I was only half-wrong.'

He crossed his arms.

'So the whole city thinks I've been basket-making with Miss Linfield,' Nathaniel said.

'The whole city thinks you've been *what*?' Arthur raised his eyebrows.

Charlotte smiled for the first time all day. Of course Arthur wouldn't know what basket-making meant. 'Yes, Nathaniel, all of London thinks you were *taking a flyer* with Arthur's betrothed.'

'That we were engaged in *amorous congress*,' Nathaniel replied, and the two of them melted into salacious giggles.

'Oh, *ha-ha*, very funny.' But even Arthur couldn't keep himself from grinning.

The doors of Somerset House stood tall and foreboding as Charlotte stepped out of the carriage. She braced herself for whatever came next, but as she and Arthur and Nathaniel walked into the building she realised that they hadn't actually come up with a plan. It wasn't as though they could simply stride into the place and tear Loretta's portrait from the wall—they'd only cause an even bigger scene and risk damaging Loretta's reputation even more.

'Should we decide what we are to do, before entering?' Nathaniel asked.

'It's been a record low year for submissions,' said Arthur. 'So expect the Academicians to put up a fight if we demand the painting's removal.'

'Enough people have already seen the painting anyway,' Charlotte responded. 'The plan I want is one that will clear Loretta's name.'

Today Charlotte was experiencing a new side of love— and it was a powerful side indeed. Whenever she imagined Loretta hearing the news her jaw clenched and wave after wave of anguish washed over her. The last thing she wanted was for any harm to befall Loretta, and this… Well, this was more than harm. It was utterly ruinous. Charlotte was sure she would give anything to make the whole scandal go away.

Anything? she asked herself.

And then she walked faster. She had her plan.

'Charlotte?' said Arthur nervously as he hurried to keep up.

He was likely beginning to notice the sudden stares and whispers as they travelled through the rooms. Charlotte moved onward, wanting to get the worst part over with: seeing the painting on the wall and knowing it was all true.

They rounded a corner and there it was. Charlotte recognised the painting by its top half—the rest was hidden by a crowd of spectators that made Charlotte sick to her stomach. A moment of intimacy ripped from its context in the dead of night. And no one had the decency to look away.

Nathaniel stood next to Charlotte. They had mere seconds before people would begin to recognise them.

'Nathaniel…?' Charlotte started, aware that what she was about to do next was heavy and delicate all at once.

'It's all right.' He nodded. 'She'll be much better off if it wasn't a man who painted her.'

'Are you sure? I know you wanted more time before we came forward and—'

'I'm sorry, Charlotte, about what I said earlier. We both knew what we were getting ourselves into. And it was always a leap to imagine that if the public discovered one of my secrets they would discover the rest as well.'

'It's understandable——'

'Yes, you're right. It is understandable. I would do anything for love.' He smiled, warm and genuine. 'And it's understandable that you would, too.'

Charlotte felt tears well in the corners of her eyes.

'Anyway...' he chuckled '...you know this lot. They'll move on from me when something more interesting happens. Most likely in twenty-four hours. But Loretta won't survive this if we don't act now.'

Charlotte reached out and squeezed Nathaniel's hand. 'Thank you,' she whispered.

And then she did something she had been putting off for years.

'Are you enjoying my painting?' Charlotte asked rather loudly.

The onlookers swivelled around, confused and intrigued.

'I finished this one only a few days ago,' Charlotte continued as she marched confidently towards the painting, the crowd parting to let her through.

If everything worked as she hoped it would Loretta would be saved on two fronts: her reputation would be far less damaged from modelling for a woman than for a man, and the mildly sensational gossip of her portrait would be overrun by the *extraordinarily* sensational gossip of Charlotte's secret identity.

'It's true,' Nathaniel said in his most pretentious voice as he strolled behind her, chin tilted up, as if he were truly above it all. 'Lady Charlotte Sterlington has been the real artist, the real "Mr Nathaniel Fletcher," this entire time.'

There was a brief moment of silent shock amongst the exhibition's patrons, and then all at once they began talking.

'This *cannot* be!'

'What kind of joke is this?'

'I always *knew* there was something strange about Mr Fletcher.'

'Surely this violates *several* Academy rules?'

'Does this lower the price of the work?'

Charlotte and Nathaniel traded sly smiles, then set about answering their questions.

Arthur stood back, watching it all, still too surprised by the whole thing to decide how he felt about it.

'Why on earth would you agree to this?' asked a generously moustachioed man with an angry finger pointed at Nathaniel.

'Oh, for the drama, I suppose...' Nathaniel replied in a nonchalant tone.

He was playing his part to perfection, and Charlotte thought how Rupert and the rest of their theatre friends would be so proud.

'With the scrutiny of being a duke's sister,' Charlotte added, 'and the pressures of being a second son, we were a natural match.'

'Are you in love?' piped up a stout older woman who was furiously fanning herself.

'What you see before you is strictly a business arrangement,' Nathaniel said.

And then, as if rehearsed, the pair of them let slip the kind of mischievous smile that implied an *Or is it...?* at the end of Nathaniel's sentence.

And just like that, Loretta Linfield was the last thing on anyone's mind.

* * *

Loretta sat on a balcony chair and read Charlotte's letter for the tenth time. She could recite it by heart, like a poem. She could close her eyes and see the curve of every letter, the dimples of dried tears on every page.

She had come outside to clear her head, to listen to the rhythmic sounds of the ocean, to decide what to do next.

I'm going to respond, she thought.

But the hours passed by and she remained on the balcony.

In the late-afternoon sun, the waves shimmered a rich cerulean blue, like the dress she'd worn that first night at the Fourth Tier.

By early evening they were a swirling steely blue, like Charlotte's eyes, inches from her own.

As the sun dipped below the horizon, Loretta finally stood.

I cannot face the dark, she resolved, *without telling Charlotte that I love her.*

She jumped at the sound of a door slamming shut. From where she sat she could see the top of a carriage, stationed outside the hotel's front door.

She folded Charlotte's letter and sat up straight as quick footsteps beat against the floorboards, coming in her direction. Peering over the balcony ledge, the better to see the carriage, Loretta spotted his family crest at the same moment she heard his voice behind her.

Wrottesley.

'Loretta,' said Cecil, his voice thick with sympathy. 'I came as soon as I heard.'

He was panting, and a few strands poked free from his heavily pomaded hairstyle.

'Heard what?' Loretta stood up from her chair.

His eyes searched her face, and the worry that sprang from his eyes was making her heart beat fast.

'Heard *what*, Cecil?'

'It seems I must be the bearer of terrible news…' He moved across the balcony with urgent strides. 'It is with a *heavy* heart that I report all of London has learned of your affair with Mr Fletcher.'

Loretta's lungs turned to stone. She stood very still, careful not to let any emotion show on her face. Confusion, panic, dread and—there it was again—*fear*. All crashed over her like an unexpected wave.

She gripped Cecil's hands to steady herself, and felt a bandage wrapped around his palm.

'Your hand…?'

'A minor fencing wound.' He shrugged. 'But I am here to worry about *you*, not the other way around. Loretta, Mr Fletcher has submitted your portrait to the Royal Academy,' he continued, his tone shifting between pity and compassion and anger. 'He has revealed to the whole world a moment of intimacy that should have remained private.'

Loretta forced herself to breathe. There was only one portrait he could be talking about, and her body turned to ice as she thought of strangers gawking at her shoulders, her knees, her bare breast…

Why would Charlotte do this? she wanted to say.

But her mouth was too dry for her to speak.

'Unfortunately, it gets worse,' Cecil said, squeezing Loretta's hands. 'As you can imagine, Colchester is furious. He is a *duke*, after all, and you know how he cares for his reputation. He could never marry a woman who…' His frown changed into a small smile. 'But, Loretta, *I* would never think differently of you. And I will stand by your side no matter what happens.'

Loretta knew she had to say something, but everything she wanted to say was about Charlotte.

'Is…is Nathaniel all right?' she tried, in a voice barely louder than a whisper.

'I'm not sure, Loretta.' A flash of annoyance crossed Cecil's face, but it was gone in an instant. 'I jumped in my carriage as quickly as I could to see if you were all right. I wouldn't be surprised if there was a duel—'

'A *duel*?'

'You know how gentlemen can be.'

Yes, she did—but Charlotte was no gentleman. Loretta could feel the presence of the folded letter behind her on the chair, as if it were a fire that threatened to catch the hem of her dress.

Why would Charlotte write any of those things, Loretta thought, *if she didn't mean them?*

'I know this is quite a surprise—' Cecil started, but Loretta interrupted.

'Why would he—' *she…* '—do this?'

Cecil sighed and let go of Loretta's hands. 'He's an artist, Loretta. He's in love with his own ambition. Artists will say and do anything to get their next masterpiece upon a wall. And then…' he tossed his hands in the air '…they move on to their next muse.'

Is that all I was? Loretta clenched her jaw. *The next muse?*

'I'll give you some privacy,' Cecil said, with a small, po-lite bow. 'But just know that I'll remain here for as long as you need me.'

He left the balcony, and even through the haze of panic that clouded Loretta's mind the implication of his words was not lost on her. If the Duke did not want her, then neither would any respectable gentleman in England.

Cecil Wrottesley would remain for as long as she needed—and that might turn out to be a very long time indeed.

Chapter Nineteen

Charlotte had guessed it would take the esteemed gentlemen of the Selection Committee ten minutes to arrive at the scene she and Nathaniel were causing.

They were there in eight.

'You really think a *man* could capture the essence of a woman quite like this?' Charlotte said with a smirk, goading the crowd as much as she could.

Three men from the Royal Academy cut through the crowd, each one looking more or less like a hawk in hunt. Ramsay Richard Reinagle, with his signature fluffy brown hair and austere face, spoke first.

'We have heard news that an act of fraud has allegedly been committed?' He turned his head to look at Charlotte, then turned to Nathaniel. His eyes widened. 'Lady Charlotte,' he said with a slight bow. 'And…Mr Fletcher? Surely there's been a misunderstanding…'

'No misunderstanding at all.' Nathaniel shook his head. 'Lady Charlotte and I have simply decided to come clean about our arrangement. She is the true painter, not I.'

The people in the crowd whispered to each other as they stared at the three stunned faces, awaiting a response.

'Mr Fletcher,' said Richard Westall, his white hair combed high. 'I'm not quite sure I understand—'

'It's quite simple, really,' Charlotte interrupted. 'I'm the artist who's been impressing all of London these past few years. The only time Nathaniel picks up a brush is to add his signature.' Realisation hit her like a bolt of lightning. 'Which is all the proof you need to know that this painting was submitted by mistake.'

She pointed at the bottom right corner: no signature.

'I refuse to believe this,' huffed Mr Reinagle. 'This would make both of you…well, common swindlers! Impossible behaviour, given your respectable lineage.'

'If people purchase my work for its quality,' Charlotte said, with her chin raised to hide the nervous energy that was building within her, 'then surely the identity of the painter shouldn't lower its worth.'

'Why go to all this trouble?' Thomas Stothard spoke up.

He was the Academician Charlotte was most optimistic about. Mr Stothard was, among other things, a playbill artist. She didn't know if he was connected with the Fourth Tier in any way, but surely he knew theatre people—and those were Charlotte's kind of people.

'We accept plenty of women each year!' he said.

'Oh, yes!' Charlotte scoffed. She gestured at the paintings all around them. 'Only they're all naked and painted by men.'

Gasps and laughter rippled through the crowd.

Mr Reinagle held up his hand for silence. 'Such deception,' he roared, 'if true, would warrant this painting's immediate removal from the exhibition.'

Hope sprang in Charlotte's chest. 'Very well,' she said with mock solemnity. 'We'll take it and be on our way.'

'*If* such deception is true,' Mr Reinagle emphasised. 'And we have no evidence to suggest that it is.'

Charlotte's breathing grew shallow. They didn't want to believe her. Of course they didn't. It would be quite the scandal to admit they had been fooled—several times over—and it would force a conversation about women's role in the Academy. There had been rumours that Mr Fletcher was likely to be offered a spot at the Academy if his Summer Exhibition submission did well, and those rumours wouldn't go away even now that everyone knew Mr Fletcher wasn't a painter at all.

'Then let her paint!' came a quiet but commanding voice from several feet behind the crowd.

Everyone hushed and turned to face Arthur Sterlington.

After a moment of tense silence, he continued. 'Let her paint in front of anyone who doubts her story. Charge a penny per viewer. Judge for yourself if the style's a match.'

Charlotte could barely see her brother through the flock of fascinated onlookers, but the glimpse she caught of his face made her stomach drop. He looked so tired.

He turned and walked away.

'It's not a bad idea,' Mr Stothard muttered to his colleagues.

He had grey hair, a bony noise and a modest smile—Charlotte searched for any clue in his eyes that he might be on her side, but he was unreadable. She glanced at the other two men, who were visibly turning the idea over in their minds.

'We'll have to discuss it further,' Mr Reinagle said. 'Until then, the painting stays.'

Charlotte's aim had been the painting's removal, but that hadn't stopped her from preparing a back-up plan.

She watched the men walk towards their offices, and she thought of Mr Westall's painting *Vertumnus and Pomona* and the woman at the centre, whose skin was so clear and lily-white it was nearly translucent. She thought of the woman's small nose and rosy cheeks, her breasts the size and shape of two perfect oranges.

She thought of that woman and all the others as she uncorked the small bottle of lavender paint she had brought in her reticule and splashed it across her greatest work of art yet.

It had taken less than twenty-four hours for the Royal Academy to set a date and time for Charlotte's live painting. The members had prepared all the necessary materials in their largest studio and sent fliers advertising the event all over town.

It was a risky move—a move entirely uncharacteristic of Arthur—but it was enough to get Loretta out of the gossip circuit by the time she arrived in London. Which, Charlotte knew, should be any moment now.

She had wanted to write to her again, to explain everything that was happening, but she knew Loretta was scheduled to leave the coast today, and there would be no way the letter would reach her in time.

Even if it might have, Charlotte didn't know what she would have said. The theft wasn't her fault, but Charlotte knew Loretta would blame herself—for being vulnerable, for jeopardising her future, for getting too close to someone so dangerous. And Charlotte, reason be damned, continued to blame *herself.* It was her art studio, her painting, her career. Loretta had trusted her. And Charlotte had failed to keep her safe.

Now Charlotte was about to turn her art—her serious, meaningful, nuanced art—into a ticketed spectacle. She wanted to feel something other than dread. Claiming true credit for her work had always been her plan, eventually, and now she could finally pursue her dream without hiding behind Nathaniel. But it was all wrong. It wasn't on her terms. Even her attempts to reclaim the moment from whoever had stolen the painting felt forced and false and hastily improvised.

And then there was the dread of knowing that whoever had done this vile thing was still out there. Charlotte didn't know if the thief had been trying to hurt her, Nathaniel or Loretta—or all three. She didn't know who it could be or what motivation they might have had, but she didn't have time to investigate. She had time for one thing and one thing only: to make that scandalous portrait of Loretta so utterly forgettable that no one would care to bring it up again when Loretta returned.

When Loretta returned...

Charlotte's dread was temporarily interrupted by a flurry of emotions—hope, worry, longing, lust—each one tripping over the other in a fight for attention. When all this was over she would tell Loretta everything. Each emotion would have its turn.

Charlotte's steps echoed through the empty halls of Somerset House—it was too early in the morning for visitors. She wore a stunning scarlet gown with an elegant foot of gold floral brocade along the hem—the kind of outfit that would command attention even under a thick beige apron.

The studio wasn't far from the building's entrance, and soon she was examining the space and weighing the borrowed brushes in her hand.

The deal was simple: she'd have three full days to paint a live model, under the supervision of the Selection Committee and a paying audience, after which point it should be obvious whether the painting was coming along in the style of Mr Fletcher or not. The room would be locked overnight, and at noon for a brief luncheon. If the Committee determined that she was the true artist—that she had for years displayed paintings under Nathaniel's name—Charlotte would be banned from submitting to the Exhibition ever again.

But that didn't matter to Charlotte. Not if it meant Loretta would be safe.

And when the spectacle ended Charlotte would be known, at long last, as something more than just the Duke's sister, or a Suffering Sterlington, or the mad girl who threw a tantrum at Almack's after her brother died.

She would be known as an accomplished artist in her own right.

'I can't believe they made *me* purchase a ticket,' Nathaniel said as he entered.

Charlotte was sitting on a wooden stool, lightly sketching the contours of her vision onto the stretched canvas.

'I can't believe they're making me do this at all,' Charlotte said, relieved to have a friend in the room.

'Oh, and suddenly you don't love a good show?' he teased from behind the rope that would separate Charlotte from her audience.

She was no stranger to performance, but she had learned to love the game of it more out of necessity than anything else. She performed scepticism at gallery showings, poking fun at her own work; she performed cynicism at balls, pretending her feet didn't itch to join the dancing; and she performed innocence whenever she found herself in conversation with the many husbands whose wives had spent the night in her bed.

As spectators gradually filled the room, Charlotte realised this was very likely her final performance. She wanted Loretta back most of all because there was no role to play when she was by her side. There was only the two of them…on an empty stage.

When enough people had gathered, she flourished her hand in the air and said, 'Shall we begin?'

The applause focused her nerves on the task at hand.

'Miss Wilson…' Charlotte turned now to the model the Committee had hired. 'Would you please rest your hands on the arms of your chair? And then—this might sound strange—can you *slouch* just a bit? Let yourself be comfortable in the chair…'

The morning trudged on in a simple rhythm of mixing

colours, painting lines, adjusting Miss Wilson and giving
to the occasional audience banter. Every so often Charlot
would glance around the room, in the hope that Loretta ha
come, or perhaps Arthur, whom she hadn't seen since he'd
left Somerset House yesterday morning.

But they didn't come, and by evening Charlotte had trained
herself to stop checking.

The gown Loretta wore on her first day back in London
was pale green, but it might as well have been raven-black for
the mournful way she carried herself. Her sober countenance,
her stubborn silence and her cleared social calendar might
very easily indicate to someone who didn't know better that
Loretta Linfield had lost herself entirely to grief.

To someone who *did* know better, Loretta had indeed lost
herself to grief—only the person she was mourning had never
existed in the first place…at least not in the way she had
imagined.

The Charlotte Sterlington she had known had been too sweet
to last, like sugar dissolving on her tongue. That Charlotte had
coaxed Loretta open with saccharine flattery and whirlwind
nights on the town, until she'd snatched away the beauty she'd
needed, until she'd and left Loretta feeling ugly and used.

Every hour something new hurt the most, and currently the
sorest spot was how Charlotte had stolen that beauty while
Loretta slept.

She should have known to keep her eyes open around
someone as blatantly duplicitous as Charlotte Sterlington.

The first thing Loretta did when she arrived home was clear
her room of any book that held even a single love poem within
its pages. She marched them down to the library shelves and
slid them into empty slots with the finality of laying bodies
in their graves. Then she retired to her room and stayed there.

air in the carriage ride home had been thick with ten-
Cecil had joined Loretta and her father, so he could
ain to the Baron everything that had transpired. The
nstaking detail of his storytelling had felt like a swarm of
ornets buzzing in circles around Loretta's head, but the look
of sorrow in her father's eyes was what had stung the most.

He hadn't even been angry. He'd just been...sad.

By the time they had reached the outskirts of London, Cecil
and her father had already begun to discuss an appropriate
strategy. Loretta had just felt tired, and weak, and hollow.

She clearly couldn't be trusted to make anything close to a
wise decision, given how she'd behaved these last two months.
Better to leave it to the men.

Their plan was simple: Loretta would steer clear of any
social engagements while the Baron tried to control the dam-
age, and within the week the Linfields would host an opulent
ball to signal to their peers that one mistake should not shame
the family name.

She'd barely spoken at all through their day-long journey
back to London. Lying had got her into this mess, and it would
have to get her out of it too—but she just didn't have it in her,
any more, so she'd chosen silence instead.

Luckily for her, men had a particular talent for filling silence with whatever story they most wanted to be true. By
the end of the trip Lord Linfield and Cecil had convinced
themselves not only that Loretta had been hopelessly wooed
by the wily Mr Fletcher, but that she had practically begged
them both to save her from the wanton whims of her womanly sensibilities.

Now she lay in bed, closing her eyes to imagine a broom
sweeping up the jagged pieces of her broken heart and throwing them away so they couldn't wound her any more.

Chapter Twenty

When news of a visitor was sent to Loretta's room she wasn't sure how much time had passed. She'd slept the night before in her clothes, and had barred even Bridget from entering her room to help her prepare for bed. Perhaps it was morning, or maybe lunchtime, or maybe a week had gone by and it was time to host the ball.

Maybe it's Charlotte, Loretta thought before she could stop herself. Maybe Charlotte had run here the moment she'd learned Loretta was back in town. Maybe she had really meant everything she'd said, everything she'd written, everything she'd done. Maybe Charlotte had some story that would make it all make sense.

But then Loretta remembered their first night together at the theatre, when they'd sat close and watched *As You Like It*.

Rosalind had said to Phoebe, *'I pray you, do not fall in love with me, for I am falser than vows made in wine.'*

Even if Charlotte had shown up at Loretta's door with a grand Shakespearean declaration of love, there would be no reason for Loretta to believe her. Their whole relationship had been a vow 'made in wine'.

The visitor, of course, was Lord Cecil Wrottesley. It was never going to be Charlotte, and it was most certainly never going to be Arthur.

Loretta's shoulders hunched inward as she thought of how disgusted and hurt Arthur must be, and how his hurt would ripple outward so that no other suitors would dare approach her. She felt rotten—like unpicked fruit withering in the sun.

Loretta forced herself out of bed and into new clothes—an alabaster gown with lace hemming and an eye-catching gold bodice. As much as she hated to admit it—and hate it she did—Cecil was now her only hope of a respectable future. He had every right to spurn her the way other gentlemen of the *ton* were surely doing—no one wanted to marry a ruined woman, especially one who had gone and lost a duke—but here was Cecil, waiting in the drawing room with a bouquet of flowers.

Loyal Cecil, childhood friend, the husband she was meant to have all along.

'I hope some time alone has brought you comfort,' he said with a bow. He handed the flowers to a maid, who placed them in a vase and then went to fetch some tea. 'I thought I might cheer you up,' he said, and gestured to the couch.

'You've always been a caring friend,' Loretta responded flatly.

Cecil placed an earnest hand over his heart. 'Such a touching thing to say. But, while I remain the caring friend you've known your whole life, I have also changed a great deal since returning from my travels. I am wiser, and nobler, capable of great things.'

Loretta nodded and retreated into her old and familiar numbness. She absently noticed the tea that was placed before her, alongside a variety of cakes and sweets. Maybe she would never be the woman in painting on the stairs again, but if she tried she could become something close.

'Given how successful I've been since returning to London,' Cecil continued, 'you've probably forgotten that I once knew the bitter taste of ruin and regret. I appear before you today as living proof that a reputation can be rebuilt—perhaps even stronger than it was before.'

Loretta nodded again. 'You are quite right.'

'Of course,' Cecil went on, 'it is harder when one is a lady.' He paused to take a long sip of tea. 'It would simply break my heart,' he said, 'to see you spend twice as many years as I did earning your way back into society.'

Loretta had a sense that Cecil didn't know the first thing about a broken heart.

'Forgive me if I am too bold,' he continued, 'but this whole ordeal has reminded me of what we meant to each other just a few years ago.'

This was her escape route. Marrying Cecil was the only path she would ever be offered to move on from the wreckage she had made of her life. She would put Charlotte behind her, along with Nathaniel and Rupert and the Fourth Tier, and all those love poems and maybe even all her books too. All she had to do was say yes, and everything would return to normal.

'Perhaps this is an opportunity to pick up where we left off,' Cecil said.

Return to normal, Loretta told herself.

'Before my embarrassing departure, I was going to ask…'

Return to normal! She begged herself to listen.

'…if you would marry me.'

The *yes* that sat ready on her tongue tumbled out as a clumsy, 'I—I don't know.'

Cecil blinked, eyebrows raised. He opened his mouth to respond, but was swiftly cut off by the drawing room door swinging open.

'I've had the most *fascinating* day!' her father exclaimed. The Baron strode into the room, blissfully unaware that he was intruding on what was supposed to be an important moment. 'Would anyone like to hear about my fascinating day?'

Loretta nodded, then glanced at Cecil. He tucked away a scowl just in time for the Baron's eyes to settle on the couch.

'Of course, sir,' Cecil answered.

'I paid a visit to Somerset House, to learn more about this predicament we find ourselves in...'

Her father stuffed his hands in his pockets and paced slowly in front of the couch. Loretta lowered her eyes, ashamed at this reminder that her carelessness—and Charlotte's betrayal—had burned more than just herself.

'And to my great surprise,' he continued, in his characteristically expressive storytelling voice, 'hardly anyone seemed to care about the painting. In fact, everyone's attention was directed not at Loretta, nor at Nathaniel, nor the Duke, but rather the Duke's *sister*. She was painting before an audience to prove that *she* was the true artist of Loretta's portrait.'

Loretta watched his feet come to a stop in front of her.

'That can't be true!' Cecil laughed.

'Oh, but it is,' the Baron countered. 'I stood there for quite some time, mesmerised by her technique, by her passion. I stood there until the Selection Committee unanimously voted that Charlotte Sterlington is indeed the real Mr Fletcher.'

Cecil took another sip of tea. 'Well, what do you make of this?' he asked the Baron.

But when Loretta raised her eyes, her father was looking only at her.

She'd anticipated anger, or perhaps disappointment, but all she could see on his face was curiosity.

'It's true,' Loretta confirmed. 'She painted me.'

Her father nodded with dramatic solemnity. 'The only part I can't work out,' he said slowly, 'is why you didn't say anything.'

'This seems a minor detail in a situation that is still very dire,' Cecil interjected. 'Our primary concern isn't the *painter*, but the *painting*. This changes nothing.'

'Oh, Cecil.' The Baron chuckled. 'You are an intelligent man, and I *do* admire your concern. But you are young, and I am not. I've seen these things play out countless times, and the fallout for Loretta in revealing herself to another woman will be much less severe.'

He checked his pocket watch, clearly satisfied with his assessment of the situation.

'And what's more, Lady Charlotte claims the painting was never supposed to see the light of day. She says it was *stolen*.'

Hope flickered in Loretta's chest. She couldn't let herself be fooled by Charlotte again—but she couldn't stop herself from wanting to hear more.

'But…but the Duke…' Cecil stood, agitation creeping into his voice. 'A failed engagement is nearly impossible to come back from—'

'He's a good man.' The Baron waved his hand in dismissal. 'From a good family. No Sterlington would end an engagement over such a petty misunderstanding.'

'It's easy to say that now,' Cecil shot back, gesticulating wildly, 'but he was out the door at once when we all thought Mr Fletcher was the painter. Surely Loretta doesn't want someone who could walk out on her so easily—'

'Cecil, your hand—'

'Loretta doesn't want someone who'll cast her aside the moment a scandal hits. What sort of a husband is that? *I'd* never have left her side. *I've* known her for years—'

'Your *hand*, Cecil,' Loretta's father said firmly, his eyes wide. A dark patch of red was forming on Cecil's bandage.

'It's nothing,' Cecil scoffed. 'Just a riding accident—'

He continued ranting, but Loretta had stopped listening.

She looked down at her trembling fingers and took a deep, shaky breath.

'Fencing accident,' she interrupted.

'What? Oh, right…yes. As I was saying, *Arthur* didn't ride all the way down to Worthing to comfort Loretta, *I* did—'

'You said it was a fencing accident,' Loretta said, with more confidence this time. 'In Worthing…on the balcony.'

The drawing room was silent. And Cecil was still as marble.

'It was both,' he said eventually, a strained smile replacing his frown. 'I—I was fencing and riding at the same time.' He moved towards Loretta, sympathy saturating his voice with each step. 'I've been so worried about you that I can hardly be expected to remember the minor details of a hand wound.'

Humility was thick across his face, but if Loretta had learned one thing from spending time with actors and liars, it was how to spot someone who hadn't honed his craft.

Cecil was hiding something.

'How *did* you make it all the way down to Worthing…?' mused her father.

'When the Summer Exhibition had only just opened that morning?' Loretta finished his thought. 'Mr Wrottesley's carriage arrived in the afternoon, yes?'

'It did indeed.' Her father met her gaze. 'And London to Worthing is a full day's journey.'

'Loretta,' Cecil implored, 'you know I have the fastest horses in all of London.'

'No horse is that fast,' she snapped.

The hope that had flickered in her chest moments ago was catching like fire on each new lie that Cecil told.

'Is it really so horrible of me?' Cecil threw his arms up angrily. The mask he had been wearing—a mask of chivalry and care—finally shattered. 'Is it really so terrible of me to try to save you from a lifetime with that insufferable Duke? I can tell you don't love him. You *fainted* the first time he proposed!'

Loretta balled her fists in anger.

'Everyone *else* said it was love, but I knew better. I *know* you, Loretta. So I made the effort to find out what was going on.' He ran his fingers through his hair, a frenzied look in his eyes. 'I've been following you. Did you know that? I've been working you out. I saw you coming out of that shed where Fletcher paints. I saw that portrait that he—or she—or whoever—did of you. It's unbecoming of a lady. It's a disgrace. No man could possibly want you after that.'

'No man but you,' growled the Baron, his face growing redder by the minute. 'I thought you'd returned to London a respectable gentleman. But respectable gentlemen do not cheat and steal to get what they want.'

'Or *who* they want.'

Loretta joined her father, her voice steely. Cecil looked between the two, opening and closing his mouth like a trout on a fishing hook. There was nothing else he could say, and he knew it.

'You may see yourself out,' the Baron said. 'Out of this house *and* out of England. If I catch word of your presence near my daughter again—and you'll find I have an *expansive* definition of "near"—I will set you on a ship myself, to the farthest country you can point to on a map.'

That was all Cecil needed to hear—he knew the Baron didn't deal in empty threats. He left the room in a terrified hurry, defeated and disgraced for the last time.

Loretta's father dropped heavily onto the couch and buried his face in his hands. 'I don't know... I just don't know,' he muttered. And then he was quiet.

Loretta had never seen her father at a loss for words. She

found his silence now rather alarming. 'Father?' she said tentatively.

For a long minute she thought he might not speak. But at last he looked up. 'Why did you let me believe Mr Fletcher was the painter?'

Loretta shifted uncomfortably in her seat. She tried to take stock of all the reasons left to lie, but this day—this *season*, really—was already so full of lies that she just didn't have the stomach for it any more.

'I wasn't sure anyone would believe me,' Loretta said, 'if Charlotte—er...*Lady* Charlotte—didn't come forward herself. I had no proof...'

She took a long, deep breath and urged herself onwards. She had narrowly escaped a life with a man she did not love—*twice* in the course of one season—and she was not about to take that escape for granted.

'I had no proof, but it's more than that. I care for her. Even when I thought she'd submitted the painting on purpose, I still wanted to protect her. And now, more than anything, I just want to find her and stay by her side. I'd like to stay by her side for a very long time. Because...' She paused, but the truth glowed within her like a lamp that would not be put out. 'Because I love her.'

Her father leaned back into the couch with a low whistle.

Loretta sat on her hands to keep them from fidgeting.

'I could get into a fair bit of trouble for saying this,' he said finally, 'but Aristotle *did* observe pigeons mating with members of the same sex.'

Loretta blinked in surprise, heat pooling at her cheeks.

'Quails and partridges too, I believe,' he continued. 'And although I say this could get me into trouble, it is simply objective scientific observation. But no study on this sort of thing would ever get funding. It's too controversial. Too *unnatural*.'

He said that final word in a mocking tone. 'I'd say pigeons, quails and partridges all seem rather natural to me. And I know a zoologist who suspects tortoises as well. But he'd be shunned if he ever suggested as much.'

'I had no idea...' Loretta shook her head in disbelief.

'Most people don't. And that's why—'

'No,' Loretta corrected. 'I had no idea you could be so genuinely enjoyable to talk to.'

Her father smiled, but it was tinged with sadness. 'I've always wanted great things for myself. And I always wanted an easy life for you. That's how it's supposed to be—great men and the easy lives they give to their wives and daughters. But after today I'm wondering if the evidence suggests you want something more than just *easy*.'

The Baron paused to catch his breath.

'I think I've nearly bored your mother to death with how easy I wanted her life to be.' He looked at Loretta earnestly now. 'And I really mean that.'

Loretta's heart ached at this sudden sincerity her father was building between them. She'd never heard him speak like this, so humbly and openly. She had always thought him a difficult and demanding man, but a great man. Sitting beside her now, he was just a man—nothing more.

She preferred him that way.

'Dear God!' he exclaimed, startling Loretta from her sentimentality. 'The ball! The ball!' He reached into his pocket, then made a twisted face at his pocket watch, as if it had personally offended him.

'What ball?' Loretta was too bewildered—and too overwhelmed by all that had transpired that day—to say anything else.

'The ball I've arranged.' He was up now, pacing around the

room. 'To remind the *ton* who you are—painting be damned. It's tonight!'

Loretta could see he was tabulating on his fingers all that was left to prepare. 'I'm so sorry, my dear, but I really must go now to co-ordinate with the staff.'

'Of course,' said Loretta. 'But perhaps we can talk like this more often?'

He stopped his pacing and smiled. 'Yes. I'd like that. I'd like that very much.'

'And Father?' Loretta was feeling emboldened. 'Perhaps you can talk like this to Mother, too? I've heard that Aristotle once observed a pigeon apologising to his mate after many years of not considering her needs.'

'Oh…' he said quietly. 'I—I think you may be right.'

He smiled at her again, then set off towards the door.

'One more thing,' he said, turning back and grinning. 'Remember to dress up. I've asked our guests to wear costumes.'

He started once again to leave, but turned back a second time.

'The sister—' He cleared his throat. 'Charlotte. She responded to the invitation. For the ball, I mean. She's coming.'

Chapter Twenty-One

The trick to Charlotte's pirate costume was making herself unrecognisable enough that no one would bother her, but not *so* unrecognisable that Loretta wouldn't notice her.

Then again, even the most recognisable outfit would go unnoticed by Loretta if Charlotte continued to hide here in the bushes all night.

Charlotte was short enough that a row of potted hydrangea and a trellis of wisteria could hide her from view while she peeked out to watch the dance floor.

Tonight she had taken extra care to pin her curls beneath her three-point hat with its ridiculous white plume. Her lips were stained deep red, and the top half of her face was concealed by a black-and-gold Venetian mask. By the time she spotted Loretta she should be able to stride over with all the confidence of a pirate king and guide her into a waltz, with no one in her way.

No one, that was, except Charlotte herself.

The longer she stood behind her wall of plants, the more she felt rooted to the floor. She was nervous that Loretta would be angry—would be too sore from nursing the wounds of the last few days to look upon Charlotte with grace. And she was nervous that her plan hadn't worked as well as she'd hoped. Maybe the live painting spectacle hadn't distracted anyone, and they had all still found time to ridicule Loretta upon her return to London.

She was nervous, yes—but Charlotte was well-known to laugh in the face of nerves. What kept her rooted to the floor tonight was shame.

Loretta's forgiveness would open the door to a future together, and that was a door Charlotte didn't feel she deserved to walk through. There was nothing she could do to earn Loretta's love, because Charlotte had found a love that was entirely unearnable. It was freely given, and it would be freely given every day for the rest of their lives, and that kind of grace was almost too much for Charlotte to bear.

She felt open, and raw, and that terrified her, but if that was what love did to a person then so be it.

Charlotte took a deep breath, then lifted a foot, ready to step out onto the dance floor.

'I do hope those flowers put up a fair fight.'

A familiar voice beckoned Charlotte to spin around.

'It's not every day they find themselves under siege by the dread Pirate King Charlie.'

Every reservation Charlotte had been clinging to melted the instant she locked eyes with Loretta Linfield.

'My queen...' Charlotte bowed, drinking in the sight of her on the way down.

Loretta stood tall in bursts of blue fabric, vibrant tulle and shimmering chiffon. She wore fairy wings as if they were truly her own—as if she might fly off at any moment and take Charlotte with her.

'I've been looking everywhere for you,' Loretta said, this time as herself.

'Really?' Charlotte took a tentative step forward and untied her mask. 'Are you glad you've found me?'

Loretta removed the delicate peacock feather mask that

was covering half her face. 'I have never been happier to see anyone in any place, at any time,' she said as she closed the gap between them.

The string quartet swelled on the other side of the flowers. Loretta reached for Charlotte's hands.

'But I—' Charlotte began.

There was so much to say—so much to apologise for, and so much to promise. But she knew she had to say the most important thing first.

'I love you, Loretta Linfield. I loved you long before I was able to say it out loud. And I will love you every day for as long as I live, and every day that comes after that.' She paused, and squeezed Loretta's hands. 'I know I've made a mull of our relationship. And I don't expect you to—'

'I love you,' Loretta said simply. 'I never stopped loving you, not really. How could I?' She laughed softly. 'I mean… have you *been* in a room with yourself?'

Charlotte smiled, and for the first time in days she felt the knot in her heart loosen. 'I told you I couldn't love you, and that was a lie. And I told you not to love me, and that was impossible. I am so sorry.'

Loretta lifted her hands to cup Charlotte's face. 'And when you finally worked that out, I wasn't ready to listen. But I am now. I'm done with pretending that I could ever live without you.'

Charlotte let her cheeks rest against Loretta's palms. She was home. She was exactly where she was meant to be.

And this time she was brave enough to stay.

Loretta brought her lips to Charlotte's. They were on the stage again. They were in the greenhouse. They were in the cloakroom, the sunroom, the library…

And they were here, behind the flowers, in the Linfield townhouse.

Loretta pulled away. 'I know what you did for me, by the way. My father told me how you painted at Somerset House, in front of all those people. I'm so sorry…' She wrapped her arms around Charlotte's waist. 'I know you wanted to share that secret in your own time.'

'That time came early.' Charlotte leaned her head against Loretta's shoulder and breathed her in. 'But I still feel it was mine.'

'I still can't believe that Cecil broke into your studio—'

'Cecil *what*?' Charlotte exclaimed, jolting backwards.

'You haven't heard?'

Loretta's eyes were wide now, the way they always were when something surprising, or frightening, or fascinating happened. Charlotte sighed in wonder. She would spend a lifetime looking into Loretta's emerald eyes.

'No, I haven't *heard*!' she said. 'I knew someone broke in, but I didn't know it was—' she scrunched her nose as if she had smelled something terrible '—*Cecil Wrottesley*?'

Loretta raised her eyebrows and nodded. 'Apparently he thought he could ruin my reputation so thoroughly that I'd have no marriage prospects left but him.'

'*Oh, Cecil…*' Charlotte sighed. 'Doesn't he know that a woman with a ruined reputation is *exactly* my type?'

Loretta laughed and pulled Charlotte close. 'I love you.'

'I'll never get tired of hearing you say that.'

'I'll never get tired of saying it.'

Loretta kissed her forehead, and Charlotte knew she would never tire of saying it back. Love had claimed its place in Charlotte's heart, and although grief would always be there too, she knew it would not devour her. It would continue to awaken in remembrance of Thomas and her parents, of past lovers who had been forced to marry, of the countless forbidden love stories that history has failed to record. But it would make peace with love and they would live side by side.

Loretta drew back suddenly, her brow furrowed in concern. 'Oh, dear! I nearly forgot to ask about Arthur! Is he all right?'

'We talked before the ball,' Charlotte said. 'He isn't here. I think he'll be taking the rest of the season off, to be honest.'

Loretta lowered her eyes, but Charlotte reassured her.

'It's a good thing, really. He doesn't fault you for anything—he was quite miffed with me, however—but this whole ordeal had made him realise that he doesn't know what he truly wants out of life. He saw me wanting you, and wanting to paint, and all that wanting was so unfamiliar to him. He's going to take some time now to just…be Arthur. To learn who that is.'

Loretta laced her fingers through Charlotte's. 'I am so happy to hear that. I know what it feels like to be cut off from your own wants…and I know what it feels like to come home to them.'

Loretta's words sent shivers deep into the core of Charlotte's body. She would be who Loretta came home to—always.

This, Charlotte knew, was as good as it got: to be wanted and to want in return, no matter the cost of those wants. She had never needed a love that she could proclaim to the world, and she had never needed a love that she could consecrate in church—but what she *did* need, and what she hadn't even *known* she needed until this season, was a love she could come home to.

'What happens next?' Charlotte asked.

There would be so much to work out.

Where will we live?

How will we support ourselves?

How can I ever be worthy of this woman?

But Loretta didn't look worried at all. 'What happens

next?' she repeated. She slipped her mask back on and held out her hand. 'We dance.'

Charlotte smiled, replaced her own mask and took Loretta's hand. They stepped out from behind the flowers.

'I think I make a rather convincing gentleman, don't you agree?' she asked.

'I think,' said Loretta as they entered the crowded ballroom, 'they're all too caught up in themselves to notice us anyway.'

Charlotte slid her hand down to the curve of Loretta's waist as a waltz began. Beneath their masks they might have been anyone.

After tonight, Charlotte would be more famous than ever—celebrated for her talent and condemned for her trickery. She and Loretta would come to be known as local oddities: two spinsters held up as cautionary tales to young girls who secretly hoped to follow in their footsteps.

They would, they would, they would...

But for now they were just another nameless couple in a sea of dancers, a fairy queen and her pirate king, waltzing away into the night and into whatever came next.

* * * * *

The Duke's Sister and I
*is Emma-Claire Sunday's
debut for Harlequin Historical.
Be sure to look out for her next book,
coming soon!*

HARLEQUIN
Reader Service

Enjoyed your book?

Try the perfect subscription for Romance readers and get more great books like this delivered right to your door.

See why over 10+ million readers have tried Harlequin Reader Service.

Start with a Free Welcome Collection with free books and a gift—valued over $20.

Choose any series in print or ebook. See website for details and order today:

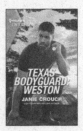

TryReaderService.com/subscriptions